PENGUIN BOOKS

NO! I DON'T WANT TO JOIN A BOOK CLUB

'Cracks along . . . Ironside writes with pacy verve' *Literary Review*

'Hilarious' *Woman & Home*

'Immense wit and charm' *Psychologies*

'Combines wise words with brilliant witticisms. A genuinely involving romp' *Easy Living*

D0243069

Virginia Ironside is a journalist, agony aunt and author. She has one son and two grandsons.

No! I Don't Want to Join a Bookclub

VIRGINIA IRONSIDE

PENGUIN BOOKS

PENGUIN BOOKS

Published by the Penguin Group
Penguin Books Ltd, 80 Strand, London WC2R ORL, England
Penguin Group (USA) Inc., 375 Hudson Street, New York, New York 10014, USA
Penguin Group (Canada), 90 Eglinton Avenue East, Suite 700, Toronto, Ontario, Canada M4P 2Y3
(a division of Pearson Penguin Canada Inc.)
Penguin Ireland, 25 St Stephen's Green, Dublin 2, Ireland
(a division of Penguin Books Ltd)
Penguin Group (Australia), 250 Camberwell Road, Camberwell, Victoria 3124, Australia
(a division of Pearson Australia Group Pty Ltd)
Penguin Books India Pvt Ltd, 11 Community Centre, Panchsheel Park, New Delhi – 110 017, India
Penguin Group (NZ), 67 Apollo Drive, Rosedale, North Shore 0632, New Zealand
(a division of Pearson New Zealand Ltd)
Penguin Books (South Africa) (Pty) Ltd, 24 Sturdee Avenue, Rosebank, Johannesburg 2196, South Africa

Penguin Books Ltd, Registered Offices: 80 Strand, London WC2R ORL, England

www.penguin.com

First published by Fig Tree 2006
Published in Penguin Books 2007

1

Copyright © Virginia Ironside, 2006
All rights reserved

The moral right of the author has been asserted

Typeset by Rowland Phototypesetting Ltd, Bury St Edmunds, Suffolk
Printed in England by Clays Ltd, St Ives plc

Except in the United States of America, this book is sold subject
to the condition that it shall not, by way of trade or otherwise, be lent,
re-sold, hired out, or otherwise circulated without the publisher's
prior consent in any form of binding or cover other than that in
which it is published and without a similar condition including this
condition being imposed on the subsequent purchaser

ISBN: 978-0-141-02583-4

For Patrick

October 3

OK. This is it. About fifty years too late, but better late than never. A diary. I know it's not January 1st, or even November 1st, but there is no time like the present. Don't we always say to ourselves: 'If only I'd written a diary when I was twenty?' Or thirty? Or forty? But in my sixtieth year (or fifty-ninth, to be precise – or, oh God, maybe it *is* my sixtieth year – I remember some tedious man explaining to me recently how even though I'm fifty-nine, I'm actually in my sixtieth year, totally incomprehensible, but I finally gave in), anyway, in whatever year it is, I, Marie Sharp, retired art teacher, divorced, one son, one cat and resolutely single after about one million failed relationships, am determined to give it a final crack. A diary, that is. Not a relationship.

Oh dear me no.

I wrote my first diary when I was ten. Riveting stuff. 'Got up. Went to school. Had maths – ugh! Came home. Did prep. Had supper. Went to bed.' I started another when I was a teenager, but that was when I had a crush on Archie, who was a year older than me and had no idea of my feelings. I still have about four exercise books covered with the words 'I love Archie', 'I LOVE Archie!', 'I LOVE ARCHIE!!!' on every page. On the cover of one of them is a huge crimson heart with 'ARCHIE' emblazoned on it.

I remember when David and I were married and had our son, Jack, we kept a joint diary, but that was just full of lies because we each knew the other one was going to read it. I had to keep a separate, secret diary, because I felt so miserable about the whole marriage. In our joint diary I wrote: 'Great day! We all went to the Round Pond with Jack and came back to tea with Hughie and James. Lots of jokes and a splendid tea!' In my private one I wrote: 'I just can't stand David and his horrible friends. I can't bear the way they all feel like a secret society I'm not part of. I want to be free! I want to dance! I want to have affairs!'

Of course, shortly after that, I did, and David and I broke up, but oddly we stayed friends. (Anyway, God knows what he was writing in *his* secret diary.) I also, even odder, stayed friends with his half-brother, James, and his partner, Hughie. *AND* I stayed friends with Archie, even though I never had an affair with him. When he married Philippa, I was at his wedding, and we've had lunch every so often over the years. It turned out that his firm in the City used Hughie as his solicitor – he works in something mysterious called 'futures' – so, as so often happens, all my friends make a complete circle.

I didn't have time to keep a diary when I was at art school, or doing teacher training, and it's only now I'm sixty – well, I will be in a few months – that I'm going to give it a go. I mean, properly give it a go. So . . .

October 8

Woke with watery eyes. Very bad sign. I mean it's OK to get them on a cold and windy day, or when something terrible has happened like flu and you think you've got ME and will never be able to so much as walk to the shops again, let alone lift up a telephone to moan to a friend about being unable to walk to the shops again. But to get watery eyes for no reason – ugh! I know a man of seventy whose eyes water so much he has a drip permanently on the end of his nose. It is, I fear, a sign of age.

It's like the time when I went to Dr Farmer recently with pains in my knees. 'A touch of osteoarthritis, Marie,' she said. 'Happens at our age.'

When I explained that it couldn't happen to me because I never take any exercise and therefore my knees ought, in theory, still to be in perfect nick, the knees of a ten-year-old, barely used, exceptionally low mileage, one careful lady owner, I could probably even dig out the original box and receipt, she explained it didn't work like that.

Rather a bore.

October 10

Have just come home, gasping with relief, from a dinner party. I was hoodwinked into accepting the invitation because my old friend Marion rang using the well-worn trick: 'What are you doing on Thursday?' and instead of saying, cautiously: 'Why?', I fell into the trap.

'Nothing,' I said.

Clunk.

I suppose the odd dinner party can spring a wonderful surprise. And Marion, being something of a wonder woman – like cheese, she's always on a board – has been known to produce interesting guests. But generally dinner parties are like the lottery. You rarely win. The problem is first of all there are never enough men, and, by now – middle-aged, I was going to say, but perhaps the phrase 'getting on' might be more accurate – the men who do attend are always spare for a very good reason: they are either completely hopeless or completely mad.

(I'm not sure that description doesn't apply to most men, actually, whether they're spare or not, which is really why

3

I've ended up so committed to being single. Doesn't mean some men aren't funny, sexy, kind and fascinating, but you can be all that and hopeless and mad at the same time.)

The second problem with dinner parties is that, as you get older, you don't – well, I don't – actually *want* to meet anyone new. There are quite enough people I know whose friendship I would like to consolidate – and other people's favourite people are very rarely my favourite people, and vice versa. The only new people I do want to meet are young people. But *all* old people want to meet young people. We fall on them like vampires.

I remember myself, when about seventeen, being mobbed by men and women who, at fifty, seemed ancient. 'Do let me sit next to you!' they'd say, floppy lips working over tobacco-stained teeth set into receding gums. 'I do so love *young people!*' And I would cringe as they hovered close, sucking into my youth, slavering over my peachy, blooming skin, my sadly immature views, my everything.

'Do tell me why you like the *messy look!*'

'Why do you like young men with long hair?'

'Do explain the Beatles to me – I do find them *fascinating.*'

'Don't you find mini-skirts rather *cold*?'

'*Do* tell me – what *is* this "*generation gap*" we hear so much about these days?'

Nowadays, I don't blame them, though I'd never be so overt in my own craving for the company of the young.

Yesterday I was talking to one of my best friends, Penny, and told her that yet another friend of mine had died – Philippa, actually, the wife of Archie who I had a crush on when I was a teenager. (She's the fourth to pop off this year. I have actually attended no fewer than five funerals since January.) And she said that six of her friends had died in the last eighteen months.

'The awful thing is,' she said, 'that now we just have to make do with the people who are left!'

4

'Unless,' I said, 'we cultivate young people.'

'Which we don't!' she said.

Well, I have to say I *do*, though the admission feels as sinful and horrifically honest as getting up in an AA meeting and saying you're an alcoholic. I mean, who is there going to be left when all around drop like leaves from trees in autumn? If I'm not one of the early droppers, I certainly don't want to be hanging around on a bare branch, flapping away all dry and brown and lonely. I want some nice young green shoots around me.

Marion and her husband, Tim, live in a poky little Edwardian house in West London, still decorated with the Laura Ashley wallpaper that had once looked so pretty in the sixties. They are one of a group of friends of mine who seem to live in rock pools – their sitting rooms could be scooped up, transported to the Geffrye Museum and displayed, along with beautifully preserved Elizabethan parlours and Georgian music rooms, as typical examples of mid-twentieth century style.

The moment I entered the room (awash with grey heads) I knew I was in trouble. You arrive at 8.15 and there is no way you can leave until after 11.00. Dinner parties can be mini-prison sentences, only you don't get out early for good behaviour.

Things weren't helped by the arrival of a guest who wore her bag across her mackintosh from left shoulder to right hip – presumably to make the chances of getting mugged less likely. To add to the general picture of insecurity, she had her glasses on strings, another sign of age and madness. If you can't ever find your glasses, say I, then wear them all the time. If you have to, push them up on to your head. But don't have them hanging down on beaded strings. It looks as infantile as a three-year-old wearing gloves that are attached by ribbons to his coat.

Because I used to teach art and so could, at a stretch, be

regarded as someone in the helping professions, my hosts had, at dinner, thoughtfully, they imagined, put, on my left, a male psychotherapist with a beard. Have to say I'm not mad about psychotherapists. They always look unnaturally serene, never cross their legs, as if they've been Alexander-techniqued up to the eyebrows, which they probably have, and they always have sinisterly caring voices. I'm not actually crackers about beards either, come to that. It's a truth, I've found, that men with beards are never remotely sexy. I think they grow beards not to hide weak chins, but to hide their weak masculinity. Men with beards often seem to have rather large womanly bottoms.

This guy also had a lot of very white hair. There's something a bit fishy, I think, about a man clearly over sixty who has a lot of hair. He looked rather like an effeminate sheep.

As we chomped our way through chilli con carne – along with the house, Marion's cooking is also stuck in a time-warp – the therapist referred occasionally to Freud. When he did, I heard myself saying, rather acidly I'm afraid, that Freud was the most frightful old nightmare, who had, during his many incarnations, once recommended the taking of cocaine to his patients. Indeed, for a while he had been a cocaine addict himself. Total fraud.

'Are you sure you're not making a "Fraudien" slip?' asked the therapist. Everyone laughed in the way English people do when given the chance to relieve the tiniest hint of either seriousness or unpleasantness in the conversation.

He chuckled in a knowing and patronizing way, therapist-style, and went back to his salad. I was very pleased when a bit of lettuce got trapped in his beard.

I'm afraid I was in rather a bad mood. I had arrived in a bad mood. And the feeling had been exacerbated long before the realization that my neighbour was a therapist by the fact that the hosts had placed in the middle of the table a huge centrepiece of giant yellow and red tropical flowers, flanked on either side by tall candles, making it impossible for anyone on one side of the table to see anyone on the other. The flowers were those weird kinds that look like penises and vaginas – only recently featuring on the floral scene and totally ghastly. I managed, with a great show of jollity and apology, to get the centrepiece moved. ('Oh, isn't it beautiful, but darling I want to *see* you when you talk!'), but felt that I could hardly make demands about the candles too, so all the guests had to dodge round them to speak. Every time I looked across the table I felt like a prison visitor in Wormwood Scrubs.

Yes, bad mood. The older I get, the more of a loose cannon I become at dinner parties. Nine times out of ten, I can shine and be good fun, but the tenth I start yelling about inappropriate things, like how great euthanasia or abortion is, or how wrong it is to give aid to Africa, and everyone gets frightfully hot under the collar and embarrassed. They say that this outspokenness is something to do with the synapses atrophying in the frontal lobes as you get older, but I think it's just the ludicrous confidence that comes with age. This time we got on to the subject, sparked off by Mrs Glasses-on-Strings revealing (as they so often do these days) that, being sixty, she had just received her Freedom Pass, and how wonderful it was travelling on public transport for nothing.

I said I would be sixty in a few months, and couldn't wait.

'Yes,' said Mrs Glasses-on-Strings, trying to ingratiate herself with me. 'You're only as old as you feel. Sixty years young!'

'Sixty going on twenty!' said the therapist.

'I really can't agree,' I said. 'If you're sixty, you're sixty. Sixty is old. I am just longing to be old, and I don't want to be told I'm young, when I'm not. I'm fed up with being young. Boring. I was young in the sixties, and once, believe it or not, I slept with a Beatle. Been there, got the teeshirt, worn it to death and put it in a bag for Age Concern. When I was twenty, sixty was old, when I was thirty, forty and fifty, sixty was still old. I'm not going to change the goalposts now.'

'I'm sixty,' said Marion, as she smilingly collected the plates. (It's an odd fact that most men never realize when empty dishes are being stacked up. The therapist, who no doubt in his work prided himself on his acute sensitivity to other people's feelings, sat with his plate firmly in front of him, unaware that major operations were being carried out that required his cooperation.) 'But I don't feel a day over thirty!'

'But, Marion, don't you realize that that's *tragic*?' I said. 'To continue feeling thirty for the whole of your life! So boring! A nightmare! I'm longing to feel sixty! What's wrong with that?'

'The great thing about age,' said the therapist, whose wife had finally leaned over the table and taken his plate, 'is that it's never too late. You can do so many things. Take an Open University degree, go bungee-jumping, learn a new language . . .'

'But it *is* too late!' I argued. 'That's what's so great about being old. You no longer have to think about going to university, or go bungee-jumping! It's a huge release! I've been feeling guilty about not learning another language for most of my adult life. At last I find that now, being old, I don't have to! There aren't enough years left to speak it. It'd be pointless!'

'Well, I feel,' said the therapist, defiantly, 'that now I am sixty-five, anything is possible.'

'I find, approaching sixty,' I replied, 'that the real pleasure is that so many things are *impossible*. I think,' I added, cruelly, putting my hand on his arm and smiling a great deal to pretend I meant no harm, 'that you're in what you therapists call denial.'

This time I got the laugh, but it was cheap and I felt ashamed.

As I drove back I was sorry for the poor old therapist, finding himself sitting next to rancid old me. Felt really guilty and horrible and wished I hadn't been so acid. Like me, the poor man probably would have far preferred to have sat next to a lovely young person instead.

October 11

Woke feeling absolutely terrible, all the 1,001 muscles in my face still trapped in a rictus of insincerity. Knew, even worse, that I would have to suffer this cramped feeling till the following morning when the poison of the ghastly evening had finally drained from my body.

To make matters worse, I looked terrible. Last night before I went to the party I saw in the mirror a raging beauty, with incredible olive skin, high cheekbones, a sensitive mouth, utterly ravishing. But when I glanced in the mirror this morning, I couldn't believe what stared back at me – I looked grotesque; Charles Laughton in a dressing gown. My face was like an uncooked doughnut. Piggy eyes, small, pursed, pale-lipped mouth, deep frown-marks, all puff. Revolting. What is it that happens in the night? Clearly Something – God knows what – Collects. Or perhaps it was the Rioja. Or perhaps, more likely, the therapist, quite understandably, had put a curse on me.

Jumped into the bath (perhaps 'jump' is not the word; 'clambered into' might be a better way of describing it, and yes, I do have a funny rubber mat with suckers underneath, lying on the bottom) and found that none of the rest of my body is puffy – just becoming wrinkly, like an Austrian blind. I can see, now, my grandmother's arms sticking out of my shoulders, my skin becoming fine and papery and shiny, like hers. As I loved her so much, I don't mind the sight. But cripes, I'm only fifty-nine. Soon I'll be sixty. And I mean soon. In the next three months. Will everything collapse even further, I wonder?

Even now, when I do my noble ten minutes of yoga a day, I see small folds of skin waiting to tumble down my thighs. They're particularly in evidence when I do a shoulder-stand with my legs in the air. They've got strange marks on them – thread veins, the odd hint of a varicose vein. My upper arms have wobbly bits hanging from them. The backs of my hands are speckled with brown spots. When did they appear? Only a few years ago, I think, when I could pretend to myself (talk about in denial!) that I was about thirty. Now, my entire body is shrieking at me that I am old. And what's so utterly strange is that I don't really mind a bit. It feels rather comfortable, friendly – and right.

OK, my skin's not young and springy with that wonderful peachy bloom and a fuzz of fine downy hair. But it's still good, like an expensive but worn old leather sofa from a gentleman's club in Pall Mall.

The older I get, I've decided, the more I am determined to look not so much like some deserted vandalized community hall in Hull, but more like a beautiful ruined abbey of the kind immortalized by Poussin – or the other painter who begins with P. Name escapes me . . . Or is it C?

When I got out of the bath and reached for the towel I remembered the time, as a child, I excitedly told my father that I had discovered a brilliant new way of drying myself.

'How?' he had asked. I showed him. With the towel around my back, I took one corner in each hand. I then pulled on each end alternately.

'Isn't it a good method?' I said.

My father smiled indulgently. 'I remember when I discovered that, around exactly your age,' he said.

It was the first moment in my life when I had the revelation – a revelation that I have again and again and again – that not only what I think is an original thought has been thought time and time again by people throughout the ages but, worse, that thoughts that I imagine are new to myself are often thoughts that I have had again and again throughout my life. The treadmillness and groundhog-dayery of it all is both depressing and, oddly, reassuring. It would be good, however, to have a brand-new thought just once in one's life. I remember only recently realizing that you could hold two feelings in yourself at the same time, that you could both like someone and dislike them in one go, that you could both want a cigarette and want to give up smoking.

As one who sees life rather in black and white – strong hates and loves – I have always tried to compromise by seeing everything in a kind of grey. The trick is not to do that at all, but to manage to hold the contrasts in oneself at exactly the same time. That results in a much more lively and invigorating approach. Very late in the day to discover that thought, but it has made relationships with people far, far easier. And, oddly, kinder.

I then got dressed. Not an easy business these days. I think I used to balance on one foot when I put on my tights. Now I sit on the bed and roll back like a hedgehog as I tug them on, legs waggling in the air.

October 20

The new lodger arrived. Well, I say lodger. Michelle is the daughter of Parisian friends, and she wants a base in London from where she can look for somewhere congenial to live. She is utterly adorable. She is young! She is blonde! She is only nineteen but, of course, being French she is more like a sixteen-year-old English girl. She clearly has absolutely no idea how pretty she is, though she dresses beautifully. I opened the door to her on a bitter, grey, West London day. She stood, wearing three-quarter-length black pedalo trousers and only a thin cotton top over a bare tummy. On the ground were five enormous suitcases.

' 'Allo,' she said. 'I am Michelle.'

That was about the sum total of her English. She says 'Sank you' a lot. She seemed very pleased with the room I offered her, despite the fact that it is painted a dark abattoir-red, is lined with my books, has space in the cupboard for only about three things to hang up and half the chest of drawers is made over to screwdrivers, pipe-wrenches, hammers, sandpaper, electric drills and old light fittings.

'Beeg,' she said.

I suppose it is rather 'beeg' compared to most of the frightful shoe boxes foreign girls are offered in London. I gave her the usual spiel, in rather bad French, about how we must live completely separate lives, we do not share anything except the bathroom and the kitchen, that she has only about two inches of space in the fridge, we do not use each other's milk, and that she is not allowed in the garden . . .

Every time I give this talk I feel such a creep, but it is honed from long experience of lodgers. Once, when Jack, my son, was two years old, I found him pottering around the house one morning in the company of a huge dog. And when I went in to find the owner, a gigantic tattooed slob who was snoring next to my lodger, I found three candles burning around the bed.

But later, as Michelle and I sat on the sofa in my sitting room, I had to really steel myself to say that we would never, ever share a meal, that although it was fine for her to ask me if she needed help with anything, I had my life and she had hers – because I could feel maternal feelings stealing through me like some kind of chemical.

Later she crept down the stairs and I could hear her standing outside the room where I potter about doing bits and pieces, terrified to disturb me. I stopped typing out a furious letter to

Then there's a strange place that advertises itself solely as Women's Clothes and Islamic Books. Everywhere is interspersed, however, with the most wonderful middle-Eastern supermarkets, including the rather ineptly named Lebanese Butchery, which cater to the local mosque.

There *is* a delicatessen in Shepherds Bush, but so few people buy the cheeses it sells that when you do buy them you find they're all covered with a strange sort of elderly sticky, smelly slime. Hope that doesn't happen to me when I get old. No, Shepherds Bush may be an 'eccentric and delightful mix of ethnic diversity' (I'm quoting from one of my many letters to the *Shepherds Bush Gazette*), but the drawbacks are that the pavements (just Tarmac – we haven't yet risen to paving stones round here) are thick with chewing gum, and the streets swarm with hoodies.

Shepherds Bush is one of those places which have always been 'up and coming' but has never actually up and come. Like those promising writers. True, it is not exactly down and going, but it has never arrived.

However, compared to Brixton, where my son, Jack, and Chrissie, his girlfriend, live, Shepherds Bush still seems to be vaguely on the up. After hearing all the rumours about Brixton, I'm scared to look anyone in the eye in the streets. Jack assures me there are only a couple of crazies about, like there are everywhere, but it's easy for him to say because he did psychology at university and knows all about body language. Recently Penny told me she's heard that there's a South London gang which goes round the streets in a car with no lights on at night and, as some initiation rite, they have to follow the first person who kindly flashes them to alert them that they are driving lightless, and kill them. It sounds like an urban myth, but she checked with a policeman and it's true.

Nov 8th

This evening Penny came round and, over red mullet and a delicious Portuguese white wine which is only 9 per cent, we discussed doctors. We are both tremendous hypochondriacs and I calm Penny down when she is convinced she has cancer of the bones and she calms me down when I become convinced I have cancer of the oesophagus on account of the fact that I have drunk so much in my life and still, it has to be said, chuck down well over half a bottle of white wine every night. At least. I'm afraid anyone who knows the alcohol content of the wine she's drinking is definitely on the way to the skids.

Of course it's fine chucking white wine down yourself when you're young, but apparently, if you do it long enough, it erodes, as I read in some terrifying health piece in the *Daily Mail*, all the tiny little wiggly bits, or fibulae (?) on the way down, and the mucus can no longer collect and settle and moisten the whole thing, and it becomes a kind of arid passage, ripe, apparently, for cancer germs or spores or whatever they are, to flourish.

I told her I'd made an appointment with a surgeon tomorrow to see about my feet. My feet are a nightmare – dry and cracked (gnarled might be a better word, actually. What is it about the 'g' in 'gnarled' that makes it such a cruel word?). I keep thinking I ought to get some Scholl's cream to rub into them. 'Has it come to that?' said Penny. 'Come to that': an expression I'll be hearing a lot more in future, I suspect.

But the real problem is the huge, agonizing bunion on one foot, inherited from my mother. Fixing the bunion will cure the pain, according to my podiatrist, one of a profession that hadn't been invented when I was born, a man who has already sucked me dry of nearly all my savings by insisting that I need special orthotics, or supports.

He's tried all sorts of things already, of course. He gave me a catalogue of special shoes, none of which I could ever dream of wearing. Most of them were 'stone-coloured' and there were lots of trainers modelled by glamorous young girls who never in a million years would wear that kind of footwear. In real life, they're worn more often by women who seem to spend much of their time in service stations, women with huge, fat swollen ankles and purple knees covered by very clean beige trousers, sporting mysterious kinds of blokish haircuts.

Penny is worried about HRT. She spends a lot of her time trying to get the balance right between oestrogen and progesterone, and is convinced that too much of one gives her panic attacks. Luckily I gave it up three months ago, and it's made not the slightest bit of difference. If anything, I think I look and feel rather better. I can now spot women on HRT – they all have a Teresa Gorman look about them, with huge boobs and unnaturally plumped-up skin.

Not sure I like the idea of hormones at all, really. I always remember when I once taught in an all-girls' school and became so freaked out on hearing that women working in close proximity menstruated at the same time that I held my breath every time I went up or down in the lift, in case my cycle started to think about getting synchronized. I couldn't bear the idea of us all bleeding away at the same time every month.

What a blessing to be rid of all that! It wasn't the blood I minded; that was a very minor bore. No, it was the endless noting its date down in my diary, I remember, and then, a week before a period was due, writing: 'Might feel weird . . .' to remind myself that any mood I got myself into should be regarded with suspicion. It is very unnerving to realize that one's actual personality can be dominated by hormonal fluctuations. But no longer, ho ho! When I was young we used to call it the 'curse', but that extremely accurate and descriptive word has been erased by political correctness, along with other essential pieces of vocabulary like 'cripples', 'loonies', 'nutters' and 'old bats', many of which apply to me.

'By the way, do you floss your teeth?' I asked Penny before she left.

'Not a lot, no, why?' she said.

'All my teeth seem to have great gaps between them, suddenly,' I said. 'My mouth looks like castellation on a medieval turret.'

'It's because your gums have receded,' said Penny. 'They do when you get older, you know.'

'Oh, God. The trouble is that when I floss my teeth, not only can I feel all my fillings wiggling about, but my gums start to bleed. You don't know a good dentist, do you?'

'Well,' said Penny, rummaging around in her bag for a phone number. 'It just so happens, that I do. This is one I went to last week . . .'

Out of her bag fluttered a couple of photographs. I picked one up. It was of a man in full leathers standing by an enormous motorbike. 'Friend of yours?' I asked jokily, as I handed it back.

'Oh, er, no,' said Penny, clearly embarrassed as she stuffed it back into her bag. 'No one. Lovely evening. Must dash.'

Later

Thinking things over I wondered about that photograph. Penny's illegitimate son? But she hasn't got one, as far as I know. Her only child is Lisa, a wayward daughter of thirty-five, who lives on benefits, much to her mother's despair, and whose biological clock is ticking so loudly you can hear it from Herefordshire, where she lives.

Then the penny dropped. It could only be one thing. A man from Dating Direct. Penny had told me she was thinking of logging on, but I never thought she'd actually get round to it. I rushed upstairs to my computer and scurried around the site, and very soon, to my amazement, found her. There was a picture of her which must have been taken before I ever knew her – it looked as if she were about fifteen – and beside it were written the words: 'Fun-loving, intelligent, good figure, likes reading, walking and singing. Vegetarian though will eat fish. Looking for like-minded non-smoker. Age: 48.'

Forty-eight! My jaw dropped. She's only a tiny bit younger than me! But mustn't say anything as it would be too humiliating for her.

I've never gone on-line for a man, but I have, on occasion, trawled through the small ads. The men sometimes sound OK in the written ads, and then it all turns to dust when you ring their box number and listen to their frightful voices.

'Hello!' they say, reading off a script which they have, it's clear, been practising at home. 'I'm sixty-five years young and have a good sense of humour and still, I hope, a sense of adventure.' This is usually said with an artificial chuckle. 'I hope I'm presentable – my female friends say that for a bloke with a bald head and a bit of a paunch, I'm very attractive! But that'll be up to you to decide! I like going to the theatre, walking, wining and dining. I love music and I go to the gym two or three times a week. I have two dogs – so if you don't like animals you're not the woman for me! I care deeply about the environment and my ideal day would be a morning walking, followed by a drink and a good meal in a country pub, followed by, perhaps, a good film or a discussion about a book we've both read. I know you're out there! Why don't you "go for it" and contact me? Whatever you feel, I wish you all the luck in the world to find that special person . . .'

Of course while I listen, I'm sitting back in my little house puking and sneering over every word. Goes to the gym three times a week? Has he nothing better to do? As for discussing books, forget it. As far as I'm concerned there are only two phrases to describe books. One is: 'Absolutely brilliant! You must read it!' or 'Total crap. Don't touch it with a bargepole.' And what exactly, might I ask, does the verb 'to wine' mean? I know about 'whining', indeed, I'm an expert, but 'wining'? 'I wine, you wine, he wines, we wine, you wine, they wine?' Surely not. Does it mean to get pissed? Or does it mean ordering a glass of warm Chardonnay or Pinot Grigio at the Goat and Duck from a bottle that was opened last July?

Oh dear, I'm such an old meanie. The awful thing is that these blokes often *do* sound rather sweet, in spite of their ghastly habits. But GSOH! OHAT (Good Sense of Humour. Own Hair and Teeth)! Preserve me!

In fact I'm often amazed by my women friends who manage to make really good sexual relationships with men. For me, they (relationships) have always been fantastically complicated affairs, like trying to set the video recorder to record in advance, and invariably end in tears. I think men must join the long list of things that I am never going to manage to master, like the stock market, the history of China, the structure of the European Union and tap-dancing. I am seriously thinking of giving them (men, that is) up for good.

These thoughts were checked by my cat, Pouncer, winding his tail around my legs, so I carefully picked off all the remaining red mullet from the bones and gave it to him. He sniffed at it and then looked at me in an angry, hurt way, as if he'd been offered a dish of arsenic. Aren't cats funny? Red mullet does cost £8 a lb after all. Whoops, I mean kilothings. There are some things I have decided I will never get the hang of, and kilothings is one of them.

Nov 9th

This morning I knocked on Michelle's door to see if she was OK.

'I am good,' she said, staring straight ahead of her. She was lying in bed in an orange bedjacket made, it seemed, entirely from feathers, and a pair of knickers, watching breakfast telly. I asked if she'd been looking for flats. 'No, not a beet,' she said. 'I like it here. You are like my muzair.'

As her 'muzair', as far as I remember her when I last met her on the Champs-Elysees, is a gorgeous and seductively slim blonde who looks about nineteen, wears top to toe leather, and has a card which reads 'Juliette Fontaine: Lady of Leisure. Expertise: Shopping and Bopping!' in French, I don't quite know what to make of it all.

(I, on the other hand, am, natch, full of quiet dignity, groan with Protestant work ethic, and rarely spend any money at all. I was born to scrimp and save, keep pieces of string, iron old wrapping paper for use a second time around, and believe it or not, even keep my tights going by cutting off one half when one leg ladders, and wearing it with another single leg to get the most wear out of them. 'You don't!' said Penny, incredulously, when I told her. 'I do!' I said. I may be a wild child of the sixties still with a penchant for gorgeous clothes from Whistles and Agnès b., but I'm also a frugal war baby – an odd combination. We both are.)

Hope Michelle will be able to cope with the house on her own while I'm away this weekend staying with Lucy.

November 10th

Got up at six and spent the whole morning putting yellow stickers everywhere as reminders for Michelle. 'Have you double-locked?' is stuck to the front door. 'Remember to feed Pouncer!!' is on the door to her room. A series of arrows along the floor leads to my sitting room, ending up by the window, with the instruction: 'Shut the shutters at night!' on the final one. The cooker features a warning: 'Turn all gas off before going out or going to bed!' On the floor by Pouncer's food is one with an arrow pointing to a bowl. 'Pouncer's water! Keep filled up!'

And on the kitchen table is a huge list of the phone numbers of Hughie and James (ex-half-brother-in-law), Penny, my mobile, my number in the country, the vet's number, the emergency vet's number . . . plus various other bits of information about where the burglar alarm is situated, who to ring if it goes off, where the fuse-box is . . . The house looks as if it's all set up for a treasure hunt.

Finally got off at midday, utterly exhausted with ironing clothes, putting things in my suitcase then taking them out again, worrying about whether one bottle of champagne was a good enough house present or whether I should take two or whether that would look flash.

I drove off, and on the way down decided to look in on my father's grave. It's in a lovely village churchyard.

Whenever I tell people that I've been to see his grave, they usually get very serious and mournful and say how 'brave' I am, or how moving it must be, or some clichéd bit of nonsense. But when I visit, I don't just think of him, and how I miss him. I also think how incredibly grateful I am to him for popping off reasonably early. He was seventy when he died, but unbelievably I know a man of seventy-five who's *still* visiting his ancient, confused mother. It must be such a burden. Staggering up to some old people's home, riddled with arthritis yourself, to visit a living corpse who doesn't even recognize you. What a life. Or, rather, what a living death.

Both my parents are dead, luckily missing the 'live for ever' generation from which I also hope to escape with a mixture of bravery and cunning. And sad as it is that they've gone, it's good, too. After all, I don't think you ever really become yourself while your parents are alive. Until they go, you're still, at some level, someone's child.

When my father died, I felt sad, but I also felt like a plant which had been struggling to survive under a giant rhododendron bush, a bush that was so abundant and magnificent, that flowered so richly every year, that spread its beautiful great green glossy leaves so broadly, that there was hardly any place for me to breathe.

So when I went to see him in his grave, it was really to say thanks for dying. It's when I know how he'd laugh if he heard me that I really miss him.

Lucy lives in a cottage deep in the country. She's a wistful-looking person, tender, funny and deeply compassionate: she runs a charity for asylum seekers, and spends her entire life, as far as I can see, visiting wretched Rumanians – or Romanians as they appear to be called these days – who live in frightful compounds all over Britain, and helping them fill in forms to get them out. Or fund-raising. Or campaigning for their rights.

Anyway, during the weekend Lucy told me she had been awarded an MBE, and when I asked how she was planning to celebrate, I was horrified when she told me that she was simply going to 'come down to London, get the award, have a pizza at Pizza Express and go home'.

I couldn't believe my ears. 'But we must have a party!' I said. I'm terrible about parties. I love going to them and giving them. Any excuse. 'I'll give one for you!'

November 14

Now, as I start writing invitations to total strangers – Lucy gave me a guest list – I begin to feel slightly anxious. It's bad enough giving a party oneself, but giving one for someone else – everything has to be immaculate. Was this, as my father used to ask, wise?

Nov 18

Came downstairs to find Maciej, my gorgeous Polish cleaner, sobbing his eyes out over the kitchen table. Turns out his pregnant girlfriend has run off with his best friend. I really love Maciej. He has fine features, like Chopin, and wonderful long hair tied in a pony-tail – the only man I've ever seen who looks good with one. He's not bad with a Hoover, either. Naturally, back in Poland he trained to be a biochemist or a brain surgeon or something, but can't get a job here so is reduced to cleaning.

I put my arms round him and gave him a hug and made him some tea, and he smoked a cigarette and told me all about it, and then Michelle came in and he quickly pulled himself together and started wiping the surfaces.

December 1

Penny helped me shop for the party at Marks and Spencer, which was very nice of her since she's not coming. She's got to go to see her daughter, Lisa, who's recovering from a broken love affair.

'Men!' said Penny, as we stared into the freezer section

hoping to find a thousand frozen sausage rolls for under a tenner. As it was, we found only fourteen 'Indian-style' cocktail snacks for a million quid.

'We'd need about a hundred of those,' I said. 'Too expensive.'

'Are we reduced to Iceland?'

'We are,' I said. 'Anyway. Men! Poor Lisa. I'm planning to give them up.'

'I didn't know you had any to give up,' said Penny. 'Anyway, this boyfriend of Lisa's, he was just so sweet! And then he says he's frightened of commitment and gives her the boot. When am I ever going to have grandchildren?'

'Well, I asked Jack the other day when I might hear the patter of tiny feet, and he just said, rather tersely, that I should get a dog, and then I'd hear the patter of four tiny feet,' I told her.

Penny said: 'I used to say to Lisa: "Wait till you're married before you get pregnant," and then I said: "Wait till you're in a stable relationship." And now I say: "Oh, darling, why don't you stop taking the pill and just have a few one-night stands?"'

December 2nd

It was a freezing cold day, but I dragged myself up to Harley Street to see the bunion man. A nice bloke – not the usual private consultant with a bow tie and a snotty voice and a bedside manner that oozes out of him like oil. He had a cockney accent and a practical manner, more like a builder than a medical man.

'Oooh, you've got a right one there,' he said, looking at my feet, in much the same way as a gardener might remark on spotting a fearful display of greenfly, or a plumber might declare on discovering a giant leak. It is, indeed, a 'right one',

25

a huge red sore lump that makes it impossible to buy any shoes other than comfortable ones. Not that I'd want to buy uncomfortable ones, but now and again it would be nice to be able to slip into an Emma Hope or a Jimmy Choo without screaming.

'Inherited, you know,' he added, writing up his notes. 'Anyone else in the family got one?'

'We all have bunions like this,' I said, not without some pride. 'It's known as the Sharp bunion. My mother, who had one, tried hard to prevent my developing one by shoving me into Start-rite shoes from an early age, and getting my feet X-rayed on those evil machines that you used to see in shoe shops before they realized that they were belting out radiation to all their customers. She even took me to see Dr Scholl, forcing me to wear metal supports in my shoes for three years. But nothing made any difference.'

The bunion man scoffed. 'Wouldn't,' he said. 'When would you like to come in?'

'Hang on a minute,' I said. I felt I was being rather oversold. 'What does it entail?'

It turns out that these days you don't have to have your leg in plaster for six weeks, which is a relief, and it is all done incredibly quickly under a local anaesthetic. Then your feet are shoved into rather weird shoes for a couple of weeks, then comfortable shoes for six, and then – 'Manolo Blanket, here we come,' I interrupted, cheerfully.

'Blahnik,' he said. 'And there's no pain, you're walking within two hours.'

'Done,' I said.

It's booked for January.

Oh dear. Is this wise?

December 3rd

The big day of the party. A grey Thursday afternoon, and I had pushed back all the chairs in my sitting room, sprayed it with something weird from Floris that someone had given me many Christmases back, put out the thinly sliced salami, shaken the crisps into bowls, distributed the trays of water biscuits covered with cream and salmon eggs, checked that the sparkly wine was cooling in the fridge, given the final touches to the flowers in the corners and polished the glasses. A thousand mini-sausage rolls from Iceland were crackling in the oven.

Glasses-polishing is very important as you get older. Jack's late godfather lived with his wife in a grisly bungalow in a private estate by the Thames, and the big drawback to visiting them, in their old age, was the filth. Cat hairs everywhere. All the surfaces covered with stickiness. And those smeary glasses. Not just that, but they used miniature plastic footballs as an alternative to ice-cubes and, in every one of the indentations of these pink and blue spheres, lay grey and greasy dirt.

As a result, I am scrupulous in the glasses department. (I'm told by Hughie that the older you get, the more important it is to be clean. New shirt twice a day, is his motto, and the tie must be checked hourly for stains. Bottoms of trousers also must be monitored in case they've brushed in the mud, and shoes must be polished every morning.)

There was a lovely expectant pre-party feeling to the room. I closed the shutters, put on the lights, turned on a low piano boogie . . . sat down and felt those confused feelings, a mixture of excited anticipation and a sinking feeling, wondering why the hell I'd thought of arranging a party in the first place. I wouldn't know anyone there, it was stupid of me, everyone would think I was pathetic, didn't have any friends of my own,

I would just be doing a skivvying job. Thank goodness Hughie was coming to help with the drinks-pouring.

The phone kept ringing. One person asked nervously: 'Could you tell me – is it *safe* to park near your house?' Clearly from the country.

The fake fire puttered in the grate. On the mantelpiece in a silver frame sat a picture of Jack and Chrissie – Chrissie looking stunning as ever, with long blonde hair and rather a sultry expression, and Jack looking pale and tense, smoking, his eyes bright red dots like Satan, and wearing, of all things, a suit. It had been taken a year ago, at his grandmother's memorial service in Ireland, on the cold, grey day when she was buried, amid lots of champagne, laughter and memories of her fey Irishness, her madness.

I had once gone round to her flat in Kensington and in the window frame was jammed a large cardboard sign, made from an old cornflakes packet. On it she had scrawled: 'Who killed the owl in Avondale Park? Murder most foul. I know who killed the owl.' When I knocked, she shouted: 'Who is it?' I said it was me, and she yelled: 'Go away, you thief!'

The phone rang again. 'What should we wear?' A bit late to ask that, I thought. I was wearing a very nice orange and green spotted skirt from Hobbs, a black teeshirt from Shepherds Bush market and a large paste brooch belonging to my mother and I looked rather mad and smart.

Outside, someone shouted 'Fuck off!' into a mobile. I think it was a mobile. There was no answer. A dog started barking and a child started wailing. 'Fucking cunt!' shouted some-one else. ''Oo you callin' a fucking *cunt?*' The arguing voices faded down the street. 'You said . . .' 'I did not say . . .' 'Fucking did . . .'

The phone rang again. It was Jack.

'Can you talk?' he asked. An odd question.

'Oh, hi, darling,' I said. 'Actually, I'm just sitting here feeling like a total wally waiting for people to arrive for a party that I suddenly wish I weren't giving. How are you?'

'Well, Mum,' he said. 'I've got some news to tell you. Perhaps now's not the best time.' I could hear excitement in his voice. I just couldn't imagine what he was going to tell me. An article he'd written for *Psychology Today* had been accepted? He'd inherited a fortune from a distant relative of his dad?

'No, tell me now,' I said. 'No one's here yet.'

'Not even Hughie?'

'No, he's late again.'

'Well. Chrissie's pregnant.'

I could not believe my ears.

'*What!*' I said, like an idiot. '*What!*'

Then a huge feeling started to creep over me. Those words were like the splitting open of a dark rock. It was as if all my life the sky had been covered with thick, dark clouds and suddenly they'd parted to let a huge, dazzling shaft of hot sun pour through. I felt as if I had been drenched in happiness – no – more than that, as if I was being totally immersed and marinated in joy. It was a completely unfamiliar feeling. The carpet had been pulled from under my feet, and had sent me cascading into a golden cavern, as if all the happiness that I had found it so difficult to garner throughout my whole life had been waiting, behind a door, which had suddenly opened, letting it burst out all at once.

'But don't tell anyone,' he said, unaware of the transformation that was going on the other end of the phone, 'because we have to keep quiet about it for three months till it's OK. But we had to tell you. What do you think?'

Perhaps my silence had rather unnerved him. 'I think . . . darling . . . I can't speak,' I said, tears springing to my eyes. 'I think it's just, just *wonderful*. Oh, how *wonderful*!'

Just then, through the shutters, I saw the security light go on, and heard the bang of the gate. Someone was staring at the door outside, wondering whether to knock or ring. What a moment to have a party.

'Let's talk later, darling,' I said. I stumbled, barely conscious with elation, towards the door and opened it to greet Hughie, who'd arrived with Lucy and her family. She was wearing a little black hat, with a sparkling pin in it, and a sparkling skirt. She looked very nervous and very happy as she came into the room. 'Oh, Marie, how lovely!' she exclaimed. 'What can we do? Doesn't everything look *charming*!'

I just grinned back like someone on drugs.

Of course the party went beautifully, but I just couldn't concentrate on anything anyone said. The problem was, I wanted to tell everyone, particularly Lucy, so sympathetic and herself already a grandmother. But I knew I could say nothing. I felt as if I were stoned. It was like the first time I ever smoked dope. My head seemed swollen with an indescribably intense feeling of – what? Intensity, is the only useless answer I can give. My whole body felt encased in cotton wool, and warmth. By the end of the party I thought I was going to burst.

Everyone had gone, and Hughie had stayed behind to help me fix some electrical fault that had blacked the party out, luckily, at the very end. Realizing there was nothing we could do, we decided to leave it and he drove me to the restaurant where we were having supper with Marion and Tim.

'Well, that went well,' said Hughie. His car is all old and glamorous and leathery (he is pretty old and glamorous too, actually, but not at all leathery), and I sank back in blissful silence. Finally I could hold myself back no longer.

'Hughie, I have a secret but I can't tell anyone and it's killing me. Will you promise not to repeat it to anyone, not even James?'

He promised, with a twinkle in his eye.

'Jack and Chrissie are pregnant!' I said.

'How marvellous!' he replied. 'Congratulations! So you'll be a grannie!'

'Grannie Sharp,' I said, trying the words out for the first time. 'I think it's what I've been hoping for all my life. It's what I've always wanted to be when I grew up. Oh, I'm so happy!'

December 14th

Christmas is coming. Always a dodgy time for us singles. Chrissie and Jack are spending Christmas with Jack's dad, David, which is sad but at least it means that I can get next Christmas with the new baby, so it's worth sacrificing this Christmas. Michelle is going to her family in Paris, Penny's going to Lisa, and Marion and Tim say they're having an open-house Christmas 'for all the lonely flotsam and jetsam who don't have a family to go to'. Not sure I really want to be categorized as a bit of 'lonely flotsam or jetsam', sounding, as it does, rather scummy and washed-up, though it's very nice of them. Anyway, I'm not going to be a lonely flotsam or jetsam because I'm going to go round to Hughie and James. So ner.

Dec 21

Got this round-robin letter with a Christmas card from an old school friend who lives in the country:

As the festivities approach, I find myself in the middle of a Christmas decoration course on Wednesdays. We all bring fir cones and spray them with glitter. When I went last time, a small bit of spray landed on our teacher. She said she looked like a Christmas fairy! We all nearly died laughing but I'm afraid it was because she is so portly that none of us could imagine her on top of a tree! On the way back I nearly slipped on a leaf – but thank the Lord, I managed to steady myself, so no damage was done!!! The key was very stiff in the door when I returned, but luckily I have the 'knack' so managed to get back to my snug home. I didn't like to think what the neighbours would have thought had they witnessed me trying to 'break and enter' my own house! I think I would have had some explaining to do to PC Plod – had he, of course, had the time to spare from catching speeding motorists to come to my aid!!!

And on, and on and on.

Think I may be getting a cold as have funny feeling like buzzing of bees at the back of my nose. Always a bad sign.

Dec 25

Oh God, oh God, oh God! Have had to spend the whole of Christmas day in bed as have such ghastly cough and cold and flu. I can barely drag myself downstairs or upstairs. I can't even drink, which is a sign of how incredibly ill I am. For the last few days have thought I was going to die and I've felt extremely self-pitying. I take my temperature nearly every hour, just to see whether I have one or not. So far it's below normal – which sometimes I think is worse than above. It is extraordinary that, even at nearly sixty, when one's feeling down, one longs for one's mum. When I'd taken to my bed a couple of days ago, I heard Michelle going up the stairs to her room to pack, past my bedroom, and realized she wasn't going to put her head round the door and say ' 'Allo'. I found myself bursting into tears. I mean, why should she? I have told her enough times that we live separate lives. And I know that if

I'd called out and asked her to get me anything, she would have jumped into loving and attentive action. But when one's ill one doesn't want to make the effort. No, we want to be cared for by people who are psychically attuned to our every desire. We want our mums.

Sky outside is awful kind of green colour.

When I went to see my grandmother, Phyllis, in an old people's home, several of the inmates were yelling for their mothers. After a few moments which I spent sitting in the hall trying to read a Waitrose magazine, I was shown into the sitting room where all the inhabitants were screaming and grimacing while, in the background, *The Simpsons* seemed to be playing on a loop. I realized I had no idea which one she was. None of the sad creatures had any teeth, their legs were all like sticks, and every one of them, except the ones who were asleep, had wild, staring eyes and white hair. Finally I worked it out (well, I think I worked it out) and my grandmother (well, I hope it was my grandmother) was wheeled back to her room to have tea with me.

Unfortunately she had no idea who she was or who I was. She made absolutely no sense whatever, and kept pulling up her skirts and trying to put Bourbon biscuits down her bra. Then, for about twenty minutes, she picked up my Waitrose magazine and stared, brow furrowed, at a picture of a mushroom risotto. I eventually eased the magazine from her grasp, and then, when she wasn't reaching over and trying to pick the flowers off my floral skirt, she attempted to make a house out of the saucers and biscuits and cups of tea on the tray with disastrous results. Finally I pushed them out of her reach saying, firmly: 'No, you don't want any more tea. It's all old and cold.'

Suddenly my grandmother looked up at me. 'Old and cold!' she said. 'Just like me!' For a moment she was at her amusing best. Then she relapsed back into gibberish. It was a dreadfully

33

sad and unnerving experience. Why did I think of this? Oh, yes. Flu making you want your mum, just like the people in my grandmother's care home. So sad.

I could think of nothing for hours, except the miseries of living too long, until the phone rang and it was James, who said he was coming by with a turkey dinner on a plate covered with foil, and a bottle of champagne, and though he wouldn't come in because he didn't want to catch my horrible disease, he'd ring the bell and leave it on the doorstep.

This time I burst into tears of gratitude and affection, and suddenly now, after a couple of glasses of champagne – funny how I can drink champagne at *any* time – and a telly turkey supper I feel on the mend at last. James is a darling.

December 28th

Had to sign a credit slip for some petrol today. My pen didn't appear to be working. When I looked closer I found that I was trying to write with the thermometer which had found its way into my handbag, using the mercury as the point. Embarrassedly stuffed it back in my bag with a hysterical laugh.

Dec 31st

Much, much better. Went round to Hughie and James for New Year's Eve supper. Must explain Hughie and James's situation. James is Jack's half-uncle – David's half-brother. Oh, dear, all the halves and sixths and steps these days. It used to be bad enough with people being second cousin once removed, but the half situation is a nightmare. I have, for instance, a half-brother. I call him my half-brother, because he is and because he was born when I was twenty-five and he is a total stranger to me, lives in South Africa, making him even more of a mystery. He, on the other hand, calls me his sister because, presumably, when he was born I was on the scene and quite naturally he sees me as a full relation. When I told Penny about my scrupulosity, she said I must suffer from Asperger's syndrome. Charming. I said she should know – she'd read enough about it in the *Family Doctor* book that is her bible.

Anyway, James is Jack's half-uncle, and a very nice, but rather over-sentimental creature who used to be in marketing but now does odd jobs, digging people's gardens, decorating, taking dogs for a walk. He says he's never been happier. He's one of the kindest people I know, always prone to tears, incredibly involved in alternative medicine and 'spiritual' things. Anyway, he's gay and he's lived with Hughie for twenty years and I love both of them to pieces.

Hughie, on the other hand, is dry and funny, and he's the sort of bloke of the two, well, more of the bloke. I never understand why they're together, nice as James is, but end up with that dreadful cliché that everyone comes up with when they simply can't understand why two people are a couple: 'It must be the great sex.' Then one's mind boggles, and very soon one has to start thinking about something else.

Hughie still works as a solicitor, at sixty-five, but you wouldn't know it, one of those sorts of people. He's always reading Spinoza and the *Times Literary Supplement*, has read Goethe twice in the original German, goes to the opera till he's blue in the face and knows all about classical music and the difference between Pliny and Plato, about which, to my shame, I know nothing.

I used to go to parties on New Year's Eve but, like most of the rest of the world, I now discover, have never enjoyed them. Why didn't everyone tell me before that they hated them? I wouldn't have felt so out of it. When I was young we never really did New Year's Eve. We never did Mother's Day or Father's Day actually, and when David and I got married we just went to a registry office, had a few people round for a glass of champagne and went to the Lake District for a week for the honeymoon. Nowadays you go to a wedding and you have to give up half your life . . . breakfasts, dinners, teas, parties, staying over at local bed and breakfasts . . . whine, whine, moan, moan, oh, stop it, Marie.

Anyway, Hughie, James and me are all around the same age and that's why this New Year's Eve we decided just to have dinner and not make a fuss. They asked Penny and we made up a peculiar foursome.

Penny and I walked round – they live only round the corner, in a big mansion flat – and James greeted us in a white apron and said he was cooking a couple of pheasants (my favourite) that he'd found at the back of the freezer, and we opened the bottle of champagne I'd brought.

James was wearing, that night, a kind of weird rubber pink thing round his wrist. That was next to one of those horrible copper bracelets that people believe cures them of rheumatism. It was obviously a statement of a kind – but what statement I didn't like to enquire since when I last asked someone what their coloured bracelet was for, they replied: 'It's for breast cancer.' A surprising answer. 'Don't you mean "For combating breast cancer"?' I asked, and then I really *did* feel as if perhaps there really might be a touch of Asperger's about me. I fell over myself apologizing.

Anyway, I've seen so many people wearing these bands – yellow, white, blue – that I'm tempted, sometimes, to wear a plain brown rubber band round my wrist so that, when people ask me what it is, I can reply: 'A rubber band, you idiot.'

Luckily James wanted to show Penny the new herb garden he'd made on the roof, and because I'd already seen it and didn't fancy staggering up a ladder by torchlight in the freezing cold, I was left with Hughie. The sitting room is all puffed-up chintz sofas and gold mirrors, very camp. He shoved some pistachio nuts at me, topped up my glass and asked me how Archie was.

'You mean how is he "bearing up"?' I replied. 'I don't know. I haven't been in touch. But no doubt in five minutes he will find some glamorous young woman to marry and, irritatingly, start a whole new family. Eligible widowers like him usually do.'

'Or someone finds *them*,' said Hughie. 'I thought you were always interested in him? Didn't you have a teenage crush on him?'

'Oh, that was *years* ago,' I said, rather crossly. 'And he never knew about it. And anyway, I'm beyond all that. It's the life of the grannie, for me. Oh, God, Hughie, I'm just *bursting* to tell everyone about this baby! I keep meeting people who say things like: "When you're a grannie . . ." And I want to say: "But I'm *going* to be a grannie! And I want to jump up and down!" Instead I have to look all sorrowful and wistful and say: "Well, one day perhaps . . ." Then there are all these people who are never going to be grannies because they don't have any children, and I feel so sorry for them!'

Hughie bowed his head and pointed to himself. 'Don't mind me,' he said, in an amused way, and I suddenly felt dreadfully insensitive and rude and cursed myself.

'Oh, I'm so sorry, Hughie, sometimes I just open my mouth and toads jump out like those princesses in fairy tales.'

'It's all part of your charm,' said Hughie. 'But don't worry. I couldn't bear to be a grannie. My role as half-great-uncle-out-law, as you would no doubt insist on my being called, will do me nicely.'

In August I shall be a grandmother. It is the most extraordinary feeling. Grandmaternal feelings are already pouring out of me like sweat. I want to take my grandchild to the Science

Museum, to the park, swimming, teach it the old songs (whatever they are), to bounce it up and down on my knee. I want to play 'This little pig went to market' on its toes, and jump it up and down on my knee saying: 'My lord and my lady went into the park, To have a little airing before it got dark . . . My lady went trit-trot-trit-trot . . .' I want to make gingerbread men, and play Pooh-sticks. I am desperate to be the kind of grannie that I had – and, funnily enough, most of us had – a woman full of cuddles, patience, treats and mischief.

It's odd – apparently a lot of women these days dread being a grannie because just the word reminds them of some tiny, bent person with a white bun shaped like a doughnut on top of her head, giving off a smell of dirty clothes, peppermint and cat's pee. But children don't notice these things. All they know is that grannie is a source of fun and love and calm all at the same time.

After delicious pheasant with apples, a recipe from the Jane Grigson *Good Things* book, it was ten to ten and Penny said she was knackered, and James said so was he, and Hughie said why didn't we pretend that ten o'clock was midnight, so we opened another bottle of champagne and toasted each other and absent friends.

'To Philippa!' said Hughie. 'I remember when she was in hospital with breast cancer and she rang me saying: "Darling, I'm in remission!" and I said: "Don't be silly, of course you're not," and she said: "But the doctors say I am, darling!" Complete rubbish of course. She was dead in three weeks.'

'Don't be so bitchy, dear,' said James. 'I know none of you liked her very much, but she was very good to Archie – and she was always very nice to me.'

'"Always very nice to me,"' said Hughie, with a wry smile. 'Not quite good enough that, really, is it? I hope they don't put the words "Well, he was always very nice to *me*" on *my* tombstone.'

'Your voice is getting very high and querulous, dear,' said James to him, querulously, as it happened.

'It happens as you get older, dear,' said Hughie to him. 'I think I shall have to apply weights.'

After that, Penny and I got up off the sofa, each saying 'ugh' as we did so, another sign of growing older, and went staggering off into the night. Very nice.

Anyway, as far as the midnight bit went, Penny and I wondered why we hadn't thought up this ruse years ago. Black may be the new white, and night the new day, and holidays the new work, as they constantly say in the papers, but what about ten, on New Year's Eve, being the new midnight? There is no one I know over sixty who wants to go to bed after eleven o'clock at the very latest.

Rang Jack rather drunkenly just before I went to bed to wish him Happy New Year on his answering machine, assuming they'd be living it up at a party, but instead Jack himself answered, sounding rather grim.

'Are you all right?' I asked, hoping I wasn't slurring my words.

'Well, Chrissie's not drinking, so I'm not either,' he replied, coldly. 'We're already in bed.' Made me feel dreadfully guilty because of course while I was pregnant I drank and smoked myself silly. And took a few drugs as far as I remember. But it was all different then.

So odd. When I was young, old people took me aside and with quavering voices told me how when *they* were young they never had sex before marriage, and could never afford more than one pair of shoes, and were glad of a shandy at Christmas, and I'd look shocked at the austerity of it all. Now I'm taking young people aside and telling them, in a quavering voice, how when I was young I tried heroin, took uppers and downers every weekend, drank so much I once passed out in the middle of Oxford Street, slept with every man who asked me without using a condom, and *they* look shocked.

Jan 1

Had a terrible dream that I was walking home where I used to live as a child in the dense fogs we had then, and on the way a half-naked man appeared, led in chains by two thugs. He was totally grey and an iron spike seemed to have been driven into the top of his head. He was about to be executed. I kissed his pleading hand, at which point the thugs put me in chains too. Luckily I woke before they could do anything to me.

Later

Had mad feeling that since it was January 1st I ought to take some exercise. Particularly as my bunion op is coming up and I may not be able to walk properly for months. Went to Holland Park and pottered about and in the shrubbery by the pond, who should I meet, walking her dog, but Philippa's sister whom I hadn't seen for years. We both said how well and young each other looked – complete lie in my case as she looked drawn and pinched. Commiserated with her about her sister's death, and then she started a sentence with the words I hate to hear: 'When you get to *our* age . . .'

I don't want to be 'our age' with anyone. I'm quite happy for it to be *my* age, but not *ours*.

Then she said how rude people were these days, and how violence was getting out of control, and wasn't it awful, and I rather meanly said that that was exactly what the oldies in ancient Rome used to say when they pushed forty or whatever age passed for ancientness when they were around, and she simply didn't listen. I got so infuriated at her moaning on about how wonderful the past was and how beastly things are today that I had to restrain myself from punching her in the face. It doesn't usually occur to me to want to hit anyone, being a peaceable anti-war-march, watering-dried-up-plants-in-strange-restaurants, picking-up-wounded-worms-from-roads-and-placing-them-on-cool-grassy-banks kind of person, but faced with attitudes like those of Philippa's sister, it's no wonder people are violent. However, half-way through her droning on about the ghastliness of traffic wardens and how unfair it was that second homes were going to be taxed, and wringing her hands generally about progress and how rushed everyone was and how they didn't have time to stand and stare, I looked at my watch, gasped and, muttering something about us all being busy people, hared off.

January 8th

Had bunion operation. I don't think it *was* very wise. I am kitted up in two great blue flip-flops and my feet are covered in bandages. It is true that I can walk, but with difficulty. When I returned home, Pouncer took one look at my feet, arched his back and spat at them. I think he thought I'd brought home two new strange pets. As I shuffle round the streets, I really do feel like a very, very old person. It's all very well to like being old, but very, very old, no thanks.

January 14th

'So, tomorrow's the big day, is it?' asked Penny, when she rang up to tell me what the last doctor she'd seen had told her about whether her white platelets were behaving themselves. Or something. Could have been the red ones. Or the green for all I know.

Tomorrow *is* the big day. My birthday.

'Is it a *big* birthday?' say friends, tactfully. I don't remember anyone asking me that when I was thirty. The truly big birthdays are 21, 40, 60, 80 and 100. 'Or perhaps I shouldn't ask,' they add, coyly. Sometimes they add, facetiously: 'Surely it can't be! You don't *look* thirty yet!' which is rather irritating.

But I am just longing for my birthday. Fifty-eight and fifty-nine are stupid ages to be. I always felt, when I said I was fifty-nine, that people must think I was lying, like some pathetic old actress. Fifty-nine was nowhere, neither fish nor fowl. If anything, in fact, it seemed to declare me a truly ancient middle-aged person. Now, nearly sixty, I feel like a young and lissom old person. I feel like a new and shiny snake who has shed a middle-aged skin that was getting horribly worn, smelly and tatty.

At last, too, my past will be truly bigger than my future. And I like it like that.

People who love life to bits hate getting older. It means death is getting nearer. For people like me, for whom life has rather resembled one of those interminable performances at the National Theatre (those ones that last all day, to which you have to take sandwiches), getting older means that at last I'm entering the final act. It means I can see freedom at the end of the tunnel. Getting older means I get happier and happier. It means that at last I can put aside those nagging guilty anxieties about whether I should take up tap-dancing (have I said this before? Am I repeating myself already?) or become an opera singer. Being sixty will mean that I don't have to worry about doing *anything* any more. I will, officially, be retired. I will pick up a pension. I will be entitled to free prescriptions. I can spend my time, as George, the black guy across the road always answers, when I ask him what he's up to, 'Tekkin' it eezee, man.'

I can't wait for tomorrow.

Michelle came in late from a nightclub. When I told her my great age her jaw dropped. 'You are as old as my grandmuzair!' she said.

January 15th

MY BIRTHDAY!

Hundreds of cards through the letterbox, one of which, from Penny, sings 'Happy birthday to you'. Hughie and James sent me one which reads 'Happy Birthday! You still look as young as ever!' Inside it says: 'Alcohol is an amazing preservative!' From Marion: 'Cheer up! Being sixty isn't too bad!' and inside: 'If you were a dog you'd be 420!'

Michelle gave me a huge box of white chocolates which unfortunately I can't eat because white chocolate is the only thing that gives me a headache, and Maciej gave me a weird ornament of a cat, with two great gobs of red glass for eyes, which is absolutely hideous. Unfortunately, as he's the cleaner I'm going to have to have it on display day and night. Aren't I an ungrateful old toad. I was touched, all the same.

And the phone hasn't stopped ringing.

'Do you feel any different?' asked Lucy, anxiously, when she rang.

'Yes, I do,' I said. 'I feel absolutely marvellous. It's clear now that I was born to be sixty. And to be honest, I can't wait to be seventy.'

When she was seventeen, my mother wrote in her diary: 'I have an absolute horror of old age nowadays; every old woman I meet, I think: "That's what I'll be like soon." I always feel uncomfortable and unhappy when I hear someone say: "What right have old people got to interfere?" or "I hate old people." And I hate to hear someone say: "Oh, she's ancient!" about someone of thirty-five. When I'm thirty-five I shan't like being called ancient. Old age is a beastly thing. Why must we get old, why can't we stay young for ever, it's so beastly to feel the days slipping past and not be able to stop them.'

But I couldn't disagree more. While other people hide their

heads in their hands and groan: 'Oh don't! How can it be that we're all so *old*?' I am hugging myself with glee thinking: At last, I can hold my head up and, instead of saying in a lowly worm kind of way: 'I'm old and I'm cowed,' I can shout (*à la* James Brown): 'Say it loud! I'm old and I'm proud!' (De! De! Deh!)

I always remember people saying, when I gave birth to Jack, that I should be 'proud' of myself. I never got it. Giving birth didn't seem anything to be proud of. But I *am* proud of being sixty. I feel I have achieved such a lot just to have got here. It's the same pride I had when I got an azalea to flower two years running.

But no one seems to be able to understand quite why I like being sixty so much. Even Penny, who popped in to make arrangements for lunch – she's taking me out. She sat down for a cup of coffee while I sat opposite her on the sofa, beaming in my Indian dressing gown.

'Now you can do all those things that you've been meaning to do for ages,' she said. 'Learn Italian.'

'Learn Italian?' I shouted so violently I spilled coffee all over myself. 'Why does *everyone* think I want to learn Italian? I only go to Italy once every three years for a week at most. No comprendo Italiano! No quiero comprendare Italiano! No, the great thing about being sixty is that I don't any longer feel guilty about *not* learning Italian!'

'Well, Open University . . .' she said.

'NO! NO! A thousand times NO! Nor the University of the Third Age! That's what Marion does. She's forever doing nodules or whatever they are. Forget nodules! I don't want to learn about anything ever again! I'm fed up with learning. Learning is for young people. Done young.'

'OK, OK,' she said. 'Modules by the way. Don't learn Italian. Join a bookclub, instead.'

A *bookclub?!* Certainly not! Bookclub people always seem to have to wade through *Captain Corelli's Mandolin*, or *The God of Small Things* or, groan, *The Bookseller of Kabul*. I think they feel that by reading and analysing books, they're keeping their brains lively. But either you've got a lively brain or you haven't. Discussing the resonances or contexts of books or whatever they discuss in bookclubs can't gee up a brain if it doesn't fire on all cylinders to start with. The thing is: I don't want to join a bookclub to keep young and stimulated. I don't *want* to be young and stimulated any more.

There seems to be a common line which runs: 'If you're old, you've got to stay mentally active, physically alive, ever fascinated by life.' You have to forever poke your brain with a pointed stick to keep it working. But I say: 'Why?' I've done fascinated, I've done curious. I want to wind down. I want to have the blissful relief of *not* being interested. I don't think those oldies who spend their lives bicycling across Mongolia at eighty and paragliding at ninety are brilliant specimens of old age. I think they're just tragic failures who haven't come to terms with ageing. They're the sort of people who disapprove of facelifts, and yet, by their behaviour, are constantly chasing a lost youth. I want to start doing *old* things, not young things.

Like slowly starting to give my property away, instead of spending my time trying to acquire it. Like seeing everything from a distance, rather than close-up and personal. Like not feeling slighted all the time or hating myself twenty-four hours a day. Like realizing that this civilization, like all civilizations, will one day come to an end and not mind. Like being able to spend a day doing nothing instead of feeling obliged to cram it with diversionary activity to avoid guilt and anxiety. Like realizing that if I can't understand an idea or a concept, it's not my fault but the fault of the person who's trying to put it across. Like being able to see things in a historical perspective and really understand that what goes around comes around. Like being nice to people, instead of scared of them.

Bicycling to outer Mongolia is for people under forty. 'Tekkin' it eezee' is for people over sixty. Well, that's how I see it. I feel relieved of that terrible Protestant work ethic that has dogged me all my life. I feel light, calm, like a great field of ripe corn, slowly swaying in the breeze, all chubby and sun-kissed. Lovely feeling.

Obviously I'm too young to get whisked away by a Stannah Stairlift, slip into a Damart vest, go on sea cruises or Enjoy the Luxury of a Walk-In Bath. Nor do I want to spend my days poring over church registers with a family tree in one hand, to discover that one of my ancestors was a medieval wood-cutter in the Forest of Dean, a pursuit that would bore me silly. (Finding out about it, that is. Probably actually being a woodcutter in the Forest of Dean had its good points.) As for joining a bookclub – no thanks!

Nick the plumber came and fixed a tiny gas leak in my pipe. He is a huge, nice black guy, about eighteen feet tall.

'You're looking well,' he said.

'I'm *feeling* well!' I said, as I brought him an orange juice. 'I'm sixty today!'

'You don't look it!' he said.

Wasn't sure quite what to make of that. In a way I *do* rather want to look sixty. Anyway, when I asked him how much I should pay him, he said: 'As it's your birthday, nothing.'

I spent all morning following up tips given me on a 'So now you're sixty' list, sent me by Lucy, which included information not only about bus passes and the like, but also the news that I might be able to get into swimming pools and sports centres at a special concessionary price. Despite the fact that several of my friends have taken up going to gyms, and spend three mornings a week bicycling, like elderly hamsters on wheels, till they are red in the face, trying all the while to listen to improving tapes that promise to teach them Italian in eight sessions, I shall not be joining them. I have done my time in gyms and have no desire to go to another one ever again, however cheap the entrance fee. So smelly! So noisy! So embarrassing! And the clothes you have to wear! It is simply impossible to look attractive, in my view, in a pair of Lycra shorts.

More interesting is the information, on Lucy's list, that being sixty I can now get my prescriptions free. Brilliant! I wonder if I could get my pills on standing order, like with bills, so I could have a constant supply of Diazepam, Migril and all the strangely creepy things I have wheedled out of my doctor over the years? When it comes to sleeping, I'm not someone for whom milky drinks at bedtime, plant extracts and natural essences do the trick; namby pamby Valerian and things you can get over the counter at chemists, with euphemistic names like Natracalm and Sleepeeze don't work for me. Instead, give me a prescription for a heavy-duty pharmaceutical knock-out pill. I get on much better with pop-out packs of goodies, things that come with leaflets listing at least three pages of possible side effects, made in laboratories by nice men in white coats.

According to Lucy, I am, apparently, also due a Winter Fuel payment of £200 a year. But *my* warming fuel will come in a bottle and not through a plug in the wall. And finally, my house insurance might be lower because old people are considered more reliable than young ones. Which is odd. Surely all old people leave the gas on regularly?

It's a funny old business. I would have thought that if the government were sensible they would double the cost of prescriptions for old people, exclude them from gyms, triple their heating bills, raise their taxes and generally do everything in their power to curtail their lives, thus saving the country billions of pounds, but no, they seem determined to keep us dragging on and on. I can see the point when it comes to animals and vets – the vets make a fortune out of keeping pets hanging on as long as possible. But what's in it for the government? Absolutely nothing.

Lucy had helpfully added telephone numbers, websites and information lines, so of course I got cracking at once and rang the number advertised as the Pension Helpline. I was taken by a mechanized voice through all the options I had, which reminded me that if I was hard of hearing I could get special assistance or, if I found it all confusing, I could get a friend to help me.

My query was finally answered by an old duck called Ernest, not a name I hear a lot these days. He spoke extremely slowly and clearly all the way through the call, and maintained a kindly smile in his voice. At the end of the conversation, he said, in a gentle, friendly, but distinctly raised, voice: 'Ta-ra, dearie. And you take care, now!'

I am now a 'concession' and can get into most films, art galleries, exhibitions and theatres at special rates. I'm told that abroad the over-sixties have an even better time of it, wandering anywhere they like, their wrinkles a passport to free entrance. The greatest perk of all is that, if I am rudely challenged about my ancient status, I shall not be offended but, rather, deeply flattered.

Tomorrow I shall apply for my Freedom Pass, which will give me free transport – whether it's for a lazy trip from one bus stop to the next, or from one side of London to the other. In the Underground I shall simply wave my card over something and sail in. None of that fiddling around with money, feeling pathetically inadequate as I stare at a blinking computer screen wondering what zone I'm in. Now I'm in the free zone, the old zone, and that's the zone I like.

I'm also suddenly in receipt of a pension – £74 a week. True, I will be taxed on it, but still, I shall be quite a bit better off. And every September the government will kindly whack £200 into my bank account to cover extra heating.

Even more fun, I then spent hours trying to cancel standing orders, get passport-sized photographs for the bus pass – all the pleasant rituals of stepping from one age into another.

As a treat, Penny had organized a birthday lunch at an incredibly smart restaurant in Piccadilly called the Wolseley. I remember it as a gleaming bank; later it turned into a Chinese restaurant, and now it is owned by a couple of people who used to own the Ivy. She had very sweetly bought me a scarf, though I am not very keen on scarves: they seem to be worn by people who want to hide lizardy necks, and if you haven't got a lizardy neck there's no point in wearing one. Wearing a scarf always seems to me rather like planting a row of Leylandii to hide a nuclear power station.

Unfortunately, as is so often the case these days, the restaurant was so noisy that neither of us could hear the other speak, and we spent an hour just mouthing across the table, pretending we could hear what the other one was saying. All I could gather was that she wanted us to go for a weekend to France as a big birthday treat, on her, which was incredibly kind.

When I got back I found a huge bunch of flowers waiting with the neighbours. It was, oddly, from the now-widowed Archie.

'Happy birthday!' read the note. Then: 'Lunch? Or dinner? Do ring. Much, much love, Archie.'

Dinner? Much, much love? Surely not. It's odd how, even at my great age, one reads so much into such things. Recently I found myself counting the number of 'x's a girlfriend had written on an email. Why only one? Why not two? Had I done something wrong? But I must say it would be lovely to see Archie again. He's always been a friend, along with Mrs Archie, the poor dead Philippa, but I haven't had a proper conversation with him à deux for a couple of years.

In the evening I went round to Jack and Chrissie's flat in Brixton for a sixtieth-birthday supper with Hughie and James.

I gave James a lift but Hughie stayed behind because he wasn't feeling well.

In the car, I asked: 'What's up? A cold?'

James looked worried. 'He's had this cough for ages now, and today he really feels terrible. I've told him to go to see the doctor, but he won't. When I ask him to make an appointment just for my sake, he gets angry. I've begged him to take arnica and echinacea, but he says it's all snake-oil. I even turned the bed round the other way because I'm certain that facing North does us no good, but he got so angry he just put his pillow down the bottom and slept the other way round so I had his feet next to my face.'

'I can't imagine Hughie angry,' I said. 'Or rather,' I added, having just imagined it and been unpleasantly surprised at what my brain came up with, 'I can. It must be horrible. Cutting and sarcastic, I suppose.'

'You have it,' said James. 'His temper is like a nuclear bomb. Very, very rarely used, but when it is, it causes death and destruction all round.'

'I'll see what I can do,' I said. 'He wouldn't get angry with me because I can do the mumsy old pal act.'

'I wish you would,' said James, suddenly turning to me at the lights, with an expression of such relief and gratitude on his face that I resolved to tackle Hughie as quickly as possible. 'Oh,' he added, 'congratulations about being a grannie-to-be. Jack told me yesterday when he invited me, but I promise I won't tell a soul.'

When we arrived at the flat – well, actually, it's more half a house – Chrissie was looking a little bit fatter, but the pregnancy's not yet obvious. She isn't giving up her job till the last minute – she's one of these dynamic women who's in charge of marketing some kind of spa therapy around the world and has been known – I've seen it – to conduct three conversations at once on different phones.

Much to my astonishment, I found Jack, once king of grunge, sitting on the sofa, wearing a cardigan, and reading the *Guardian*. The realization that one's child is not only an adult, but a responsible adult who is about to become a father, is quite astonishing. Phrases like: 'Don't you think, darling, that you might polish your shoes now and again?' seem to dry up before their bony fingers even start plucking at the vocal chords.

They had ordered an Indian take-away, with extra poppadoms, which was delicious, Chrissie had baked a totally scrumptious chocolate cake, and everyone sang 'Happy Birthday'. They had all clubbed together to buy me a DVD player. Can't quite think when I will use it, as I am never in, but I was incredibly touched. Perhaps they imagine that every night I curl up with a video and a crossword puzzle. I also got a whole pile of special soaps and bath gels which Chrissie got from work, none of which I can use, unfortunately, because I am at an age when I am allergic to every single product with scent in it and have to stick with boring old Simple soap. But it was a nice thought.

Nicest present of all was a pedometer, which I'd asked for. Since I'm now out of the bunion shoes, armed with this gadget I'll be able to find out if I am remotely fit. Feel a bit nerdy wanting a machine to tell me whether I'm taking enough exercise or not, but after five minutes pottering around the flat and going to the loo once, I'd already clocked up about 100 steps, so I felt delighted with myself. I think I'll have to keep it on somehow in bed because these days I must go to the loo about three times a night, and it would be a shame to miss out on a few steps. Though it might be a bit uncomfortable trying to sleep with it under my nightie.

'What do you want to be called, Mum?' Jack asked. 'When the baby arrives.'

Having been brought up by two people who tried to insist

I call them by their Christian names, I long for everyone to be called by their proper family names – from Daddy and Mummy to Auntie and Uncle. Then, when a friend at school refers to their own grannie, they can join in the conversation with chat about their gran, too. Not their own 'Annabel' or 'Chris'.

So, naturally, I replied that I wanted, if at all possible, to be called 'Grannie'. Obviously if the baby couldn't manage it, I'd be happy with 'Moo moo' or 'Grandy' or whatever it came up with. I wouldn't even mind being called 'Grungy' or 'Grumpy'. When Philippa was alive I remember she couldn't bear the word 'grannie' and even balked at the word 'grandchild', insisting that hers was always referred to as her 'daughter's baby'.

'I think you ought to be called "Glammy",' said James. 'You'll be the most glamorous grannie I know.'

'Glammy!' said Jack and Chrissie in horror, together. 'How naff!'

'Well, it's better than "Gaga",' I said, not that I'd like to be 'Glammy' of course.

'The five ages of man,' said James. 'Lager, Aga, Saga, Viagra, Gaga.'

It was my first night of being sixty and I slept like a baby.

Feb 4

Went to a 'cosy birthday supper' with Marion and Tim which was much jollier than the last time. Just us, and not a therapist in sight. Tim had written me a beautiful poem which he read out, rather drunkenly, over pudding.

> Oh, how you do defy the years
> You're half the age of all your peers

In fact you're only twenty-five
Compared to you, we're half-alive
So clinging to your skirts we go
While you disdain Time's stupid flow!

Very flattering and sweet, of course, but that preoccupation with being young unnerves me.

I'd have been very happy with a poem that went:

At last you're free of youth's cruel chains
With time to sit and count your gains –
Experience, peace and lack of fear
Are gifts of this, your sixtieth year.
So celebrate the past unroll'd
And cheer the fact that now you're OLD!

Or something like that. I would never have made a poet, clearly.

Slightly worried to find that, driving back, I couldn't see a thing. I stopped and cleaned my glasses but still everything seemed incredibly fuzzy.

Feb 5

Rang up Penny and asked if she could see. She said yes, she could. I then asked her if she could see in the dark and she said no, only vampires, owls and moles can see in the dark, and I said but seriously, I can't see when driving and I can't see to read in bed at night. So she looked the problem up in her book *Eyes: Problems Of* and it turns out that after sixty, people need two-thirds more light to read by than they did when they were twenty. Made a date with the opticians at once.

Penny has booked a jaunt to Nice for us in June.

Feb 6

Is there actually something wrong these days with the word 'old'? I wonder. I was in Waterstone's today and saw a book which was a compilation of quotes from people over sixty with the unbelievable title *Late Youth*. What are all these euphemisms? I've even heard people talk of the 'autumn of life'. I'm starting to think that 'old' is becoming a dirty word, like 'niggers' or 'mongols'. While I quite understand why we should avoid using those particular words, not using the word 'old' seems as coy and ludicrous as Victorians putting skirts on their piano legs because they felt so uncomfortable at the sight of them.

Though I was rather touched by Hughie who the other day described James's aunt of ninety-five as '*very* grown up indeed'.

Feb 7

Had lunch with Lucy in her London *pied-à-terre*. She gave me a lovely pot of hyacinths. She does yoga and showed me the Sun Salutation on her carpet. Luckily, I managed to do it too, though I didn't like it when your leg has to be stretched out behind you.

'We've got to stay fit,' she said, worriedly, 'or we'll fall to pieces.' She dreads becoming sixty because she thinks that something terrible will happen to her.

'You know when teenagers reach fourteen they go to bed the night before their birthday perfectly sweet and amiable, and wake up on their fourteenth birthday sulky, slamming doors, spotty and telling you they wish they'd never been born,' she said. 'Well, I believe that the day before I'm sixty I'll go to bed perfectly normal, and wake up on my sixtieth birthday ranting about the state of the world, shouting that teenagers have no respect, and complaining about the amount of rubbish left on my street.'

I assured her that I'd been complaining about the rubbish left on my street from the age of about forty. But, of course, living in Shepherds Bush it's difficult not to complain about the rubbish because often it is hard to get out of one's front door for the piles of old fast-food cartons, chicken bones, half-drunk Special Brew cans, broken television sets, mattresses, bags of what look like dead babies, oozing car batteries and old sofas that clog up the pavements.

Feb 8

I am plagued with spam. I think it's because someone once sent me an all-singing, all-dancing birthday card via some company in the States and now I am deluged with ads for Viagra and penis-enhancement, not to mention desperate requests for money from Nigerians. This is the latest, which I rather liked:

Minister Charles Simpson has the power to make you a LEGALLY ORDAINED MINISTER within 48 hours!
WEDDINGS
MARRY your BROTHER, SISTER, or your BEST FRIEND!
Don't settle for being the BEST MAN OR BRIDESMAID
FUNERALS
A very hard time for you and your family
Don't settle for a minister you don't know!
BAPTISMS
You can say 'WELCOME TO THE WORLD! I AM YOUR MINISTER AND YOUR UNCLE!'
What a special way to welcome a child of God

WANT TO START YOUR OWN CHURCH??
After your LEGAL ORDINATION, you may start your own congre-
gation! Since I know how much you want to help others, you're
going to receive your Minister Certification for under $100.00
... Not even $50.00 ... You are going to receive the entire
life-changing course for only $29.95.

For this you will receive:
1. 8-inch by 10-inch certificate in colour, with gold seal
(Certificate professionally printed by an ink press)
2. Proof of Minister Certification in your name
3. Shipping is free

How about getting a certificate and then, during the
christening of this little person, suddenly bursting out with:
'Welcome to the world! I am your minister and your grandmother!'

Perhaps not.

Feb 19

Went to opticians. At sixty, I now have free eye tests – brilliant!
– but rather irritatingly, being sixty, my sight barely changes
(except at night and in front of the computer). So just at the
time you don't need them, you get them for nothing. Typical.
When I arrived, the man behind the counter, the nephew of
Mr Ahmed, who runs it, was complaining about the smell of
drains. As far as I could make out, the manhole for the drains
for the entire block of flats above opens in the basement of
the opticians. Mr Ahmed himself came up looking very peeved,
rubbing his hand as if he'd had a nasty encounter with a piece
of slime, or worse, down there.

He tested my eyes and told me that my sight hadn't changed

at all – but, he revealed gleefully, he could see cataracts growing already. He gave me the news as if he'd spotted the first crocuses coming up in spring. I felt a bit depressed. Then I got cross, because if my sight hasn't changed, why can't I see?

I've never been really able to see with my present glasses. I can't see the words on my computer screen unless I crane my neck right back. I have tried sitting on piles of cushions, so the computer is lower than me. I have tried putting dozens of ancient Victorian volumes of *Punch* underneath it to raise it, but nothing makes any difference. Mr Ahmed says the problem could be one of two things. First, it could be floaters. Certainly, so many dark floatery shapes pass my eyes I sometimes feel as if I am walking through an autumn forest in a storm. Or, more likely, it could be that the line of mid-vision is bad because of the fashionably tiny glasses I have.

Mr Ahmed and his nephew stared at my line of vision, made marks with a special pen on my glasses, garbled optical jargon to each other, and finally said that if I were to pay £575 for a new pair I would be able to see perfectly well. I gulped. No reaction. Then I gulped again, more loudly. Nothing. Finally I said: 'Golly, that's *frightfully* expensive!' and got a result.

'For you, £500,' said Mr Ahmed's nephew.

It is still 'Cripes!', however much money they take off.

When I left I had a sudden thought: could the smell in the drains be due to all the old cataracts they flush down them? Yuk.

I then went to Sainsbury's to buy some fish, and some special food they do that Pouncer likes. At least he liked it last week. It's funny with cats. They'll refuse to eat anything but Whiskas Turkey in Gravy for about three months and then, just as you buy a whole crate of it wholesale, they'll suddenly turn up their nose at it and eat nothing but Sainsbury's Select Cuts of Chicken and Tuna.

A fat man in front of me in the queue was wearing a teeshirt on which was written the word: WHATEVER.

Later
When I got back James rang to tell me that his aunt Jane – yes, the 'very grown-up' one – has gone into a home, kicking and screaming at first but not for long because apparently the place is stuffed with what he calls 'wingcos', slang for 'Wing Commanders'. Even if the blokes in question have lost every single marble they ever had, Jane, who retains only about half a marble, is still galvanized and rejuvenated simply by the presence of a man. Exactly, in fact, like me. Funny that. I have no interest in men at all these days on the sexual front, thank God, but I can still get flattered out of my tree by a man, any old man, turning his eyes on to me and twinkling and flirting.

Asked Hughie round for a drink to help me with the DVD – not that he knows anything about such things but I thought he could read the instructions out to me while I followed them. More importantly, I wanted to tackle his cough. He dropped by but, instead of looking five years older than me, which he is, he looked pretty washed-up, more like someone of my father's age.

'Are you losing weight, Hughie?' I asked, when I let him in. 'You're not looking quite as – er – well-covered as you were the last time I saw you.'

'Well-covered! What a word,' said Hughie. As he came in he coughed, which was lucky because if for some reason he hadn't coughed I would have been up a gum tree. 'Doesn't everything look lovely?' he said, admiring the room as he sat down. 'You're so lucky to have Maciej. He's so good-looking, too. James and I have to put up with a terrible old duck called Lilian who does nothing but call in sick.'

We tried to work the DVD but drew a blank. It involves something called a scart plug, and whenever I hear those words my brain goes kind of dead. I don't know what a scart plug is and I never will. When I rang Jack, he told me it was a fat thing full of prickles, so I then had a vague idea of what it looks like and he told me that we had stored several of these in his old room upstairs.

'Mum, you've got dozens of scart plugs,' he said. 'In that chest. In my old room.'

I thought about it. Jack's old room was now lived in by Michelle. I could just imagine the daunting piles of CDs, beauty products, DVDs, plastic bags and cast-off handbags that Michelle would have stuffed on top of my assorted collection of wires. So I decided that enough was enough for that evening. I'd got the DVD out of its box, and that was scary enough. I will tackle the scart situation tomorrow.

In the meantime, it was easy to tackle Hughie about the doctor, since he coughed all the time.

'Hughie, what are you going to do about that cough?' I said. 'It's terrible. Have you seen the doctor?'

'No,' he said, 'but you're right. I must. James keeps nagging me. I'll make an appointment tomorrow. I swear on my mother's grave.'

'Your mother was cremated. She doesn't have a grave,' I said, Sherlock Holmes-like in my eagerness to stop up all the loopholes that Hughie might use to avoid seeing the doctor.

'So she was,' said Hughie. 'But I will. I've got to get it sorted out.'

But I had a very strong feeling that he wouldn't do anything about it at all. He looked like a man who was deceiving himself. However, I couldn't press him any further, so I left it at that.

March 4

A late birthday lunch with Archie at a restaurant called Pulli in fashionable Clerkenwell. It was very nice of him to organize it, because he must still be feeling pretty grim after Philippa died. It was only six months ago, too. I imagined him thinking: 'Why should I be celebrating Marie's birthday when poor old Philippa never even got to sixty?' That's how my mind would work, anyway. But Archie's probably too nice to think like that.

He is wonderfully self-effacing. The message on my answering machine to invite me for lunch, went: 'Could you *bear* to give me a ring if the idea of having lunch with me isn't absolute *anathema* to you?' When he rang to make the date, he'd said: 'Let's meet on Thursday – if we live that long . . .'

God knows how Archie booked a table, because Pulli is a restaurant in which you have to kill to get one, but no doubt he tips like a trooper. (Do troopers tip? Or do they swear?)

I must say that catching sight of him waiting outside the restaurant did rather make my heart lurch. I know lots of people adore chunky blokes in vests or simmering young Italians with tumbling black curly hair, but for me the sight of a tall, svelte, middle-aged Englishman wearing a long well-cut tailored coat, open down the front, standing in a London street, is something to capture my heart – if my heart were capturable, that is.

When he was my First Love (though he never knew it then and still doesn't now, thank goodness), he can't have been more than fifteen, and I'd met him at a bottle party I'd gate-crashed. From then on nightly I would walk past his parents' house in Chelsea and stare in at the lighted window, wondering if he were inside. And yet, as I sat down at the table, it seemed quite extraordinary that my two roles could exist in a single lifetime. Once, when I was sixteen, shy, terrified, miserable, I used to crawl by his window like a stalker – and now, nearly forty years later, I was sitting with him in a Clerkenwell restaurant, confident and relaxed with no designs on him at all, and simply deriving pleasure from being in his nice company for lunch. How wonderful not to be driven by a longing for company and sex.

'Would you mind passing me the menu if it isn't the most *frightful* bore?' he said to me. Then: 'Oh, how *splendid!*' to the waiter when he brought the sparkling water. 'How *frightfully* kind!'

Obviously, I'd written to him when Philippa had died, but I felt I had to acknowledge her death again, couldn't really avoid it after all, and he said, in that rather sweet way that some men have when talking about something that really matters to them but they don't want to show it: 'Yes, absolutely *rotten* luck, wasn't it? Still makes me blub now and again.'

Anyway, the dishes were incredibly expensive and I felt very guilty ordering one veal sweetbread in mushroom sauce and some polenta because it cost about £21. Archie ordered lobster and black pudding cappuccino, and the waiter said: 'Eez that all? Here we advise our clients to order at least three things each.'

When the food arrived, mine was a sweetbread the size of a thumbnail with what looked like three sliced beansprouts and one chopped-up button mushroom in a teaspoon of sauce – all served on *a piece of slate*! Archie's lobster and black pudding cappuccino was a tiny bowl like a children's tea-set cup, half-filled with broth.

Over lunch we naturally talked of old age. Our first topic was the fact that everyone we know is dropping like flies.

'Yes, we're getting to the difficult age,' he said.

'What do you mean?'

'Well, when I look in the obituary columns, it seems that everyone's either between fifty-eight and sixty-five or between eighty and ninety,' he said. 'Poor Philippa was fifty-nine, when you think of it. I believe that if we can get through these next few years, we're probably in for a long stretch.'

'You mean like in the Grand National, getting over Butcher's Leap or whatever it is?'

'Exactly! How *frightfully* well you put it!'

Of course we got on to the subject of retiring as well, and he revealed that he had started to lose his nerve when it came to investing huge sums of money or whatever he does. And I agreed. When I've occasionally done the odd bit of supply teaching recently, a task that I would usually take in my stride, I can feel all wobbly. I know how an acrobat must feel when she reaches thirty. OK, she's leapt into the air thousands of times since she was sixteen, but suddenly it's scary.

'But we should get *less* frightened as we get older, not *more* frightened,' I said. And indeed one of the brilliant things about old age is the ludicrous confidence that it bestows.

'I think we're like old stags, frightened by new young bucks coming up with great antlers,' he said.

'I don't feel like an old stag,' I said. I was wearing a very nice Vivienne Westwood top which I got in a sale, and high-heeled boots and thought I looked rather glam.

'You don't *look* like an old stag! You look, if I may say so, like a frightfully *young* stag. A most attractive and *beautiful* young stag.'

'Surely not stag, Archie . . .'

'Of course not! How *frightfully* foolish I am.'

My feeling is that there is a moment when too much experience works not to our advantage but to our disadvantage. We have found, during our lives, so many things that could happen, so many frightening possibilities, that we are constantly trying to avoid them, and that makes us nervous.

'My parents, who when young thought nothing of driving across the world, and nothing of getting on a train, became petrified of travel when they got old,' said Archie. 'Just going to Oxford was this huge production and put them into a total funk. That's why old people are earlier and earlier for trains.'

'I'm getting *terribly* early for trains,' I said. Instead of telling old people how young they look, perhaps the biggest compliment would be to say: 'Oh, you look like someone who catches trains by only a couple of minutes.'

'What about gardening?' I asked.

Archie nodded gloomily. 'Yes, very much into that, I must admit,' he said. 'Partly the nurturing instinct – there's no one left to look after when the children have flown the nest – but partly, surely, the realization that everything is recycled, it grows, it dies, it grows, it dies . . . just like us. Did you know,' he suddenly said, rather irritatedly, 'that apparently that runner, Linford Christie – wasn't he the one with the lunch-box? Anyway, he won something when he was the great age of thirty-two and he said that "Age is only a number." What did he mean "only a number"? I bet if someone said he'd taken three and a half minutes to run a mile instead of two and a half minutes, and when he complained replied: "But it's only a number," he'd be *frightfully* put out.'

After the tiniest main course known to man, the sort of thing one might prepare for a goblin, I asked for a cheeseboard to finish off as I was starving, and three pieces of cheese, transparent with thinness, like inch squares of net curtain, arrived; Archie's chocolate mousse, a thin tube the size of half a pencil, was served on a piece of mirror. God knows what the bill was.

But as he paid it, he said: 'Well, we won't be coming here again. Perhaps we should pop in to a Burger King before we go back?' Then he said, looking at me rather intently, 'We must do this again soon. Let's make a *habit* of it.'

Soon? Habit? What on earth did he mean? I feel all peculiar. *Surely* he didn't mean . . . ? Of course he didn't.

Anyway, I'm giving all that up.

Later

Got back and popped into Michelle's room to get the scart plug. Discovered that she has completely redecorated the place in dark pink. How I didn't smell the paint I don't know. Penny says that as one's sight and hearing go down the drain as one gets older, so one's sense of smell gets more acute. Clearly total rubbish. Michelle has also fastened gold stars to the ceiling and erected a kind of deep blue chiffon canopy above her bed, which is covered with stuffed toys; it looks like a mixture of a tart's boudoir and a ten-year-old's bedroom. I was just about to be furious when I realized that actually it looks fantastically pretty.

Noticed, to my horror, a couple of empty bottles of wine in her wastepaper basket. Surely she isn't a secret drinker? Wished I'd never gone in at all.

Odd, that. All right for *me* to be a secret drinker, but not OK for her to be a secret drinker. I say secret drinker. The problem is that increasingly I need one glass of wine before I can even go out and have a drink with someone. Did I say 'need'? Did I say 'one' glass of wine? Oh, Marie, AA, here you come.

March 6

Jack and Chrissie have finally had the scan, which means that at last I'm able to tell people. Unfortunately it is no fun at all, because those who already have grandchildren aren't remotely impressed and those who haven't got them look so pitifully envious that I feel a complete creep for sharing my good news with them. In fact I feel like someone walking about the slums of Bangladesh carrying a huge bag of cream cakes which I stuff into my mouth, one by one, with a hand covered with diamond rings.

It is, apparently, a boy. Ever so slightly sad, because having had a boy I'd love to experience something different, and, of course, be able to dress it up in all kinds of girlie things. But there you go. As Jack says, at least it's not a rabbit, which would be very unsettling.

One of Jack's friends asked him why they wanted to know the sex of the baby and didn't they want to keep it as a surprise, and Jack replied, rightly, that just having a baby would be quite surprise enough, and anyway, when they were told the sex after the scan, that was a surprise in itself.

I'm going round to see them both tonight, so I'd better get cracking with the DVD – I can't arrive saying that I haven't got round to working it yet.

Later
Spent the entire day struggling with the DVD. I got the scart plug sorted out, and then the telly went blue and the words DVD came up . . . so clearly it was all working. But when I put a disc in, it kept saying that there was no disc in. I eventually drew a blank and had to ring Jack.

'I've put it in, and nothing happens,' I said.

'Mum,' said Jack, with that cautious note in his voice that I know means: 'I can't believe you're such a total idiot.' 'Which way up are you putting it?'

'The right way,' I said. 'Silver side up.'

'That's the wrong way up,' he said, and I could practically hear his eyebrows crashing against the ceiling.

'But the other side's got all writing on it,' I explained. 'And pictures.'

'That's the side you want,' he said.

He was right.

What would I do without a son? If I hadn't had a son, I would still be writing letters, rather than emailing. It was only because he screamed and begged me to get a computer, back in the eighties, that I ever got weaned off the typewriter in the first place, and I still remember him, at eleven years old, with his curious middle-sized hands, unpacking the entire thing and setting it up and explaining it all patiently to me as if I were some total imbecile.

'This, Mum,' he said, showing me a piece of plastic attached by a wire to a sinister-looking box, 'is a mouse.'

Already frantic with tension, I burst into tears, saying: 'But it *isn't* a mouse! That's the whole thing about these horrible computer thingies! I can't understand it! I can't understand any of it! I'll never understand it! I wish we'd never got this horrible thing!'

And I remember him putting his arms round me, laughing and comforting me, and my thinking for the first time: This is the beginning of getting old, when my son comforts me. When my son teaches me. When my son looks after me. Today it's when we're sorting out computers, but this is the first day of many, and it's a huge stage in our lives, and although I don't like it right now, it's a necessary stage and a normal stage for him and for me.

Anyway, by the time I went to supper with them, I'd got the hang of the DVD, though I still think videos are better because you can fast forward through videos, and it's all peculiar with DVDs, but there you are.

'There you are.' That's an old-age expression if ever there was one. I don't think I've ever used such an expression so much as this year, and I don't think I ever used it when I was younger. When I was younger the whole idea of 'There you are' was anathema. 'There you are *not*!' more likely. 'There you are' is an expression of complete resignation combined with gnomic acceptance. I like it.

I scampered from the car to avoid the gangs – 'scampered' not being quite the word; perhaps 'hurriedly shuffled' would be better, because the feet are still not totally up to scratch after the op – and Chrissie came downstairs absolutely bursting out of her clothes looking exhausted. They cooked me a lovely supper and I had the dubious pleasure of being shown the scan.

Of course scans are things we never had in our day . . . there was no chance of knowing the sex of the baby, either. The best predictors we had involved friends hanging our wedding rings over our tummies suspended on pieces of cotton. If they went round one way it was a boy, and the other way it was a girl. Or vice versa. Oh, Lord, that doesn't make sense. Anyway, now the scan apparently shows everything. Well, it does to some people.

All I could see, and that was both with my glasses and without my glasses, was a kind of weird blobby thing like a pool of petrol on the surface of a pond. Or, rather, like a photograph in the *Daily Mail* I saw last week of what was apparently a picture of Jesus discovered in a potato crisp. Though I couldn't decipher it myself.

Jack kept saying: 'Look at his little head!' And I kept saying I couldn't see it, until finally I had to pretend to see it.

'Oh, I *see*!' I said. 'Oh, how sweet.'

'Can you *really* see it, Mum?' asked Jack, suspiciously.

'Yes, well, I can vaguely,' I said.

'It's not vague, it's perfectly clear,' he said, rather snappily.

As I drove home, I had a sudden worry. Would it be autistic? Where the fear came from I have no idea, but I knew that once I'd got this fear it wouldn't leave me. Odd, because when I was pregnant with Jack I had no such fears. I think the whole idea of having a baby was terrifying enough, and occupied the worrying section of my mind sufficiently for there to be no room for anxiety about whether it would be OK or not. But

I suddenly had this terrible fantasy of this baby being weird. And me being the only person who could spot it being weird, from the word go. And everyone else thinking it was fine – except me . . .

'Now, stop it!' I told myself as I got out of the car my end. 'Stop it at once!'

I may have left my job, but there is still a sixty-year-old schoolmistress alive and well inside me. Forget about inner child. What you want is an inner, sensible schoolmistress, who stops you getting things out of proportion. Unfortunately, when it comes to truly mind-blowingly upsetting, irrational worries like babies and autism, the schoolmistress in me often seems to have retired into a locked study to correct exam papers.

March 20

Have just seen an ad in a colour mag for a 'classic retro-style manual typewriter'. It is, claims the ad, a 'rare classic'.

Save £1,000 on the cost of buying a computer – it's only £49.99.

There's nothing more satisfying than the click, click of a traditional typewriter . . .

Makes a fabulous gift for those who remember the good old days . . .

Anyone who thought it was a fabulous gift for me would get short shrift, I can tell you.

Those 'good old days . . .' how well I remember them. Sheaves and sheaves of carbon paper interlaced between stuff rather like Bronco lavatory paper (another thing I'm happy to say goodbye to) known as 'flimsies'. Any time you made a mistake on the top copy, you'd have to go through all the back copies correcting the mistake as well. No ability to cut and paste meant that if you were writing anything of importance, you really *did* have to cut and paste.

I remembered my first secretarial job, before I became a teacher. I sat in a room so cold that I had to wear gloves to type – and copying anything in quantity had to be done on an enormous machine called a Gestetner. All the copies to be reproduced were typed on to wax . . . and mistakes had to be repaired by strange pink stuff and retyped. I still remember the groaning sound it made when it was in action. I also remember the groaning sound that I made while I was trying to work it.

Who on earth would buy an old typewriter now? Oh, I know . . . Philippa's sister. She'd love it. Something for people of 'our age'. Grr.

March 30

James came over to help me hang a mirror that I'd bought at a car boot sale the other day. He was adamant that the place I wanted to hang it would drive away all the good spirits from the house because it was opposite the front door at the end of the corridor.

'It just reeks of "Go away!", my dear,' he said. 'You don't want to come in and the first thing you see is yourself coming in! Looking all shopped-out and haggard!'

'I see the reflection as welcoming me in,' I said, defiantly. 'Not shoving me out. And it will reflect the light, making this squinny hall look much bigger. I think that light,' I added, with false confidence, 'keeps out bad spirits, anyway, not good ones.'

'Light, yes, but mirrors are strange things, Marie,' said James. 'They are our negative opposites. Bad karma. Not good for chakras.'

'There's nothing wrong with my chakras, whatever they are,' I said crossly. 'They sound like water biscuits. Anyway, are you going to help me or not?'

When it was up, James admitted that it looked so nice it couldn't possibly do anyone any harm, which was a relief. Although I don't believe in any of his crazy ideas, there's always a bit of me that thinks . . . but what if it's true? What if, at night, there is a chakra under my bed, waiting to pounce?

April 10

For the last week, I have been convinced I have throat cancer. I have woken at three in the morning, quaking with fear that first my tongue will have to be cut out, and then my vocal cords, and soon I will be able to communicate only in grunts, via notebooks and eventually in a strange American voice like Stephen Hawking.

Luckily this morning I remembered that I had had this fear before and, after extensive tests, it turned out I had an inflammation of the throat, due to something called acid reflux. Some valve that used to shut off at night to stop the acid hurtling up one's windpipe or whatever it is doesn't work so well, and I have to take some special valve pills for a while till everything settles down. It is just one of the very minor cracks and creaks that come with early old age.

Took a couple of anti-valve-shutting pills (or was it pro-valve-closing pills?). And it seems to have done the trick.

April 11

Since I can't worry about throat cancer any more, I've now got time to be pre-occupied with my other big worry, whether the baby will be OK or not. I woke at four in the morning, fantasizing myself into the most terrifying situation. The baby had been born hideously disabled, and mentally a vegetable. Chrissie and Jack loved it, but their lives were being destroyed. They wished, I knew, that it had not lived. One day when babysitting I took a pillow and smothered it. I then rang the police, was arrested and ended up in Holloway. Naturally Jack and Chrissie never wanted to talk to me again, and yet I knew they also were grateful for my releasing them, and the baby, from this terrible life. I was certain I'd done the right thing . . . By 5 a.m. I had set up an art class in Holloway, and was helping the entire prison with their social and educational problems . . .

April 12

Will these worries never end? Last night I woke at three in the morning and started panicking about getting old, I mean really old, and being in a chair in an old people's home tied in with blankets with wee pouring down my legs. The telly would be on all day, Jack and Chrissie would have got fed up with visiting me, and anyway would think I was a vegetable so it didn't matter, and every time I got pneumonia I would be resuscitated with powerful antibiotics to live another million years till I finally popped off aged 150. I started sweating with panic. Why am I having all this anxiety? Must be something to do with this baby's arrival. I am sure of it.

Or maybe it's to do with spring. Oddly, people get more

anxious and depressed in spring than at any other time of the year. And certainly everywhere is bursting with crocuses, and daffodils, even the hideous concrete pots on the pavement by Shepherds Bush station.

Later
Rather irritated by whistling from Maciej. He now has a new girlfriend. He showed me a picture of her. She works in a Nail Clinic and looks absolutely stunning. 'I in love,' he said, touching his heart.

April 13

Slept all through the night, thank goodness. In the morning I weighed myself. Found I was 67 stone 8 pounds. Extremely worried, and wondered how, if I were ill, I would ever fit into the ambulance, but then realized that Michelle had got there before me and switched the knob underneath the scales to kilowatts, or whatever, damn her.

I keep my scales in the bathroom next to a tall mahogany chest of drawers inherited from my grandmother. She used to keep in it letters, bits of ribbon, magnifying glasses, all kinds of knickery knackery ... I, on the other hand, keep pills, ointments, bandages and quantities of out-of-date old prescription drugs. Experience has told me that though some drugs go off after their sell-by date, most don't. Found myself suddenly wondering if sleeping pills, which had lost all their power over the years, could kill you, if you believed in them enough.

I have a box of whacking great sleepers left over from the sixties, bright blue capsules, hidden in a drawer for suicidal emergencies. It would be awful to swallow the lot and wake up still alive. But, on the other hand, if I believed strongly enough that they were still incredibly potent, would I die, whether they were strong or not? In other words, could one be killed by a placebo?

These thoughts were prompted by a mysterious email from a total stranger who had apparently got cancer, gone to Africa and met a witchdoctor, who asked if he could bring on his next visit:

3 young cats, I blackbird's egg, I dove, I black cock, a medium-sized calabash and plenty of soap, 8 candles and a bottle of Gin. I followed this to the letter and with these items the Old Man performed a ceremony and this time gave me my own Voodoo, which was black soap with a single corey shell in the middle. I was given strict instructions to use the soap every day and repeated in my mind, while washing, all that I had written down in previous ceremonies.

All this has been followed as instructed and as a result I feel as good as new. I feel so much better and went to see the oncologist at the Marsden and he was amazed at my progress.

Now I look closer, this email appears to have been forwarded by Philippa's sister. Very irritating. She requests that I send it to ten of my friends who can pray for this bloke, whoever he is. I shall do no such thing.

All the same, the story is very seductive. Longed to rush off to the witchdoctor with several bottles of gin and get instantly cured of everything – arthritis, bad dreams, incipient alcoholism . . . Might have a problem with the young cats, though. I fear they came to a sticky end.

Having retuned the scales, I found I was 10 stone 9 pounds which is far too heavy. I moved them about six inches away only to be told that I was 10 stone 11 – even worse. Now I am paranoid. Maybe I am really 13 stone 5, and don't know it. Or maybe I am anorexic and about to die. Dream on.

Later

When I got down to the kitchen I found that I had no milk left. I have an awful feeling that Michelle took my last drop. I felt enraged. First because I had no milk but secondly because I find it so irritating to get upset over half an inch of milk. It is not the milk I mind, but the fact that I have to get dressed and go to the shop to buy more supplies in order to have a cup of tea. In the event I tied my nightdress up tight with my dressing-gown cord, put my coat on over it, stuffed my bare feet into a pair of shoes and staggered round the corner to the supermarket. Apart from my hair sticking up on end I didn't look much different from how I always do.

It was pouring with spring sunshine and, in the street, the Imam of the local mosque bowed to me and said: 'Good morning!' He is perfectly charming, with a long grey beard, and he was wearing a cricketing jersey over his dress and had a lovely embroidered hat on top of his head. So I didn't feel too embarrassed about my own weird attire.

Last week, when I was sweeping leaves away from the road outside my house, he took the broom from me and insisted on doing it himself.

'As-Salaam Alaikum,' he said. I replied, feeling very proud of myself: 'Wa-Aleikum Salaam.' But this does not mean that I am learning Arabic. Those three words are going to be the very limit to my foreign-language learning in later life. And who knows, they might save me from death when I am kidnapped by terrorists in Iraq.

I am very lucky to have the mosque so close. It means that a) I will never get hit by a terrorist bomb and b) I have the pleasure of looking out of the window in the summer and seeing all the congregation out in the garden praying facing my house, it being in the direct line to Mecca.

I noticed to my surprise that the Kwik-Fit garage on the corner of the street had been boarded up and was for sale.

Immediately went into panic mode. Just hope it's not bought by someone who wants to turn it into a rock-music venue with twenty-four-hour drinking. Will have to alert the Residents' Association, of which I am chair. I was chairman until someone said it was sexist, so I had to turn into a chair.

I thought I had got away with my disguise and was hurrying home with my milk, when I was stopped by George, the black guy across the road. He is very tall, with two teeth missing and one gold one.

He has two very nice tearaway sons. But this time he had a terrible tale to tell. The man downstairs, he said, had threatened him.

'My neighbour,' he shook his head. 'He mad! You know what he do the other day?'

'No. What?' I asked. I knew this neighbour. A nasty piece of work of about sixty-five, covered in tattoos, with a bald head, who lives below George. Once he asked me to come in and measure his curtains for him 'because my daughters won't 'ave nuffink to do with me'. He is thick, whingeing, tough and lonely. When I wrote a few days ago that any man who turned his attention on me would set me sparkling and simpering, I was not including this creep across the road. Nor, actually, bearded counsellors.

'A policeman came for one of my boys,' said George. 'And my neighbour he let them in the door! So I came down next day and I say: "When policeman ring my bell, you don't let them in, you leave it to me to let them in, you hear?" So he get most unpleasant and that night, you know what, he bring a friend with a baseball bat and they come upstairs and they beat me op!'

'But he's disabled!' I said. 'He's got a sticker on his car!'

'Disabled – nonsense,' he replied. 'He's a bad man. I don't speak to him no more.'

When I got back I found that my dressing-gown cord

had come adrift and my nightdress had been trailing on the pavement like a ball-gown. God knows what they thought in the shop.

May 10th

Went to the Tate where I was meeting Hughie for lunch after going round the Turner exhibition.

'Can you face it?' asked Hughie. 'I mean all those sunsets and ships at sea, was there something wrong with his eyesight, all that old rubbish?'

'Lovely!' I said.

As I stepped into the tube station I was quite bowled over by the idea that I no longer had to pay. Ever. 'Freedom Pass!' – the very words are like the entry to a new life. On the platform I sat in a kind of dream of coddledness waiting for the train to come, thinking how lucky I was. I haven't been on an Underground train since I was about forty. I waited, and waited . . . and then it turned out that the service had been halted because someone had committed suicide. Not that we were told that, of course, but I knew it because they said it was due to 'passenger action' and a train driver I know told me that that was a euphemism for what was known in the business as a 'one under'.

Felt very sad that anyone could want to die like that and imagined that he was probably young, youth being one of the most depressing times of life in my experience. At the same time felt fantastically irritated that whoever he was decided to commit suicide on the very day that I was taking my first free trip on the Underground.

When I arrived at the Tate (and no, I will not call it Tate Britain, whatever the marketing men say), Hughie looked even older than I remembered him from the DVD evening.

He said that on his way a pregnant black woman had even got up for him in a bus. 'Everyone is very keen on old gentlemen,' he says.

Of course, he *is* older. He is sixty-five and the gap in our ages oddly seems far greater than between me and someone of, say, forty. Or, come to that, thirty. The thing is that those people who did National Service and missed out on being young in the sixties simply don't share the same common cultural language as those of us who, like the young today, were into sex, drugs and rock 'n' roll. Five years older than me and a man is still into suits. Hughie wears a jacket and tie wherever he goes. And yet, these people imagine we are the same because we both know all about thrift and pen hospitals and Lyons Corner Houses and ration books, etc.

What makes my generation so utterly distinctive is that we had one foot in an almost Victorian generation, and another in the new technological revolution. We're much more geared to big changes in our lives than the generation just before us. We were brought up by a pre-pill, washing-sheets-by-hand-removing-the-water-by-putting-them-through-a-hand-turned-mangle generation, but then we lived through the affluent sixties and later through the plunge into microchips and huge advances in technology, experiencing a seismic shift which has made us far more adaptable to change than either those who were young before the sixties or those who were young after them. It helps, too, that it's hard for us sixties survivors ever to shake our heads worriedly about today's youth and say: 'Ah, they aren't like the young people of our day.' The young today *are* like the young of our day. If anything, they're possibly less adventurous and more responsible.

Anyway, off we went into the exhibition. Going to an art gallery these days is like entering a rather civilized old people's home. Everyone is nearly 100 and smelling of pee, and they're all bent double on walking frames and listening to the talking guides with the volume so high that you can hear every word leaking out between their ears and the headphones.

'Oh, dear,' said Hughie, looking around in rather a depressed way. 'Pictures by dead people being looked at by nearly-dead people. I *do* hope I don't live too long. The idea of another thirty years – what total hell.'

Then, looking down at me, he suddenly asked: 'What have you got on your feet?'

I explained that once I'd got out of the blue flip-flops I had to wear sensible shoes for a few weeks and had got rather addicted to them. Sensible shoes from Ecco, no less. There's a funny moment when you're sixty and thinking about shoes, when someone (everyone in fact) suddenly reveals there is a special shop for old people's comfortable shoes. It sounds glamorous – Ecco. Ecco! Behold! But rather than continuing with the theme: 'Ecco! Da beautifulla shoes for the lovely matura ladya! Flattera your beautifulla feeta!', the words following Ecco should, in my view, run: 'Ecco! Atta lasta! The hideousa but comfortaballa shoesa for the olda batsa!'

'They're delightful,' he said, gallantly. 'I do hope you can walk, though. Would you like me to hire a wheelchair? It might be rather fun . . . Then you could be at the level of the captions and near enough to read them out to me – very loudly of course – and we wouldn't have to get the Big Print version of the catalogue for oldies with fading sight.'

On our way out we saw a man's big black hat lying in the corridor. 'Oh dear, I saw the owner of that hat earlier on,' said Hughie.

'Show me a man in a big hat and I'll show you a cunt,' I said. It's a joke Penny told me.

'Marie!' said Hughie, shocked but unable, despite himself, not to laugh.

We both imagined this wretched man going around pompously, imagining he'd got his ludicrous hat on his head, and then going home and looking in the mirror and finding to his horror that he'd been strutting around all day just an ordinary person with a small bald head.

Hughie bought me a scrummy lunch in the restaurant which was fearfully expensive but it was good because over the saddle of hare (oh, dear, too yummy, poor old hare) I was able to bring up the difficult subject again.

'Now, what did the doctor say about that ghastly cough?' I asked, in a no-nonsense kind of way. Hughie'd been coughing his head off all the way round the exhibition, narrowly avoiding exploding all over Turner's *Thames above Waterloo Bridge*.

He looked at me, slyly. 'I think you know I haven't been,' he said. 'You've been talking to James, I can hear it in your voice.'

'I have absolutely *not* been talking to James,' I said. 'I swear on my mother's grave. And what's James got to do with this anyway? Is James worried too?' I said. When I lie, though I say it myself, I lie well. Anyway, my mother, like Hughie's, was cremated. So ha!

Hughie looked rather uneasy. 'Yes, yes, I must go to the doctor,' he said. 'I know. And I will. I'm just putting it off, but I will, I promise.'

'You're not one of those ludicrous men who's frightened of going to the doctor, Hughie?' I said. 'Please don't tell me you are. I'd lose all respect for you.'

Hughie grimaced. 'Stop it, Marie. Don't use cheap tricks on me. I will go.'

'I don't believe you,' I said. 'I can see it in your eyes. They've kind of clouded over as if someone's drawn a piece of cheesecloth over them.'

He laughed, then paused, thinking.

'I'll tell you why I don't go, Marie,' he said, eventually. 'If I've got cancer or something – and I frankly don't care if

I have – I've lived long enough. Sixty-five isn't a bad age, quite honestly, and I've still got all my faculties. But if I have got something sinister, I'll have to start having all that chemotherapy, last strand of hair falling out, feeling utterly wretched, James in floods of tears, you wringing your hands. I've got better things to do with the end of my life than lie in hospital on 800 drips, a living corpse surrounded by people discussing whether I'm well enough to have a lung transplant. It's not the doctor I'm frightened of. Or the diagnosis of cancer – which is probable, as I've smoked for fifty years now. It's the curative treatment that scares me. Or, most likely, the non-curative treatment. All that hoo-ha.'

'But it might be just a chest infection,' I said. 'Which could be cured by a few antibiotics. Who says you've got cancer? You're letting your imagination run away with you! You could always say no to treatment anyway, if it was.'

'Don't talk nonsense,' he said, rather brusquely. The waiter arrived with a second bottle of wine which Hughie sampled before nodding. 'How could I say no? The pressure on me would be unbearable.'

It struck me again, the difference between us because of our ages. Hughie was brought up in an era of public schools, the army and distant parents, and as a result has this totally inappropriate respect for authority. He could no more say to his doctor that he didn't want any treatment for whatever it was, than fly.

'That's true,' I said. 'I do understand.' And I did. Understanding people is rather like lying. You simply have to believe you understand a person's point of view – and I really thought I did – in order for a declaration of understanding to be accepted as true. I scrabbled around in my brain for something – just something – that might push him into going to the doctor.

'But I think there is one factor you haven't taken into account,' I said, hit by a brainwave. 'Your cough is very public.

If you were suffering some kind of internal private symptom that you could shield from people like James and me, fine. Bleeding stools. Stomach cramps. Mad voices in your head telling you to kill everyone. None of us would be any the wiser. And I'd understand your point of view. But, Hughie, this cough is so public. Every time you cough I bet James is just suffering agonies. He must experience, if this morning is anything to go by, about 150 knife-wounds of anxiety per day. Either stop coughing,' I concluded, sternly, 'or get it checked out.'

It's rare that I hit the spot with Hughie, but I could see he was listening to me and absorbing what I'd said. You can always persuade rational people to do anything as long as you have the logic ready. Terrible really. Emotional people are far less easy to win round.

There was a long pause.

'I hadn't thought of it like that,' he said. He coughed again. I mimed a stabbing motion into my heart.

'OK, OK, OK,' he said. There was another pause. He pushed his plate away, and coughed again. He then held his forehead in his hands, thinking. Finally, he rummaged in his pocket and brought out his mobile phone and his address book and started dialling.

There was a pause while it rang. Then he said: 'Dr Evans's surgery? It's Hugh Passton here. I want to make an appointment. Yes. Yes. Fine. Nine o'clock. Next Thursday. I'll be there.'

He put his phone away and I felt my eyes filling with tears. I don't really know why. Perhaps it was something to do with wondering if he was dying, but I think, rather, that it was to do with having made a connection with someone else at such a deep level. It seemed to be something to do with love, but I couldn't quite define it.

Hughie put his hand to his mouth and blew me a kiss.

'Now can we change the subject?' he said, pouring me out a glass of red. 'Can we have some pudding? Can we . . . oh!' he said, looking over my shoulder. 'I wonder what's going on over there! I think I see Penny and it looks as if she's having lunch with someone *most* unsuitable!'

I turned and there, sitting in front of the Whistler mural, between a fawn and a small painted bridge, was Penny, deep in conversation with a bloke I had never seen before. His back was to us, but as far as I could see he had red hair. And then he turned slightly to reveal – yes, a beard! How could she! Do hope she won't fall in love with him and put off our weekend in France.

The Underground was working when I finally made the journey home. By the way, who on earth ever buys or eats those repulsive grilled nuts covered with sugar that they sell at stations? Are they a cover for something? Like those sinister Nail Bars? Do hope Maciej's girlfriend isn't a member of the Mafia.

June 1

Turns out that Michelle does. Eat those nuts I mean. I caught her nibbling from a bag in the kitchen, at the same time as she was poring over all the so-called healthy food she has stored in the fridge. Funny how people who are into health foods, soya milk, organic bread and fresh juices so often go mad and break out into the most revolting food imaginable. I once caught Marion guiltily eating an unspeakable raspberry ripple from Iceland. And she has the nerve to say I'm not a healthy eater! I may buy creepy identically shaped vegetables from Tesco occasionally, but I'd never eat a raspberry ripple if you paid me.

June 4th

Last-minute plans from Penny about our trip to France. But as my computer seemed to have crashed I had to go round to Lucy's to look at the options that Penny had sent me. Luckily she's working in London this week.

Lucy asked me, rather oddly, I thought, whether I had broad beans. I said that no I hadn't and wasn't it a bit early for them, anyway? Turned out she'd asked me whether I'd got broadband.

June 12th

Three slight problems with the journey to France.

One was that you are compelled, now, to check in by yourself. It was bad enough, quite honestly, booking tickets on-line. I can't see what's wrong with people doing the work for you. They get a job and I get an easier life. But now you have to be your own travel agent, instead of having someone do up your itinerary in a nice little plastic folder and give it to you with the words 'Have a lovely holiday!'

To have to check yourself in as well was a bit much.

I noticed some kind of official hovering about, and continued to goggle at the self-checking-in machine helplessly.

'How does this work?' I asked him. I could tell, already, that he was trained not to do it for you. He pointed to various buttons and I then declared that as I hadn't got the right glasses on (total lie) I couldn't see which buttons he was pointing to. I was, I explained cunningly, very *old*. In the end he had to do it all for me and I felt totally victorious. Why *should* I check myself in? Soon supermarkets will be forcing you to make your own ready-made meals.

I paid for all this, of course, by appearing to be a fool, but it was a payment I was delighted to make. Because one of the great pleasures of age is helplessness. If my tyre blew on the motorway, I wouldn't, now, lose any pride in flagging down a bloke to help me. The days of struggling with a jack and a handbook, with one's hands covered in oil, just to prove something, are completely over.

Penny checked herself in with no problem at all and I think rather disapproved of my scam.

Another blight was that going down the corridor to the departure gate (I was reeking, as usual, of about a dozen scents I'd squirted on myself in the Duty Free) an Italian girl asked me if this was the way to Turin. I couldn't help her, but did rather wonder why she'd asked me rather than Penny – or someone else. Was it because I looked Italian too? I preened myself. So chic! Or was it because I looked old and therefore safe? Again, I felt a maternal glow coming over me. But then I caught sight of myself in the reflection in the glass that divides the white drained people from the healthy bronzed people, walking in the other direction, and discovered the reason I'd been targeted. In my black stockings, black flat shoes and long grey jacket, I looked just like a gloomy old Italian widow, rather a different kettle of fish.

Third problem was that sitting next to me on the plane was a man with a very black beard who read the Quran to himself in a low mutter all the way there, making me sick with anxiety. I tried to smile at him in my 'Hey, I'm just a harmless old sixty-year-old!' way, but no response, just a glare.

Only plus was that at least none of the loos had been modernized at the airports. At Schiphol airport in Amsterdam, you go in, sit down normally, then stand up, and then you just can't find anywhere to flush the loo. So, being a decent middle-class human being, you try to pull a couple of sheets of loo paper from the inexplicably heavy loo-paper machine, and lay them neatly over whatever you've done, and leave, expecting to murmur apologetically to the next person in line that the loo doesn't flush. Only to find that, as you open the door to leave the loo, it explodes into a huge flushing *all by itself*.

I do think modern technology has gone too far when you can't even flush away your own poo.

Anyway, we checked into a funny little hotel in Nice – totally unchanged since when I'd been there with my mother in the fifties – plonked down our bags and went down to have dinner.

'Now, I want to ask you a question,' I said, after I'd ordered my *bouillabaisse* and *boeuf grillé*. We ate in one of those typically French dining rooms, full of thick-leaved plants in brass pots, with oak tables covered with plastic tablecloths, and big paper napkins with dolphins on them. 'You're not, by any chance, internet dating are you?'

Penny's eyes popped out of her head. 'Do you have second sight?' she asked. 'I didn't tell you one day, did I?'

'You said you were thinking about it,' I said. 'You didn't say you'd started, though.'

'Does it *show*?' she asked.

'It's simply that you've been looking rather anxious recently. And I have to admit I did see you at the Tate with a most peculiar-looking man who just couldn't have been a friend.'

Penny screwed up her face in horror. 'Peter!' she said. 'He was the most horrible little man who'd brought a whole kit of ghastly sex toys down to London and wanted us to check into a hotel to try them out! I told him I wasn't remotely interested. He was such a creep. He said he was fifty-six but he must have been at least seventy.'

'Is this wise?' I asked her. 'Aren't you heading for trouble?'

'I suppose so,' she said. 'But I never meet any men these days. And I'd like to. Do you think it's awful? I mean, just because one's old, doesn't mean one has to give up sex, does it?'

'Rather you than me,' I said. 'But do tell.'

Her next hot date is with a retired philosophy professor – an Aquarian, apparently, whatever that means – who lives in Northumberland and sounds immensely civilized. For a moment I felt envious and wondered: am I right in thinking that there are no sensible men around? Hughie's a sensible man. And, I have to say, so is Archie. Then I gave myself a slap on the wrist. I've heard the argument before. 'Maybe there's just one . . .' But there isn't.

On our list of Sights to See was the church decorated by Jean Cocteau at Villefranche, just down the coast. But what made it particularly uncanny was that I remember clearly being ten years old and literally being *dragged* round it by my mother, finding it all unutterably boring.

Who is the real person, I wonder – the ten-year-old being dragged or the sixty-year-old going round full of admiration and appreciation? How many other characters can I expect to be before I die?

One of the funny things about being old is that when you're four years old, you can only imagine yourself as a one, two or three-year-old. But when you're sixty, you've got a vast range of eras to choose from. So one day I feel like a miserable three-year-old, the next like a girlish 25-year-old, hop straight into feeling like a mature sixty-year-old and back, before you know it, to being a precocious twelve-year-old. The cast of selves increases and increases until eventually you've got a veritable Wagner opera of people on stage to pick from.

June 13

What a great place France is. The countryside is just like England used to be fifty years ago, all wildflowers and bees and butterflies; you're knee-deep in shrews and otters. And there are all these lovely individual shops. In England we're just a mass of Body Shops, Starbucks and Tesco Metros, while in France there seem to be no chains at all, except, of course, Monoprix, where charming clothes of all descriptions can be purchased for virtually nothing.

Oh, dear. Suddenly realize I'm sounding exactly like Philippa's ghastly sister.

Bought Chrissie a very nice black and white pregnancy top which I thought was extremely smart.

Pottered around Nice and, as always in foreign cities, I find, we ended up going down those strange back streets, full of electrical repair shops, and places selling kitchen equipment, and tyres, but finally got into the main drag, where Penny rather unnerved me by declaring that whenever she passed a hat shop, she always wondered which one she'd choose for when she had to have chemotherapy. She doesn't even have cancer for heaven's sake!

Sent Hughie and James a postcard saying: 'Yesterday we went to a tiny restaurant in the old town and had scrummy lamb shanks in gravy, salad, pears cooked in red wine and a bottle of wine. The bill was seven pounds each. Yum! Yum!'

Sent a card to Archie (about whom I've been feeling rather guilty since I completely forgot to thank him for the delicious lunch) saying:

So sorry not to have thanked you for the best birthday present of all. Always lovely seeing you. Meet when we get back?
Much love from Marie.

I mean, it would be nice to see him again. Oddly found myself wondering rather like a teenager whether to put 'Much love' or 'Lots of love'. 'Lots of love' is something to write to everyone now, even the milkman, and it's got rather debased. 'Much love' sounds more considered and meaningful.

June 14

When I got back, I took the top round to Chrissie, full of exhortations not to wear it if it wasn't right, and I was amazed that not only did she look wonderful in it, but that, despite very polite murmurings, she clearly didn't like it at all. It slowly dawned on me that all pregnant women these days like to have their bump showing, bursting out of a tight teeshirt. What makes it all even more weird is that they like to show their tummy button sticking out, like a third nipple.

I was rather blown away by the fact that Chrissie didn't like it. I am usually spot on when it comes to fashion. But I really felt I had egg on my face when it came to pregnancy fashions. I suddenly realized what it must feel like to be an out-of-date old duck who buys some frightful twin-set for a daughter-in-law and finds that yes, she does want to take it back to the shop to change it. Very humiliating. And yet I know – which is what is so odd – that were I Chrissie's age, and pregnant, I, too, would want to wear tight teeshirts with my tummy button sticking out.

Rather unnervingly, she asked me about birth.

We sat at the kitchen table, over a cup of coffee, and I honestly didn't know what to say.

'It's not brilliant,' I said, in the end, hesitantly. 'But it's not the end of the world, either. And you do forget it very quickly.' Forget it quickly my arse, I felt like saying. Well, I doubt if I would have actually said 'arse'. I try not to be the sort of person who says 'fuck', 'shit' and 'arse' too much because I think it's a bit undignified for a woman of sixty, like wearing a mini-skirt with varicose-veiny legs. But that doesn't stop me thinking 'arse'.

'Tell us what happened when I was born,' said Jack.

I cast my mind back. It was an absolute nightmare. Some junior doctor stitched me up wrongly, I was in agony all through the night, had to have an emergency operation under anaesthetic the next day, and was in excruciating pain for two weeks. Not only that, but my breasts were so engorged that the West Indian nurses came round and flicked them. 'Like concrete, darlin',' they said. Occasionally, when Jack cried, great squirts of milk came shooting out of my nipples like some dreadful ejaculation. It was really horrible.

'Oh, it wasn't that bad,' I said, lightly. 'Well, the birth itself was fine, let's put it like that.' And the very last bit was. I always remember watching my stomach deflate, like a landed parachute, once Jack had popped out the other end. 'And these days you're drugged up to the eyebrows.'

I refused to be drawn. Birth is so strange you just can't predict how people will feel about it. 'Why don't we go shopping and get some stuff for the nursery next week?' I suggested, to change the subject.

Chrissie's already painted the room they've prepared for the baby, and lined a little Moses basket. The walls are covered with frescos of ducks, elephants and cats. Lying across the basket is a beautiful lacy white shawl with yellow daisies embroidered into each corner, knitted by Chrissie's grannie. And suddenly I feel completely inadequate.

Will it all come back to me, like riding a bicycle? Will there be new ways of child-rearing that I won't understand? Will I be of any use to Chrissie at all, or will I be an old lady, all fear and fingers and thumbs and forgetting that above all, you *must support the baby's head* at all times? Will I be stuffing bottles of boiling milk into his little mouth? Will I get the mixtures all wrong? Will he choke on a grape that I've given him? Will I forget to read the crucial label: *May contain nuts*? Worst of all, *what if I don't I love him*? And yet I'm the one who's meant to be experienced and calm. And I'm not!

Help! Help! Help! HELP!

June 15th

Supper with Lucy, whose London base is at the top of a mansion block in Belsize Park. She said, on hearing my voice through the intercom: 'You might find it easier to take the lift.' I notice, when I get up to her flat, that she does not say this to any other guests.

Latest email:

> Spur M is the latest of all natural male-enhancement formulas which guarantee: Rock-hard Erection like 'steel.' Strong ejaculate like a porn star! Cum again and again! Up to 50% volume. Cover her in it if you want!

Golly, men are weird. They always were and they still are.

June 16th

Went to a movie with Penny. It was so truly dreadful that we walked out half-way through. The truth is that having seen so many films in my life, I now know exactly what is going to happen in most of them. I know how they're going to be shot, I know everything. When I was young, movies were still experimental – and every time you went to the cinema you experienced some new thought, some wizardly fresh idea.

Now, apart from the odd foreign film, about one every couple of years, they all seem the same.

'I knew who the murderer was, didn't you?' I said to Penny.

'Yes,' she said. 'It was the hero. Or "protagonist" as heroes are now called.'

We checked on the mobile with James who'd seen it, to see if we were right.

'Hughie walked out after ten minutes,' he said. 'He knew who did it like you. But I think it's got something to do with Rupert Sheldrake's theory of Morphic Resonance.'

'What's that?'

'Oh, you must know. I gather the general drift of the theory is that the reason you find a crossword puzzle easier to do the day after than on the day it's published is because so many other people have done it on the day it came out and their knowledge is pooled in the great subconscious, which we all tap into.'

'So the more people who've seen a movie, the less surprising is the ending?'

'Precisely.'

'It's Morphic Resonance,' I told Penny, when I'd said goodbye.

'Oh, God,' she said. 'Is it catching? What's the cure?'

Turns out that she has her date with the prof from Northumberland on Thursday. I fear for her.

And still, I have to admit, I envy her. Just a speck. Despite all evidence to the contrary, I still can't help having a fantasy in the back of my mind that somewhere, just somewhere, there might be a bloke who isn't a complete screwball.

But, of course, there isn't.

July 1

I have been keeping the old white-painted wooden high chair of Jack's for . . . well, it must be thirty years. And I've been keeping it, let's be honest, for a grandchild. Now, at last, I can offload it, so I barged into Michelle's room and tried to reclaim it. Unfortunately she has used it as a spare dressing table and the little tray, the seat and the flat piece of wood at the bottom are all completely covered with things that she calls 'products'. What she wants 'products' for I have no idea, since her skin is in full bloom, the skin of a nineteen-year-old, but there they all were, facial scrubs, lotions, anti-ageing cream for her neck (I could do with some of that – she certainly doesn't need it). Everything seemed to be made from camomile, avocado, aloe vera . . . an evil-looking plant with treacherous spikes, illustrated on every label. I tipped them all on to her bed, and staggered downstairs with the high chair.

I bet they don't like it. I bet they want a plastic, wipe-clean affair, which turns into a baby trampoline at the touch of a button and doubles up as a sling. But this is far, far nicer. It was second-hand when I bought it, and made in the forties . . . it converts into a kind of weird seat with wheels, featuring a few faded coloured beads on a rod of metal.

Rather surprised to find that it didn't look as if Michelle's bed had been slept in last night.

Later
No Michelle and no post either. The post has been completely terrible recently. I met a postman in the road who couldn't speak English and was trying to find the police station. He was standing right in front of it.

Maybe Archie didn't even get my postcard, which would

account for silence from him. But who cares about Archie? I don't. No, I don't. No, I really don't.

July 2nd

No sign of Michelle today, either. I have rung her mobile but it's just an answering machine. And anyway, when I went back into her room to look for clues, I found her mobile was actually on her bedside table, charging up. And her handbag seemed to be there as well. I suddenly had a dreadful vision of her just popping out to the shops to buy some more 'products' for her face, and being lured into a van by a bunch of Romanians who were, at this very moment, gang-raping her in a dank concrete cellar.

Later

Still no sign of Michelle. I am out of my mind with worry. I rang Penny and she said not to worry, it would surely be OK . . . these things always are. But she didn't sound totally convinced when I said that Michelle was completely naïve and hardly spoke any English. I know it seems mad, but I'm going to ring round the hospitals.

Later

No sign of a stray French girl at any of the hospitals. I finally rang her 'muzair' in France, but that was an answering machine too, and before I knew it I'd burbled out an anxious message, with no way of retracting it.

Finally I rang the police and to my horror they took it quite seriously. Anyone, they said, who was young and had been missing for over twenty-four hours could be treated as a missing person. Much to my astonishment I found myself sitting on the sofa downstairs, actually in tears I was so worried about her. Honestly I feel like a bird out of the Conrad Lorenz book in reverse. He was the naturalist who hatched out a bunch of ducks and because he was the first live thing they saw, they all went honking and waddling after him on their baby feet, thinking he was their mother. I, on the other hand, simply open the door to any young girl and immediately think she is my daughter. Crackers.

Later

Had just made a date with the police for them to come round when the door opened and a happy voice sang out ''Allo!'

I hastily dried my tears and pretended I'd only been slightly worried, begging forgiveness for ringing her 'muzair'. She couldn't have been more apologetic. She'd left her mobile at home and had stayed with her cousin for two days. Well, that's her story. Anything but the Romanian gang.

When the policeman came round, five minutes later, I had to hustle him out hurriedly because I couldn't bear Michelle to think I'd been so silly.

July 17th

Baby due next month. Jack and Chrissie have been thinking about names. Jack says that they're considering Stanley or Alfred – or Lester or Igor. Or Gene. Stanley and Alfred are OK, but Lester? Gene? *Igor?* They must be joking.

Each one fills me with horror. I suppose I could get used to Lester. (Or is it Leicester? Surely only people in Shakespeare plays are called Leicester?) Gene sounds quite weird. It's a name that must belong solely to the Vincent and Pitney families. Gene . . . cripes.

Jack tells me on the phone that Stanley has been knocked out 'because Chrissie's grannie says she once knew a horrible little grocer in her village called Stanley'. Gene is still on, and when I suggested that Eugene might be a better name than just Gene, there was a long silence and I had to retreat before he had summoned up a withering reply. But Igor is still a strong contender. Surely Igor was the mentally disabled assistant of Frankenstein? They *must* be joking. But apparently not.

'And what is your grandson's name?'

'Igor.'

'*Igor?*'

'Yes, I'm afraid so.'

'As in Frankenstein's assistant?'

'The very same. But' (lamely) 'we prefer to think of him as Igor in Stravinsky.'

'Well. Er. How original. I do hope he won't get teased at school.'

The same old wish – the hope that he won't get teased at school.

I do remember Jack, five years old, once coming out of school in tears. 'Mum, why am I called Jack?' he said. 'I *wish* I were called Wayne. I wish, I wish, I were called Wayne.' At that moment, of course, I wished, too, that he were called Wayne.

I rang Jack's dad, who lives in Devon. 'What do you think of Igor?' I said.

'*Igor!*' he said. 'As in Frankenstein's assistant?'

'Or Gene?'

'Gene! As in Harlow?'

Oh, God, I hadn't thought of Harlow.

'It *is* going to be a boy, isn't it?' he said. Then he recovered himself. 'Well, I suppose we could live with it,' he said. 'I suppose we'll *have* to live with it. There's nothing we can do about it. Well, blow me. Igor or Gene.'

August 1

Yesterday garden totally dried up. Lawn looked like the Gobi desert. Put sprinkler on today and totally forgot about it till now hours later, and garden is a mushy swamp.

August 20th

The baby is due today. Wondered whether to ring Jack and Chrissie to ask what's going on. I remember how boring it was when I was pregnant with Jack and just before he arrived, the phone ringing every five minutes with people desperate to hear the news. But I am on tenterhooks! I long to know the latest! I rang on the feeble pretext of asking if Jack wanted me to post on a piece of junk mail that had arrived that morning offering him a loan.

'No, Mum, nothing has happened,' he said tetchily when he realized it was me on the phone, before I'd even opened my mouth.

'Oh, sorry,' I said, feeling rather idiotic.

There was nothing left to say.

I feel so weirdly stressed. Lucy and Marion and James and Penny and everyone are constantly ringing me up asking if anything's happened. This is a precursor, I can see, to the feelings of being a grandparent. No control. Then there's the added problem of love. Might love him, of course, or might not. No love. That ghastly possibility that always lurks treacherously in the background. Oh, Lord. What if he's just one of those frightful lumps with no hair? A great big white blob with an expressionless face and eyes that look like pissholes in the snow, as my father used to say. I mean, it could be possible.

More likely, however, a grandchild will result in a case of extreme love combined with extreme powerlessness.

Cripes, what a ghastly idea. Just as you consider giving up men, and find yourself free from the dreadful addictions of love and lust, another addiction creeps into your life. A grandchild. Like giving up wine, and then finding yourself hooked on beer.

I felt utterly miserable all day, longing, just longing, for news. Any old news. News that Chrissie was feeling well. News that she was feeling ill. News that she was feeling happy. News that she was feeling down. The longing for contact was overwhelming. Never since I was twenty have I waited with such longing for the phone to ring. Tried to do the crossword, but in the end felt I was staring at a Bridget Riley. Rather sick.

Luckily Jack put me out of my misery in the evening, saying sorry. 'I didn't mean to snap this morning,' he said, 'but five people had already rung and we're getting a bit stressed out. We'll let you know when anything's happened, you know that. You'll be the first, the very first to know.'

So funny this reversal of roles. It was always me, in the past, who would console my son. Now he consoles me, reassures me, looks after me. And yet all the time he is also reassuring, looking after and consoling Chrissie.

If I ever come back on this earth, God forbid, I don't want to come back as a man. Actually I don't want to come back as a woman, either. If I had to come back (and please, please God, not that you exist, just snuff me out like a candle) – if, as I say, I had to come back, I would like to be re-incarnated as an olive.

Why an olive? Well, first you grow on a lovely tree in the sunshine in Italy, which is fine by me. Then you are picked and spend some time in a vat being soaked in oil so that all your bitterness comes out. Couldn't be better. Then you are served up at a cocktail party and eaten by some lovely young thing. A perfect ending. And the whole cycle lasts only a year.

Aug 24

Jack rang me this morning. He's born. And he's Gene. Sounds a terrible birth. Chrissie went through hell and finally, as the heartbeat monitor showed that the baby's heart was wildly out of control, the doctor told Jack that he would have to decide whether Chrissie should have a Caesarean or not. When Jack asked what he advised, the doctor said: 'It's up to you.'

'But what if it were your wife, what would you do?'

'I can't say,' said the doctor, smugly. 'It is the patient who has the say in all this these days. All I can do is tell you the facts.'

'But if she didn't have a Caesarean would the baby die?'

'It's a possibility,' said the doctor.

Luckily the midwife was miming 'Caesarean' behind the doctor's back, by making all kinds of slashing and snipping signs over her stomach, so Jack said: 'Let's go for the Caesarean, then,' and he did.

I felt curiously flat about the whole thing. I was hoping for a leaping of the heart, a repetition of the feeling I had when I heard that Chrissie was pregnant, but whenever I looked into my heart there was just a sign up saying 'Shut'. An awful blankness. I wondered if my lack of emotion had anything to do with the dreadful feelings I'd had when Jack was born, and made the great mistake of looking in my diary. Oddly enough this was written exactly thirty-two years to the day before Gene was born.

After the birth, which was OK, I had the horrors a few times in hospital – sufficiently bad for well-meaning doc to allow me out to 'stop you feeling like a prisoner', the result of which was a nerve-racking trip on my own round Hammersmith which resulted in me staggering fainting back into the ward, trembling with fear and terror of the cars, and collapsing into hysterical tears.

Then I am *always* bursting into tears because I feel that all the good old days are gone, and that I'll never be able to feel that Elvis is God any more or get crushes or listen to records because they're all unreal feelings – just an awful wallowing in nostalgia. I had a horrible feeling the other morning of suicidal depression with the awful vision of life continuing as it had done before, the only difference being this sort of pet animal I have around in the shape of Jack.

Then, two days later, also from my diary:

I just worry about how I can cope. This morning I was feeling I'd got enough on my hands with me, let alone having to cope with Jack as well. I should never have had him, I know, but I suppose now he's here I'll have to go through the motions of coping. I was so depressed this morning that I just felt like jumping out of the window. I know I won't be a good mother. I feel nothing for him, poor wretch.

Thank God all that changed after a year or so. After reading it, and various other grisly entries, I found I was crying with pity for myself. I snapped the book shut. Such a case of post-natal depression! I'm amazed no doctor picked it up – but then PND was hardly recognized in those days.

99

August 25th

It is so hot I could pop. But since I can't allow my upper arms to be seen, I had to wear a cardie over my sleeveless linen dress. But have to keep up the standards, whatever.

Went to see Gene with Hughie and James, who were full of the news that Archie has found love.

'Too late,' said Hughie. 'I told you you should have got in there quick.'

Apparently he has a young Swedish girl of thirty-five, whom he absolutely adores. But I was in such a state I couldn't sum up even the tiniest twinge of jealousy. I couldn't think straight. I took a bottle of champagne and James told me that it was Krishna's birthday, and therefore Gene was specially blessed, and we went into the poshest hospital known to man, quite unlike the run-down affair that I had Jack in, all white corridors and stainless-steel lifts – and there was Chrissie, radiant.

'Well, well, well,' said Hughie, wryly, staring down at Gene, who was lying, like a pink prune, wrapped in a little white shawl, in a cot by Chrissie's bed. 'Imagine that when you're an old man like me, the number of people over the age of sixty-four is expected to have grown from 9.5 million to 15 million. It's a ghastly prospect, little chap.'

I looked at Gene but unfortunately could still feel nothing for him at all. He is absolutely tiny and has little puffy bits under his eyes, like a minuscule alcoholic. I made all the right noises, but the sight of him left me cold. I felt such a creep. Even after we'd had champagne, I couldn't think of anything to say. It was as if my brain had shut down and my heart had just left the building. It all seemed like a dream. I suppose I shall have to pretend to rave about him. It is all so embarrassing. What is the matter with me? I felt dreadfully sad and different since James was beside himself and started crying with emotion.

Later I told Hughie how I felt and he said: 'Yes, babies leave me cold too. Ghastly things. Can't see the point. But I bet you'll change your mind.'

'I won't,' I said, mournfully. 'I know I won't.'

August 26th

Penny has just rung me saying she thinks she's got prostate cancer. I only just stopped her making a doctor's appointment.

August 31st

The next day the bell rang. Thinking it was a friend I was expecting, I was horrified to find my opposite neighbour, the man who had beaten up my black friend.

'Why hello!' I smiled, welcomingly, hoping he didn't have a baseball bat behind his back. 'How are you? How nice to see you!' Lies, lies.

He stood there, like the Incredible Hulk. But his eyes were more hollow than usual. He seemed a bit thinner. He was wearing that most repulsive of male garments, a white polo-necked sweatshirt made of cotton and polyester, worn tight across his chest, showing his nipples.

'I got bad news for you,' he intoned.

'Oh dear, I am sorry,' I said. 'What's up?'

He drew his arm from behind his back and proceeded to pull on a cigarette.

'The doctors told me,' he said, 'that I got lung cancer. Only got six mumfs to live.'

Much as I feared and loathed this man, I couldn't help being touched by a spark of compassion.

'I'm so sorry,' I said, suffused with a mixture of pity and at the same time a vicious feeling that he had got just retribution for his frightful behaviour.

'Yeah. Well,' he said. 'I'm going to fight it,' he said. 'That's all I can do. Fight it.' He turned away, and as he walked across the road he looked diminished, more like a padded skeleton than an old bully boy.

From then on I have seen him every day, sitting at the wheel of his parked mighty maroon four-wheel-drive car, smoking his cigarettes, 'fighting it'.

Don't think Hughie will do much 'fighting it' if the worst comes to the worst. He *did* go to the doctor's and was put on a course of antibiotics, but James tells me his cough is just as bad as ever, so he's going to go back to see what else is on offer.

September 2nd

Went round to see Jack and Chrissie, who is finally out of hospital. I thought these days they barely dragged the placenta from the womb than they chucked new mothers on to the streets, but, perhaps because she'd had a Caesarean, Chrissie seemed to be in for days. This afternoon she went up to have a sleep just after I arrived, and Gene lay quietly on my lap.

Jack is clearly overwhelmed and overjoyed. They are talking of having a 'head-wetting' in a pub rather than a christening, which is fine by me. Jack asked me about what songs I thought ought to be sung and I just sat, stroking Gene's head. No, I didn't feel any love for him, I thought, but there was no question: he was awfully sweet. The panic I had felt when he had just been born seemed to have disappeared. And what struck me, as I touched him, was how my own hands looked so fat, puffy and middle-aged, like my mother's hands. And Gene's hands are, like all baby's hands, so utterly tiny and moving. It is what everyone says when they first see a new-born baby, after all. 'Oh, look at his tiny fingers! His tiny fingernails!'

Jack made me a cup of tea, and Chrissie came down, exhausted, but still radiant and incredibly happy. I held Gene and patted his warm little back after he'd been fed, supporting his floppy head. He made little sucking movements with his mouth. He looks quite baffled to be here. I went up with Chrissie to change his nappy. Everything quite different to how it was in my day, of course – throw-away nappies, with kind of Velcro fastenings, none of those terry-towels with nappy pins. No buckets full of Napisan. And all kinds of different creams and unguents to put on his tiny bottom.

'Why don't you have a go?' said Chrissie.

What was so peculiar was finding how familiar it all was. How my right hand went instantly to his ankles, to lift him up, how I wiped his bottom with the back of the nappy, then gave him a good clean, and blew him dry, and covered him with cream and powder, and then lifted up his oddly thin bottom again, and slipped the nappy into place – it was like riding a bicycle after one hadn't ridden one for years. Then I picked him up and held him close, his head and weak little neck resting on my shoulder. His baby smell, a mixture of sharpened pencils and talcum powder, gusted over me like fairy-dust. Later, when I looked at my watch, it was half past six, but I didn't really want to leave.

I drove home feeling very peculiar. And then I realized. I was so heavy and sodden with adoration for Gene that I could hardly change gear. I seemed to have acquired a great burden of love that hadn't been with me when I had left the house. I finally made it back to Shepherds Bush, staggered in through the door and sat for a few moments, regaining my strength. I rang up Jack's dad. It was the most extraordinary experience. When you are sixty, you don't expect suddenly to discover that someone new has come on the scene for whom you feel overwhelming love. And instant love, as well. Not the slow-growing affection you feel for friends.

'He is absolutely lovely,' I said, on the verge of tears. 'I can't wait for you to see him!'

'And have they decided on a name?' asked David, nervously.

'Gene,' I said. 'And do you know,' I added, meaning every word of it, 'it's a *wonderful* name! It suits him down to the ground. He looks like a Gene, he breathes like a Gene, he just *is* a Gene . . .'

David burst out laughing.

September 3

Rang Penny to ask if she'd like to come with me to see Gene some time. Oddly, she didn't seem terribly keen, though she's agreed to pop in one day when Jack brings him over. Simply cannot understand why anyone would *not* want to see Gene, since he is so incredibly interesting and charming. Hughie says that all babies look the same. I say that all babies look the same – *except for Gene*, who, oddly, is the only baby I've come across who is so exceptionally lovely-looking with such intelligent eyes, such a kindly face . . .

Managed, after hours of chatting about Gene, to remember to ask how Penny was, and she said she'd just come back from the Family Records Office.

'Why on earth did you go there?' I asked.

'I wanted to find out how old the philosophy professor really was,' she said. 'He certainly isn't the age he says he is, that's for sure. I was going to go back today to look him up in other years in the directories, but you won't believe this, I suddenly couldn't remember his last name!'

'A senior moment?' I suggested.

'A CRAFT moment,' she said.

'What's a CRAFT moment?' I asked.

'Can't remember a fucking thing,' said Penny.

September 4th

Having taken Pouncer to the vet last week and discovered he has an overactive thyroid and kidney problems, I have spent the last few days trying to shove pills down his throat. It is extremely difficult to do this on your own as it involves completely disabling him with one hand and, with the other, opening his mouth and throwing a pill into the far regions, and then shutting his mouth and stroking his throat till he gulps. I've already got two nasty bites like that and last year, when I was involved in the same pill-chucking procedure, got a wound which went septic, and then I had to go on antibiotics.

No one to stuff them down *my* throat, though, luckily.

I've tried sneaking the pills into pieces of fillet steak, but he has an amazing way, even when I bury the pills deep inside, of managing to remove them before eating the meat.

However, today I have discovered some cunning camouflage chaps, called Tab Pockets, soft little squidgy cat treats with slits in them in which you conceal the pill.

Today Pouncer ate one.

Poor fool!

September 8

All these dreams. I am being driven crazy by them. Last night I dreamed that I was in some kind of work camp. I had two babies and I was given a syringe with which to inject them with some lethal poison. When I'd finished, I said to a passing woman who was wearing a green, flowered, ragged dress: 'I am so unhappy. Please put your arms around me and squeeze me like an orange.' After she had done this she gave me a chain that her husband had given her, which turned into a piece of green soap, shaped like a baby's hand, which melted in the bath.

Where do they come from, these dreams? I once went to the most frightful counsellor, when I was feeling I couldn't cope, as we all do at some point in our lives, and she always wanted to know my dreams, which she would interpret in weird ways. Once I dreamed I was trying to work out the VAT on a new fridge and she assured me that really I was dreaming about vats of wine. Pretty peculiar leap, if you ask me. I think, as counsellors so often say in their soft, knowing voices, that it said more about her than it did about me. Ha!

Unfortunately far too late to reveal this interpretation to her which would have reduced her, I like to think, to complete pulp.

I wonder if all this anxiety I'm suddenly feeling isn't a kind of post-natal depression? Can grannies get post-grannie-depression? PGD? I certainly don't feel 'myself'. Though what on earth 'myself' actually is, I have no idea. Suddenly starting to worry terribly about dummies, which I think are an essential part of a baby's emotional health. Have a horrible idea that Jack and Chrissie may consider them naff.

September 9th

In order to get all these horrid thoughts out of my mind and to throw a bit of reality on the situation, I went to see Gene. Not as simple as it seems, of course, since I have to disguise my visits so I don't appear too desperate to pop in.

'I was thinking of going to Tate Modern this afternoon,' I

said, when I rang Jack. 'And as it's only half-way to you, I wondered if I might drop by?'

Two days ago I'd rung saying: 'I've got to go to Chelsea . . . just wondered if you were in, as it's only a few minutes away.'

Yesterday 'I had ten people to dinner last night, and have a lot of stew left over. Would you like it for supper? I'm going to be your way . . .'

Jack and Chrissie must think I spend all my time in South London. It's tragic. Particularly tragic as, in order to make my excuses vaguely valid (excellent as I am at lying to other people, I just can't lie to Jack) I do indeed have to 'do something in Chelsea', or whatever, on my way. So far this has involved going round the most ludicrously expensive wallpaper shops and even dropping in to Peter Jones, purely in order to give my journeys some kind of authenticity. And I suppose, today, I will be obliged to see something at Tate Modern – groan.

Later
Not that easy when you're in a car because you have to park miles away, practically in Greenwich, and walk. By the time I got to the Turbine Hall, I was so bad-tempered I stumped around the Rachel Whiteread installation in a very cross mood. Then I found that I couldn't get to the second floor of the shop through the bottom floor of the shop – only out of the door and up some other stairs – and my mood worsened. Then the exit that would have taken me out to look at the river was roped off with ribbons and arrows. And the loo was on yet another floor.

Finally staggered up to the fourth floor to see the Henri Rousseau. At the door, the girl said: 'Tickets for sale on the lower ground floor.'

So I simply stumped out and back to the car. Stump. Stump. Stump. Who wants to see Henri Rousseau anyway? Just a lot of old tigers in jungles. Probably seen them all in France years ago. One of those painters who's just as good reproduced in books. Grr! As one of his tigers might have said. Though actually quite relieved to have an excuse to get down to see Gene rather earlier.

'You needn't pretend, Mum,' said Jack, kindly, when I arrived and he rumbled my pathetic strategies. 'Come over any time you want.'

'But if I did I'd be here all the time!' I said. 'I'd be living with you! I'd never go away!'

At that moment Gene suddenly woke up, screaming. Jack held him and jigged him about but nothing helped. Finally I took him and stuck my finger in his mouth. He latched on to it and nearly sucked the nail off.

'He can't be hungry, he's just been fed,' said Jack, wearily.

'What this little chap needs is a dummy,' I said.

'A dummy!' said Jack. 'But they look revolting! Chrissie would never allow a dummy in the house!'

'Now you've got a baby you can't start worrying about aesthetics, for God's sake,' I said. 'I had to put up with going out with you wearing nothing but a dreadful Bri-Nylon Spider-man suit for six months when you were small, darling. Dummies are essential. Babies suck on them for comfort.'

Oh dear. I just can't stop looking at Gene. I can't stop thinking about Gene. I'm like a lovelorn teenager pining for Cary Grant. Well, not Cary Grant. Who used I to pine for? Ashamed to say it was Richard Burton, a man whose very pock-marked face now gives me the creeps.

Get back to find a message from Penny saying she has some amazing news to tell me.

September 10

It was a completely different Penny who rang on my bell that evening. She was all of a flutter, giggly and, I have to say it, rather irritating. I spent about twenty minutes telling her all about Gene and how brilliant he was, until I finally remembered to offer her a drink and allowed her to get a word in edgeways.

'I've got a boyfriend!' she burbled. 'And he's only thirty! And he knows my real age! And he doesn't mind!'

Horrible as it is to admit, I felt rather put out. I always felt she was a loyal friend, and to find she's now got some bloke is extremely irritating, happy as I am for her to have found someone. I mean, she is going to be sixty next month, and thirty is on the young side. It can't last. And I found myself telling her so rather too quickly. We sat down in the garden (on the nice new stripy chairs I got from Tesco last week) catching the last of the September sun. Pouncer was sitting staring out of a bush, watching the woodpigeons on the lawn.

'I *know* it can't last,' she said, rather irritably. She picked at a piece of salami I'd got from the slimy delicatessen. 'I'm not a complete fool. But I actually met him last weekend, and he said he fancied me and I just can't believe it.'

'And what about the philosophy professor from Northumberland?'

'Oh, dreadful man. Turned out he was seventy-seven. Hair growing out of his nose,' she said, dismissively. 'But Gavin, he's totally wonderful!'

'Married?' I asked. 'Unspeakably unattractive? Looking after four severely disabled children? Mentally ill?' I ticked off all the likely pitfalls.

'No . . . isn't it extraordinary?' she gushed.

'Look, if he fancies a woman of nearly sixty, there's got to be something wrong with him,' I reasoned.

'I know, I know,' she said, half-sobbing with delight. 'But I don't care. He's just so-so-o sweet! He says I'm his soulmate. And we have everything in common. He's got exactly the same ideas about interior decorating as I have, and has got the most wonderful taste. And guess what he was reading – *Death in Venice* . . . the most wonderful book in the world, as you know, and he used to stay in exactly the same house where I used to stay in Norfolk when he was small, he even knows the PR agency I used to run, and says it is brilliant. He just *loves* Eartha Kitt who, of course, is magnificent, and Lena Horne, and has seen *The Wizard of Oz* ten times. I've just never met anyone I've had so many connections with. I feel as if I've met my long-lost brother. *And* he fancies me!'

'Well, good for you,' I said, but my heart wasn't in it. I was sort of jealous – and sort of annoyed because I knew it would all end in tears, and I would be on the receiving end of countless miserable phone calls, and partly terribly sorry for her. Thirty years' age difference just doesn't work.

Apparently Penny met this guy on some weird writing course where he fell for her hook, line and sinker. He runs a crystal healing shop in Glastonbury and she's going to spend the night with him next Friday.

'But what will you do about sex?' I asked.

'I don't know!' she said rather desperately. 'I've gone to the doctor to go back on HRT and she's given me some Ortho-gynol cream to shove into myself, which apparently makes the vagina more lubricated, but I'm sure it's going to be agony.'

'I'm sure it is,' I said, remembering the last time I'd had sex. After the menopause your vagina gets all dry and miserable and having sex is like having oneself rubbed down with sand-paper on the inside. 'I'd use KY jelly as well, if I were you. I think I may have some upstairs.'

And I went up to my grandmother's old chest of drawers and rummaged around among the death pills. Sure enough, there was some ancient KY, long past its sell-by date, but it looked to me as lugubrious as ever was. If that's the right word. Lubricious? Lubricative?

'Why on earth have you got this?' asked Penny, when I brought it downstairs.

'Never you mind,' I said. 'But you bung that up yourself and I'm sure you'll be fine.'

'His mother's only forty-eight!' moaned Penny. 'Oh, it's so awful, and so wonderful. And it's doomed, all doomed. And I'm going to be so miserable. Oh, Marie, why did I get into this fix? I wish I were strong-minded like you.'

'Don't worry,' I said. 'Have a good time. I'll "be there for you" when it's over.'

'Oh, Marie, it's "come to that"!' moaned Penny, 'You'll "be there for me". This doesn't look promising, not promising at all. It's just that he's such, such a darling . . .'

I didn't like the sound of this 'darling' one bit, but tried to appear light-heartedly enthusiastic about the whole business. The trouble with Penny is that, although she's quite sensible and feet-on-the-ground most of the time, when it comes to men she can suddenly tumble down a black hole and then it's chaos and the seventh circle of hell. And who is the one who's sending baskets down on ropes to try to haul her up? None other than yours truly, sensible old Marie.

'The funny thing is that when one's young one thinks, "Oh it can't last because the man *doesn't* want marriage and children," and when one's old, one thinks, "Oh, it can't last because the man probably *does* want marriage and children," and one can't give them to him!' said Penny. 'And honestly, Marie, you're right. It has no future. There's no way we'll be together for longer than three months at the most.'

'Archie's got a young Swedish girl of thirty-five,' I said.

'Only minutes after Philippa died.' I was surprised to find that as I said it, I felt a pang of something.

'But you know it's completely different for men,' said Penny, rather crossly.

'Barbara Windsor married a man twenty-six years her junior,' I said, trying to be consoling. 'Joan Collins and what's-his-face, thirty years younger?'

'Marie, don't bullshit. You know and I know that this is going to end in tears,' said Penny with a flash of her old self. 'And the other awful thing is that because I, like you, am a sixties girl, I go straight back into that servile "yes-you're-a-man-I'll-do-anything-you-want" mode when these days all that's changed.'

'Maybe that's what he loves about you,' I said.

'Marie, I'm depending on you, during this whole disastrous caper, to be my sensible self,' said Penny. 'I rely on you to pour cold water on everything. Don't start encouraging me in my madness. Please. Though thank you,' she added, changing like Eve (as in *The Three Faces of*, the movie), getting suddenly all girlish and fluttery, 'for the KY. Oh, I can't stop thinking about him! It's awful!'

There was a pause while she stared at her empty glass. I suddenly caught on and rushed to the fridge to get the bottle to top her up. When I got back I was astonished to see tears had come to her eyes.

'You should feel happy, not miserable,' I said, putting my arm round her.

'But I know already that the relationship hasn't got a hope,' she said, rather sadly. 'You see, you've got Gene to love. But I don't have anyone.'

And I suddenly realized how selfish I'd been, always talking to Penny about Gene. It must have been much more painful and envy-making for her than it was for me hearing her talking about this bloke.

But Gavin! Glastonbury! Practically half her age! How could she?

Later
Pouncer has discovered the Tab Pocket trick, and now refuses to eat them. Back to the throat-stuffing.

Later
Went to the shops and coming back was amazed to be met by a woman in a burqa speeding towards me on one of those disabled motorized chair things. She had slowed down just before my house and as I passed she waved angrily at a man who'd obviously insulted her in the street. 'Fucking Irishman!' she shrieked in a strong cockney accent, from inside her black shroud. 'I'm more fucking English than you are!'

Later
Penny rang with a query: 'What does KY actually stand for?' she asked.

Sep 12

Rather worried because yesterday Michelle hurried up to her room with a man in tow – and not just any man: a man twice her age (but probably half mine). I only glimpsed him on the stairs, but I saw that he was missing one tooth, had a ring through one ear, was half-shaven and his jacket smelled strongly of dope. Having been around so many addicts in the sixties, I have one of those noses that can sniff dope out at twenty paces. In fact, if I were paid enough, I'd be happy to shuffle round Heathrow on my hands and knees checking suitcases for drugs.

When, later, I asked her what he did, she looked very

dreamy and told me, simply, that Harry, for that is his name, was 'a genius'.

'What do you mean, a genius?' I asked, immediately suspicious. He hadn't looked like a genius to me.

'He ees poet,' she said. 'He ees writer, film director, designer of gardens, photographer, he write plays, he ees performance artist, he create installations . . .'

The poor girl thought that the more professions she laid on this wretch, the more impressed I would be, but quite the reverse. Being old and experienced, with every new talent this man went down in my estimation rather than up.

'Darling,' I said. 'I think he's a bullshit artist.'

'Bullsheet?' said Michelle. 'He ees certainly artist,' she added, her face suffused with admiration.

'Well, next time he comes round, introduce him to me,' I said rather sharply. She said she would. One look at my knowing old bat face, I knew, would keep this creep away for good. I've fallen for my fair share of 'geniuses' in my time. Been to bed with them. Lent them money. Believed them when they said it had fallen down a drain and could they have some more. No "genius" can fool me.

Sep 13th

Just read today that grannies are more likely to get heart attacks than people who aren't grannies. Can't understand it. Total tosh. Far from courting a heart attack, being a grannie, for me at least, makes me feel there is even more reason to go on living than before. And these days the irrational worries I used to have about Jack have practically disappeared – because I know that now he has to take charge of someone else, he, too, will become even more responsible than he was before.

September 20th

This afternoon I just sat in my garden with a cup of tea doing absolutely nothing. I say nothing. A lie. I was eating a delicious gingernut – oddly the presence of Gene has got me back to biscuits. Chrissie keeps a tin of biscuits and offers me one with coffee whenever I go over, and today I took the big step and bought some for myself.

Pouncer was lying on his back on the grass in the golden September sun, his eyes closed in bliss, his velvety paws resting in the air. So vulnerable. On the cherry tree sat two woodpigeons as fat as grey cushions, and hopping on the lawn was a blackbird looking for worms among the daises. Towards the back of my garden, where there is a forest of trees and shrubs, it was green darkness, from which, amazingly, emerged a grey squirrel.

I had one of those really weird moments when you feel like St Francis. Not only do you feel like St Francis, but you also feel peculiarly at one with nature. I never used to feel like this: it feels like another age thing. Nature is saying: 'Now you're getting on and coming to the end of your life, come and join us. We're your friends. There's nothing to fear.' It was definitely a presentiment of death, but not a creepy ghoul-like-figure-in-a-black-cape-clutching-a-scythe kind of presentiment but, rather, a beautifully peaceful and seductive kind of pre-sentiment, a call to a world where the phrase 'Go for it!' and other such unpleasant prods to do an Open University course or live for three months with a Masai tribe in Africa have no place at all.

These things can never be repeated, of course. Today, I made my cup of tea and got out the last of the gingernuts, and sat down in the garden with my Sudoku puzzle – a fatal addiction that was introduced to me by Lucy, who is a demon at it. They say it keeps the brain active, but it just drives mine into a frenzy of fury, mental cross-eyedness and frustration until the final stage when it all works out, and you're flooded by this ludicrous sense of achievement, swiftly followed by a terrible sense of inner emptiness. Anyway, I'd just got going and done all the 3s and the 5s, when over the gardens the raucous noise of a football match commentary blared out through the trees.

Instant fury. Telling myself to calm down, I went back into the house and sat in the cool, but half an hour later it was still going on. I rang up Penny.

'Can you hear it?' I asked.

'Can I hear it!' she said. 'It's deafening! It's that idiot across the way from me. I've asked him to turn it down, but he won't.'

'Let me see what I can do,' I said grimly. I put on my Furious Old Bat face (a face that is all too easy to summon up, I'm afraid) and stomped round to Penny's. Into her garden we went, with the noise getting louder and louder, and there, over the wall, sat a huge, elderly yob, covered with wrinkly tattoos; his head was shaven and he wore shorts, over which spilled a vast beer belly. He was barefooted and he appeared, to make things worse, to be fast asleep.

On the table beside him were three empty cans of Special Brew, and a transistor, turned up at full blast.

'Excuse me!' I shouted. No response. 'Excuse me!' I felt like such an idiot. I wished I had the kind of voice that was able to say: 'Oy! You there!' but I don't. After the fourth 'Excuse me!' he looked up.

'Yeah?' he said drunkenly.

'I wonder,' I shouted, forever polite, 'if you would be so kind as to turn down your radio.'

'Why?' he said, staring sullenly at me through drunken eyes.

'Because not everyone in these gardens wants to listen to the Arsenal v. Chelsea match. Or whatever it is,' I added, as he strove to correct me. 'I live ten gardens down and I can't hear myself speak.'

'It's a free world,' he said, aggressively.

'It is indeed a free world,' I replied (oh dear, that 'indeed' – it doesn't come across well in a shriek). 'But,' I added, 'I am chair of the local Residents' Association, and I am speaking not just for myself, but for dozens of other residents who have complained about the noise to me.' (Not true, but what the hell.)

'Fuck off,' he said, glumly. 'You're not tellin' me what to do.'

I upped the ante slightly. 'If you continue, I'm afraid I will have to complain to the Shepherds Bush Housing Association, which owns the house you live in. I don't want to go down that route. I want us to be friends.'

'Wha'?'

'I want us to be friends,' I shouted. 'And by the way, I'm not telling you to turn the radio down, I'm begging you!'

At this point a window flung itself up from across the way and a woman leaned out.

'Here we go,' muttered Penny, who was hiding in a bush behind me. 'Now we're for it. It's Sheila the Dealer.'

I'd never come across Sheila the Dealer but she is a known drugs supplier in the street. Actually drug dealers are so common in the streets round here that there isn't a street that doesn't have one. They've become like corner shops, an essential attribute of every neighbourhood.

'Oy! You!' she shouted. Both the man and I looked up. Her voice was piercing.

'Not *you*,' she screamed. 'Fucking *you*!' Neither of us was any the wiser. I was terrified she was going to gang up with the man against me, this appalling old middle-class complainer.

'Look, you fuckin' arse-'ole!' she yelled. 'Can you 'ear the lidy? She's not fuckin' *tellin*' you to turn your radio orf, she's fuckin' *beggin*' you! You deaf? So fuckin' turn it off, you cunt, and give us all a fuckin' bloody break, OK?'

Her outburst startled the man so much that, without a word, he took the radio off the table, and marched indoors. Just as I was about to give Sheila the Dealer a friendly thumbs-up sign, the window banged down and that was that.

'Wasn't that just amazing?' I said to Penny.

'Astonishing!' she said. 'Cup of tea? Or perhaps, as it's five, it's not too early for a drink?'

For the next half-hour we discussed whether we would like a tattoo ourselves, and discovered that we'd both always longed for one but thought that now it was too late. Penny wanted a flower, but I wanted a bird. 'Or what about a brace-let which would read: "This is my wrist," Magritte-style?' I suggested.

We then wondered why we had taken drugs when we were young when it is surely *now* that's the time to take them. If one went totally off one's head it wouldn't matter terribly. Penny said that she'd read that a combination of Red Bull, aspirin and Coke can make your brain sharper. But the mixture sounds about as plausible as the recipe we used to try in the sixties, when, before we got on to the harder stuff, we tried to get high by smoking dried banana skins.

I long to take an E. Penny says she's up for it if I can find any. Will ask Jack – though maybe he'd disapprove of his old mum taking drugs? Perhaps, I suggested, she could ask Gavin, but she says Gavin only smokes dope. Typical.

At the mention of Gavin she went all quiet. Then she told me that apparently after a blissful day during which they had made love, laughed, walked, sung songs together, read poetry to each other, and found they had everything in common, he had become completely unobtainable. Not a peep.

'He hasn't texted or emailed or rung,' she said. 'I'm starting to wonder if he's dead! Had some frightful accident!'

'You and I know,' I said, firmly, 'that unfortunately men are never dead or lying in hospital in a coma. We are experienced old ladies, who have acquired a certain bit of wisdom. The reason that a man – or anyone come to that – doesn't contact one is very simple. Either they are terrified to do so or they don't want to. Or they are married. If I were you, Penny, I would settle for the terrified option. It is, quite honestly, easier to bear.'

She looked so sad and frail, like an elderly five-year-old, if there is such a thing, that I put my arms round her and gave her a hug.

'You're very brave,' I said. 'You're braver than me. I couldn't do it any more. I'd be too frightened of getting hurt. You've done it once. You'll do it again.'

Penny's body shuddered with sobs. 'The trouble is that with this love business – or whatever it is – just because one's old doesn't mean to say it isn't just as agonizingly painful as it was when one was seventeen,' she said, through her tears. 'Oh, I wish I hadn't started it. I must have been mad.'

I rather wished we could go round to Sheila the Dealer and score some drugs right there, but perhaps it wasn't such a good idea.

September 26th

The sight of the awful cat that Maciej gave me for my birthday made me feel so ill that I have taken it off the mantelpiece and put it into a drawer. Will he notice? That is the question.

Later
Decided that putting it in a drawer was too hurtful to Maciej. Hit on brilliant idea and asked if Michelle would like to have it in her room. That way Maciej will see it when he cleans her room, and I can say that she liked it so much that I let her have it till the end of her stay. To my delight she was enchanted with it.

Later
Hughie rings. It turns out that after trying a course of antibiotics, the doctor has finally given up, and Hughie's waiting to have a chest X-ray. He asks if I've heard the one about the man who was visited by an angel one night. I say I haven't and he says that the man asked the angel if there was a golf course in heaven. The angel replied: 'Do you want the good news or the bad news?' 'Good news,' said the man. 'OK,' said the angel. 'Yes, there is a golf course. It's a brilliant green, wonderful grass, superb scenery, dozens of caddies and endless sun.' 'And the bad news?' said the man. The angel said: 'You're due to tee off at 9 a.m. tomorrow morning.'

'So I'm getting my golf clubs polished in readiness,' adds Hughie.

Find Hughie's preoccupation with death rather gruelling sometimes. He seems to have got it all taped, but no one around him has, that's the problem. Anyway, who said anything about dying?

September 28th

Was delighted, when I went round to see Gene today, to find that he was contentedly sucking a large see-through purple-and-yellow-striped dummy. Not only that, but there appears to be a spare one with red and blue spots, on the kitchen table. Could they have come from the Design Museum?

Poor Chrissie is shattered with getting up and feeding Gene, though now he has a supplementary bottle. What is it about feeding babies? It is just so lovely to sit with him on my lap, his little head cradled in the crook of my arm, and watch his tiny lips just sucking away at the teat, his eyes closed in a kind of blissful meditation. His eyelids are transparent and blue, and he smells of warm cotton wool. He only has a small bit of hair, so the shape of his head is quite clear, with the little soft fontanel at the top, and the skin in the triangle moving slightly, bomp bomp bomp, to his tiny heartbeat.

He's got to the stage when he stares at you with what can only be called a quizzical look, not a word I often use, and studies your face as if he's searching for something he's lost. I look back at him, also searching for something I've lost.

Have to say that I feel slightly nerve-racked carrying him upstairs. And I don't think I'd be very happy having to lift him down a flight of concrete steps wearing high-heeled shoes, in case I dropped him. I don't feel quite the same confidence with him as I did with Jack, simply because he isn't mine. And yet, what is so immensely rewarding and fulfilling about being with him is that my love for him is pure and clear, unclouded by all the guilt, panic and anxiety that I experienced with Jack when he was tiny.

When he cries, I don't have any of those feelings of 'Oh, Lord, he's shouting and crying, he must hate me . . . oh dear, if I do this or that it will affect him for life . . . oh, why did

I bring him into such a terrible world?' I just think, quite simply: 'Ho hum, he's crying. He'll soon get over it.'

Some other grannies, talking about their grandchildren, give a fearful wink as they end up with that well-worn cliché: 'Yes, aren't they lovely! And the best thing is – you can give them back at the end of the day!'

But I can't go along with that. For me, the only thing I have against being a grandmother is that, sadly, I have to.

October 1st

Oh dear. Today I called Jack 'David' (his dad), Chrissie 'Mummy', and Gene, 'Jack'. Am I going mad?

October 2nd

Maciej said how kind it was of me to have lent the dreadful ceramic cat to Michelle.

'Beautiful cat for beautiful girl,' he said. 'But I will bring you new cat!' he said, his face lighting up in the most lovely smile. 'Beautiful cat for beautiful woman! My brother he import them, actually. I will bring you one with green eyes! Bring good luck! If you want more for your friends, I get!'

October 7th

Archie left a message on my answering machine. He asked if I could bear to come for the weekend next month, as he's having some kind of house-party. God knows how he'll manage without Philippa who used to organize all that, but good for him for making the effort. I can't imagine that Ulla or whatever ghastly name the Swede's got will be able to cope with organizing a house-party in the same way that Philippa used to. Anyway, surely she won't have any time for the Marions and Tims of this world – of whom Archie knows plenty. They're like barnacles that you suddenly find you're stuck with, whether you like them or not, simply because you've known them for so long.

Still, rather wish Archie hadn't got hitched up to this creature quite so soon. Anyway, when – and if – she goes he'll certainly find another bimbo person just as fast. So unfair that older single men can take their choice of women from twenty to eighty, while all us female oldies can get are either weirdos like Gavin or, worse, ancient old gentlemen who want someone to wheel their bath chairs for them.

Can't go, however. Next time. And actually quite relieved. It's not that I'm remotely interested in Archie, but to see him with a succulent young blonde draped around him might, I'm afraid, make me feel rather ill. Makes me all the more determined to give up men for ever.

October 9th

Penny rang and while we were talking about Scotsmen, she asked me if I thought it was true that they wore nothing under their quilts.

October 10th

Today I took care of Gene all day while Chrissie went off and did some work at her old company. She seems to have to fly off to Brussels and back in one day. My plan was to take Gene shopping in the morning, then bring him back and give him his lunch, then make some phone calls and do some bits and pieces when he was asleep, and finally take him to the park in the afternoon.

I was almost sick with fear as I bumped him down the steep steps that lead down from Jack and Chrissie's flat, tightly gripping on the handle of the pushchair, visualizing a dreadful Potemkin scene in the middle of the road. I wasn't only sick with fear because I might let go of the buggy handles, but also because before I'd set out, Jack had warned me: 'Remember to take care, won't you, Mum. There's only the odd maniac and mugger, but it's old ladies like you who stop and make mobile phone calls in the street who are a natural target. Not that you're old . . . And that handbag looks rather inviting.'

I could hardly imagine that the battered old black object into which I cram all my possessions could even pass as a handbag, let alone be an invitation to anyone for a quick mug, but I suppose no one has handbags these days, only rucksacks, so I duly transferred my mobile, purse and wallet to a little string pocket thing on the pushchair, and covered it with the white shawl that Chrissie's grannie had knitted. She is one of those knitters who just whacks out a couple of jerseys in an afternoon. Very annoying as I am only half-way through the hat I decided to knit, and have yet to tackle the little socks that go with it, a four-needle job. Though I think four needles might be a bit of what my builder calls, when the RSJ he's just put in falls down, a 'challenge'.

I wheeled Gene into the chemist – I say 'wheeled'. One thing I'd completely forgotten was how to manoeuvre the pushchair, so I charged at the door like a ram and couldn't understand why it didn't open. Then it all came flooding back. You have to turn yourself around, shove the door open with your *bottom* and then go in backwards. I needed some Nurofen Plus – everything in my body is aching these days – and couldn't resist saying to the surly man behind the counter:

'This is my first grandchild. Aren't I lucky?' He peered over the counter and broke into a gloopy kind of smile.

Gene, who had fallen asleep, gave a yawn, his tiny mouth forming that curious long and perfect O. An adult's yawn is a hideous thing, showing fillings, bits of old cabbage, coated tongue, wrinkled lips; a baby's yawn is so vulnerable and enchanting. I longed to lean down and smell his warm milky, silky breath.

When I got back with Gene intact, I felt fantastically pleased with myself.

He had his bottle and went to sleep, and I spent the next hour and a half sorting through nappies, emptying the washing-up machine, generally tidying up, and was just mopping the kitchen floor when Gene woke up and we skipped the park and just frittered the afternoon away. Everything went like clockwork and Chrissie was very sweetly grateful when she returned from Brussels. Then she looked sternly at a bottle of milk in the fridge. It turned out that I should have given it to him when he woke up from his nap.

From being grannie *extraordinaire*, I then felt like someone who would be pretty pushed to get an NVQ in can-opening. I have visions of him starving to death. After a brief brush with therapy, there is always a bit of me that thinks: 'Is that what I'd like to do secretly? Starve him to death?' That's the sort of thing the therapist would have said.

I keep worrying about Gene being harmed in some way. Worse, I keep worrying that *I* might harm him. That I might go round there and stab him with scissors. Or throw him out of the window in a fit of madness. I used to have these feelings when Jack was just born. I couldn't tell anyone then or he'd have been taken into care and I'd have been carried away by the men in white coats (or so I imagined) and I certainly can't tell anyone now. But I find myself torturing myself with these thoughts.

Despite all these anxieties, which I kept to myself, Chrissie was extremely forgiving about the milk-forgetting incident, and I drove home with a feeling of huge relief. But as I got to Victoria I found I was so tired I could hardly pinch myself awake. Had to go into a mews by the station, park and have a little snooze. Will it always be like this? I have never felt so exhausted in my entire life.

Oct 25

Latest email:

> *Gorgeous European girl forcing a dildo in. Extremely hot Hungarian, Czech and Russian girls having fun with wild objects.*

God, how depressing.

October 26

Am finding it very difficult to get out of bed in the morning. Not the old teenage reason, because I can't face the day, far from it. Not because of my knackering days with Gene. No, it's just that everything hurts. I'm fine lying down but then, the minute I get up, my knees hurt, my hips hurt, my neck hurts, my shoulders hurt and my feet are agonizing. It can't still be the bunion operation because it's the other foot that's so painful, which was untouched, except for a couple of toenails being narrowed.

Could it be the weather? Walter Gabriel of *The Archers* used to be able to tell the weather by the state of his feet, I seem to remember, and it's just starting to get nippy. Anyway, my feet are such agony that when I saw an advertisement for Companion Stairlifts ('My stairlift is more than just a FRIEND, it's a Companion'), I started to wonder whether it might not be rather pleasant to glide up and downstairs in a sitting position day and night.

I made another appointment to see Dr Farmer and found, to my horror, that she had retired. She is the person who saw me through my depressions before I married David, my anxiety after I'd given birth to Jack, my being a gibbering wreck when Jack finally bought his first flat and moved out – not to mention curing a whole pile of unspeakable diseases from thrush and cystitis to eczema and piles. You go to these people thinking you're going to be with them for life, and then you find that they've retired and some young whippersnapper barely older than Gene is sitting in their place. It's happened with all my props. Even the vet now appears with a young man in tow, whom he's clearly briefing to take over the practice when he finally retires, and my favourite librarian suddenly revealed that he had to leave his job because he was sixty-five the other day. It's odd – one's life is changing not only because of the death of one's friends, but also through all the familiar faces retiring.

Of course it's always a problem with doctors. Does one want them to be old and experienced or young and up in all the latest techniques and research? I don't want them to be like the ancient old geezer I took Jack to once when he had a tummy ache before going to school. 'Give him some oranges!' he barked. 'That's what the lad needs. Exercise and oranges!' But then nor do I want them to be someone who, whenever one goes to see them with, say, a small green spot on one's toe, immediately diagnoses stress and depression and whips out a prescription for Prozac.

In the waiting room a girl of about twenty in a track suit was telling her friend about a visit to her grandmother in an 'evening' home: 'She's shrunk! Soon she'll be shorter than me!'

I wonder if, when we are all old, we'll say to other old

people: 'Oh my, how you have shrunk! I remember you when you were so high!'

The new young doctor was a pleasant girl called Dr Green. I like my doctors to be 'pleasant'. I'm not sure I would welcome the adjective if applied to myself, but when it comes to doctors, 'pleasant' is just fine. She wore scruffy jeans and an old teeshirt and looked like someone who had just arrived from a weekend in Glastonbury. Come to think of it, she probably had. No doubt staying with Gavin, the creep.

'The osteoarthritis has spread,' she said, after examining me. 'It happens, I'm afraid, at a certain age. But one thing – it's known as a present that's given to you on your fiftieth birthday . . . and although the bones don't get back to normal, the inflammation only lasts a short time, at the most fifteen years, so,' she added, looking at my notes and seeing when I last came round complaining of aches and pains, 'although the damage will still be there, you shouldn't have the pain.'

In the meantime she gave me some anti-inflammatories called Arcowreck or something like it. She said that if those didn't work, there were plenty of others I could try . . . 'whole families of new pills'. Wonderful idea. I could see them all queuing up to cure me, these families, with cousins, nieces, step-daughters . . . grannies in stone-coloured shoes.

'By the way,' she added, and I knew what was coming. 'How much exercise do you take?'

'Why? Do you think I'm fat?' I asked, quickly. I have been rather freaked out as Hughie described me recently as 'stately', James as 'statuesque' and Tim as 'strapping'.

'Not at all. You're, you're . . . well, well-formed. And you have a very good posture. But a bit of exercise would do no harm, you know. How much did you say you took?'

'None,' I told her.

'None?' she said. She seemed surprised. I expect she was amazed to get an honest answer.

'Don't you swim or jog?'

I shook my head.

'Well, you must walk. If you go upstairs, or run for a bus, do you get puffed out?'

'I walk up stairs very slowly,' I said, rather pompously, 'And a) I rarely go on a bus and b) if I do, I never run for it.'

She took my blood pressure, and took a blood sample, and said I should try to get at least twenty minutes of brisk walking in every day.

I am so busy pottering about and mooching around, I would never have time to get in twenty minutes of brisk walking. And brisk walking where? No one in their right mind would want to walk anywhere in Shepherds Bush – though of course, it being knee-deep in hoodies, if they did want to walk, 'pretty briskly' would certainly be their pace.

Doctors and care-givers are so arrogant. They always think that the advice they give you is the only advice you're given.

The bunion man told me to exercise my feet and ankles. 'Just five minutes a day,' he said.

A man I did yoga with said: 'Just ten minutes a day will do you no end of good.'

A physiotherapist suggested I did a daily ten minutes of stretching exercises to prevent back pain.

A book on meditation recommended twenty minutes' meditation.

Then my dentist thinks I should clean my teeth for at least a couple of minutes three times a day, and not only that, he's given me no fewer than three kinds of toothbrush to do it with: an ordinary electric one, a small hard bunch of spikes on the end of a plastic handle, and a vile little thing like a wiry caterpillar that I have to insert into all the spaces in between, every night. It is a clearly important procedure, I have to say, particularly when one sees what emerges after a good going over. Sometimes entire meals.

So far I've got over an hour's worth of keeping myself trim every day, which seems a ridiculous amount. That's seven hours a week, practically a whole working day. No thanks.

October 27

Very surprised, this morning, when turning on the radio, and hoping to hear the acid tones of John Humphrys grilling some poor politician about his latest policies, to find heavy metal music blaring out. For a moment I imagined that John and the team had gone mad, and fantasized about them all cavorting around in black leather with skulls tattooed on their foreheads, but on inspecting the radio I found that Michelle had been at the dial the night before and had failed to turn it back to Radio Four.

Later

Hughie, James and Penny to dinner for Penny's birthday. I had bought some scrummy salmon egg 'caviar' from Waitrose and served it with sour cream on blinis, followed by an amazing fish stew from a recipe in a book I've kept for years – Robert Carrier's *Great Dishes of the World*, which was given to me in the seventies as a wedding present. James brought the pudding – an amazing trifle bursting with brandy.

But unfortunately it was rather a sad affair because firstly Hughie is still coughing like mad, and the X-ray showed up something that was clearly rather creepy, though they won't say anything definite. He is now waiting to have something called a bronchoscopy. He's clearly not well. He has to do his trousers up with a belt, gathering them in slightly at the top, which doesn't look good on a man whose clothes used to fit him perfectly. James is worried sick, and trying to make him follow some kind of carrots, yoghurt and wheat-free diet, which Hughie is having nothing of, and as a result is behaving rather badly, smoking even more cigarettes than usual, stuffing himself with cream and butter, and drinking at least two bottles of wine a night. He is starting to look rather red in the face.

And Penny is still grieving over the wretched Gavin who has not replied to phone calls, emails or texts. After the night of passion, she *still* has terrible cystitis, of course, and is now on a seven-day course of antibiotics, and gulping down cranberry juice by the bucketful. A couple of days ago I tried to ring Gavin to make totally certain he wasn't dead and, much to Penny's misery, I'm afraid, when he saw it was a strange number, and not Penny's, he answered it, sounding perfectly healthy. He had rather a high, piping voice when he said: 'Hello! Gavin here!'

'I'm ringing to ask you whether you are worried about global warming, the state of the world, lawlessness in our society, 24-hour drinking laws, and the general lack of spiritual health in the country,' I said. 'Could you answer "yes" or "no"?'

'Yes!' he squeaked.

'Congratulations! You have won a prize of £50,000. Please ring this number immediately.' I rattled off twenty random numbers and hung up. 'Little creep!' I said. Of course there was hardly any point, really. He must have received so many unwelcome calls from dumped girlfriends in his life that unpleasant ones must roll off him like water off a duck's back. Or perhaps he has some ghastly crystal he uses to protect himself against hurt.

'Remember, Pens,' said James, as he opened a bottle of champagne, 'that it is *he* who is the loser. He is a frightened, terrified man, who doesn't know what's good for him. He's a total, sad little wanker, and he's much unhappier than you. Even if he doesn't think he is. Inside he is.'

Hughie nodded his agreement, even though I knew that

he, like me, found this theory, though extremely comforting, exceptionally unlikely. We thought he was a go-getting creep who was laughing up his sleeve and probably telling everyone down the vegetarian café what it was like screwing an old lady.

But 'Scared stiff,' agreed Hughie, loyally.

'And anyway, you've got *us*!' said James, brightly. 'It's friends you want, not lovers!'

Penny said tremulously: 'But now I'm sixty, and no one will ever want to have sex with me ever again! They'll be repulsed when they see my horrible wrinkly old body! To think that when I die, the last person I had sex with in the whole of my life ever will be frightened Gavin from Glastonbury!'

'Nonsense,' said Hughie. 'Go to the Gambia and if you pay them a fiver you'll find a guy on the beach who will sleep with you no problem. Even someone of sixty! Mind you, make sure they use a condom!'

Oh, dear. Suddenly I did rather wonder whether the idea that the synapses shrivel in the brains of over-sixties, making their social inhibitions wither, might have some truth in it.

'Anyway, what was he up to? Surely he could find someone his own age?' asked James, inquisitively. And as Penny started to explain the scenario, I could see Hughie and James become more and more interested, particularly when she got on to the sex bits.

'Very good at sex?' said Hughie, thoughtfully. 'Doesn't sound like a heterosexual to me.'

'Why on earth was he reading *Death in Venice* anyway?' I asked. 'Isn't that rather a gay book?'

'Did you say he adored Eartha Kitt? And Lena Horne?' said James.

'*Wizard of Oz*, I seem to remember, was one of his favourites,' said Hughie. 'Judy Garland. Gay icon. Bet he watches the *Eurovision Song Contest*, too.'

In the end we decided that Gavin was one of those gay men that are the scourge of older women.

'They decide they want to go straight and have children,' said James. 'They find an older woman to practise on, and they discover they can't hack it. Even though they can just cope with sex with a woman, it doesn't really mean anything to them. You had an affair with an older woman once, when you were young, didn't you, Hughie?'

'I certainly did,' said Hughie, shuddering rather, and coughing as he shuddered. 'She was lovely, I adored her, but while I gave her great sex, I can't explain, my heart wasn't in it. Also there was something slightly disgusting about all that wet squishiness.'

Penny burst into tears. But luckily, as she was crying, I noticed that she was also shaking with laughter. 'Gay Gavin from Glastonbury!' she said. 'Oh, fuck him! What a weirdo!'

'To Penny, on her birthday,' shouted James. 'And to Gavin's amazing sexual prowess! May it shrivel and shrivel until finally it drops down a drain!'

Penny and he raised their glasses, but I noticed that Hughie, though smiling vaguely, was reticent, and barely sipped at his drink. Like me, I knew he found the whole toast slightly repellent. After all, even if Gavin were a creep, you don't want to curse anyone in that way.

That's one of the wonderful and terrible things about being older. You can see, even in the most repugnant people, the god in everyone, as they say (even if you don't believe in God) and it becomes less and less easy to sneer at them. Well, hold on, Marie. One can sneer, but when you get down to it, you're only sneering at their surface pretensions. Increasingly, I do believe that the most horrible people, even the bearded counsellor, were once fundamentally good. Their judgement became clouded as they grew up, but baby beard was probably just as lovable as Gene himself. OK OK – and the vile man across the road.

Sometimes I think that Gene (though I can hardly bear to say it, it sounds so utterly sentimental, trite and generally yucky) has taught me to love.

Anyway, enough of that. Even though the schoolmistress in me found that particular bit of the evening slightly repellent, at least everyone cheered up, and in the end I enjoyed myself.

As she left, Penny groped for her mobile. 'Oh,' she said. 'I've got a text!' She read it out:

Is it your birthday? I think it is. If so, have a wonderful day. Will you come down again next weekend? Can't wait to see you . . . love, Gavin.

'Oh, shit,' she said.

October 28

I took Pouncer to the vet today to have his teeth cleaned, poor chap. When I picked him up the bill was £225!!! He has been given a toothbrush, special teeth-cleaning chews, a gel, teeth-cleaning biscuits . . . for God's sake. *And* he was given a follow-up appointment, which I certainly don't want to take advantage of. His teeth aren't even particularly white, for heaven's sake. And he is, let's face it, much as I love him to pieces, only a cat.

(I once tried to get my own teeth sparkling white, with the aid of a curious plastic gum-shield and some special gel, but it turned out that had I stuck it out, my two crowns would have been left as yellowed stumps.)

Pouncer had a little letter accompanying him saying that as he'd had an anaesthetic, I must keep him warm, let him sleep . . . and rest . . . not let him out, give him soft food . . . fish or chicken . . .

He came back and scoffed a tin of Whiskas, went straight out into the garden and has been generally prancing around.

October 29

Went round to Hughie and James for a drink, and to deliver back the trifle dish they'd forgotten to take home.

'Hughie, darling, what's the latest?' I said, as I sat down on the lovely squishy, chintz-covered sofa. Over the top, but so, so comfortable. I wish Jack and Chrissie had a sofa like theirs. They have a curious thing that is only about three inches off the floor and you need a couple of ski-ing sticks to hoist yourself out of it. 'Have you heard from the hospital?'

The minute I'd spoken I felt the room freeze slightly.

'Yes, he has,' said James. And as he spoke instead of Hughie, I realized, just in that sentence, that something not terribly nice was coming. I felt cold and prickly. 'He's on the waiting list for an MRI. Aren't you, dear?'

'I am indeed,' said Hughie. 'I can't tell you how I long to be in that long tube of darkness. Everyone says: "Aren't you frightened?" but I say I'd like to stay there and never come out. I am looking forward to it immensely.'

'But I'm not,' said James.

'My dear,' said Hughie. 'You will, I hope, be on the outside, singing wonderful alluring songs like a siren – perhaps the hits from *Oklahoma*? – enchanting me, reminding me of the wonderful world outside.'

I knew he was speaking cynically, but James didn't seem to understand. 'Don't let's talk about it,' he said. 'I'm dreading it.'

'You're dreading it,' said Hughie, 'because you're the one who, if I die, might be left behind. I don't envy you. In your position, I would be the same. And to be honest, it looks more like when rather than if. But then, of course, it is *always* when.'

'So what was the result of the brontosauroscopy or whatever it's called?' I asked, trying to sound casual, but listening like a hawk. I could almost feel my eardrum tightening, in case it missed a vital word.

'Cancer. Of course,' said Hughie quickly. 'I think we all knew that long ago, didn't we? I knew, anyway. But so what? Lung cancer, schmung cancer.'

'So what will the MRI show?'

'How far it's gone. How long I've got. Whether to give me chemotherapy. But since I'm not going to have it, it seems fairly pointless.'

'You *might* have chemo,' said James.

'I am *not* having it and that's that!' said Hughie, loudly and sharply. 'It would just drag it out. And if I did have it,' he added, 'I certainly would not refer to it as "chemo" as if it were some kind of friend of mine. Anyway, I've got to go one day, my dear. Why not now? As Proust said, "We are all but dead people, waiting to take up our posts."'

We laughed, in rather a forced way, and said no more about it. But I knew we were keeping quiet for James's sake. And, in a way, for mine. I left rather earlier than usual. I know nothing about lung cancer. But I do know some people with cancer can carry on for years. Perhaps I need to consult Penny, the great amateur doctor.

Oct 30

In anticipation of buying a bicycle, to stop people calling me stately, statuesque or strapping, I borrowed a bike from Lucy, who's in London this week, and we went off to the V and A together.

What a mistake!

'I hope you're going to wear a hat!' said Jack, when I told him on the phone.

'Certainly not!' I said. 'It would make my hair go all funny.' I've got rather perky hair and after taking off a biking hat it's all flat and hideous and the top of my head looks like the warming plate on an Aga. Or, worse, I look like one of those awful short-haired elderly betrousered and asexual-looking American women you see in art galleries, who exist as a warning to everyone over the age of sixty.

'What do you mean, no?' he said. 'You always insisted I wore a hat when I was small, so I'm insisting you wear a hat now. And a yellow jacket,' he added, rather spitefully, I thought.

No question, those 'hey-look-at-me' bright yellow jerkin tops just don't suit me. Added to that, because I always wear three-quarter-length skirts, which get caught up in the wheels, I'm forced, on a bike, to wear trousers which make me look fright-ful. One of my old boyfriends once told me that I have what he called a 'Japanese bottom' and I never wore trousers again.

So off I went to this Lighting exhibition at the V and A and arrived, having had exhaust fumes blowing in my face all the way, looking like a sweaty old lesbian, which never does the morale any good. Lucy, who'd bicycled ahead, was waiting for me in the café. She looked very cool and collected. But she also looked very low.

'When I married Roger, he was a working man,' she com-plained over a lightly done calves' liver. ('I'm going to be naughty,' she said, as she chose. 'I know I should have a salad, but what the hell.' The idea of anything but a salad being 'naughty' baffled me. If she wanted calves' liver, have calves' liver. Nothing naughty about it. But she was behaving as if she were some kind of secret shoplifter. Naughty chocolate cake. Naughty bread and butter. The whole idea made me cringe, but I smiled indulgently as I ordered a steak and chips. 'Oh, you're being naughty, too!' she squeaked. 'I'm not being naughty,' I said, irritably. 'I'm just having what I want . . . but anyway . . . go on . . .')

'But now he's retired, he's driving me utterly bonkers,' she said. 'He's there *all the time!*'

The idea of having Roger, a sandy-haired man with hairs growing out of his ears, around even part of the time made me flinch, but the idea of Roger around *all the time* was an unspeakably unappetizing prospect.

'He never goes out,' she said. 'And at around twelve o'clock every day, you know what he says?'

'No,' I said.

'He says "What's for lunch, pet?" I just can't bear it.'

I bet also, when they're out and she's telling a story, he interrupts and at some point in the conversation one or other of them turns to the other and says: 'Now, who's telling this story, you or me?'

Now, let's be completely honest. I do have moments when despite Gene, despite my infatuation with the onset of age, and despite my increasing conviction that I should give up men altogether and never even fantasize about them, I can trail around the house feeling like a lost soul, longing for someone to chat to, longing for some kind of connection with A.N. Other, longing, I suppose, for a partner and a soulmate. But then, when I look back, none of the men I've been with would I be happy to have in the house with me now. And God knows I've had enough.

Anyway, I only have to think of Lucy and Roger or, indeed, Penny's dreadful experience with the frightful Gavin, and the realization of how lucky I am comes roaring home. 'I married him for life, but not for lunch.' That's what Lucy was really saying. Men just can't cope with retirement. While women are quite happy pottering about reading and getting the shopping and cooking and gardening, your average man just gloops about doing sod all when he's retired.

I've seen these wretched creatures on walks in the country. You're going along a lane minding your own business and suddenly, round the corner, comes a retired man, his wife and a dog. The wife has obviously given up all pretence at being a sexual being, since her hair is cut in a weird cut (the same style as mine after I've been wearing a bicycle helmet; yes the American-woman-in-art-gallery look), she's wearing trousers and ghastly stone-coloured shoes. He, on the other hand, has clearly had to retire from the important role he used to play in the office, for which he has substituted a wretched dog and a pair of binoculars.

You barely have time to say hello before he's stopped and yelled at his dog, often a mild-mannered spaniel or sometimes even a dachshund: 'Sitt! Sitt! No!! SITT!!' As he says this, he struggles to attach the animal to a lead, as if it were some kind of man-eating dragon. Then, as you pass, he retreats very obviously into the bushes to let you by, pulling on his dog so that it is nearly strangled, and says: 'Good AFTERNOON! SITTTTT!!!'

I hate to find myself one of the aren't-all-men-a-load-of-wallies brigade, but sometimes it's hard to resist it.

So whenever I'm feeling a bit lonely, I just have to say to myself 'SITT!!' or 'What's for lunch, pet?' and the desire for a man completely vanishes.

Very pleased to read, when I gasped my way back from the V and A, that apparently, after the age of fifty, our chances of a serious bike accident increase . . . they rise 5 per cent every decade after fifty. It's not just because our reactions are slower, but because we have such stiff necks we can't turn them far enough to see what's coming up behind.

Think I'll give up bicycling.

October 31

Saw, this morning in the bath, that my knees are covered in scars anyway from old bicycling accidents I had when I was twelve. Really weird, these visual voices from the past.

Michelle put her head round the door before I went to bed to discuss the latest with Harry, whom I still have to meet properly. Like Gavin, he hasn't rung for days. It is absolutely agonizing to hear all this, particularly having been through it all myself, and knowing that Michelle's got years and years of it before she's old enough to settle down. It is her birthday and she is only twenty, poor girl. All that misery ahead.

Since Harry isn't going to take her out on her birthday I suggested she come to the Thai round the corner with me. Privately I thought it would almost be more fun for her to sit alone in her room watching telly than going out for a meal with her ancient sixty-year-old foreign landlady, and hedged my invitation round with all kinds of get-outs like: 'But of course, if you get an invitation to go to a party or a club or out for drinks with your friends, just tell me, I won't be offended . . .' but she said she would like to have supper with me.

I rather hope, for her sake, that she gets asked out.

Later

Angela, my other aunt, has just rung, saying she is eighty-three, all her friends are dead, she is so upset about her husband who has just died – he was such a lovely old duck – she doesn't want to live, why do they do all this research on keeping us alive, she asks?

Later

Michelle's friends never called, so I took her to the Thai. What constantly surprises me is the selflessness that comes with old age. I don't mean one's selfless in some noble or admirable way. More that nothing matters any more. I used to have a nervous breakdown if I wasn't facing outwards in a restaurant, if the water they brought was still and not sparkling, if there was a draught . . . Now I feel I've drunk enough sparkling water to quench my thirst for ever, I've faced outward so many times I'm bored with the view. I suppose, also, there's that feeling that if something really bugged me, I have enough confidence to ask for things to be altered, quite nicely and without causing a scene.

We talked about love, and I said that the direct pursuit of love is one of the most destructive aims in the world. She said that, though she was full of ambition, she didn't know what she wanted to do in life.

'I know, darling,' I said. (This use of the word 'darling' is getting too frequent. I'm starting to sound like some frightful old actress.) 'Like an arrow in a bow all quivering to go, with no target,' I said, demonstrating as I did so and knocking over the soy sauce.

'*Exactement!*' she said, laughing. 'You know,' she added, 'I tell my friend at work I leeve on my own with a woman of sixty!'

'Oh yes!' I said, trying hard to smile lightly and finding all my muscles had seized up.

'But she say: "Ees eet not borr*eeng*, leeving with one old woman?" and I say: "No, ees not bor*eeng*. Yes, she is vairy, vairy old, but she is also vairy, vairy cool."'

I practically fainted I felt so flattered.

Nov 1st

Listened to *Desert Island Discs*, with my least favourite man, Bill Nighy, and he chose a Rolling Stones record called 'Winter' and it took me straight back to running along the cobbled streets of Liverpool when I saw the Stones in the sixties, hand in hand with an old lover by whom I had two abortions. (As he said at the time: 'To have one abortion, Miss Sharp, may be regarded as a mistake, but to have two looks like carelessness.') I could smell him, remember the greasy hotel room we stayed in, recall the inky, dark, glowing evening light as we ran . . . it was like a drug trip – that sudden surge of memory and emotion, an emotion that, oddly, I don't remember feeling at the actual time.

November 2nd

Penny rang saying she'd been shopping in Fenwicks, had seen a counter selling scent she used to do PR for so went up to look at their literature, and the assistant had gathered up some bits and free samples, put them into a bag and handed them to her, saying: 'Something for you to read on the train home, dear.'

'She thought I was from the *country*!' said Penny, horrified. '*Me!* She probably wouldn't have a job if it wasn't for my company. The cheek!'

November 3

Rather a nasty surprise as I came running down the stairs to get the post. Have to say those new anti-inflammatories really do the business. I spend my entire time turning my head round like an owl to show how supple and pain-free I am. Of course at about forty-five degrees it gets a bit ouchy, but what the hell.

Anyway. The nasty surprise. A letter comes from the Planning Department to the Residents' Association (me, basically) saying that someone has bought the Kwik-Fit garage down the street and they want to turn it into an evangelical church called Praise the Lord! Inc. My heart absolutely sank. The only reason the Residents' Association was created originally was because of an evangelical group which set up in a house nearby and spilled out into the garden in the summer. You couldn't go into the garden at all in the evening without hearing the preacher's frightful curses of hellfire and damnation for anyone who was homosexual or who had had an abortion, and as for anyone divorced like me (or who had had two abortions), we would roast in the fire for eternity. Not much fun as you're sitting having a drink and a crisp in the evening sun.

So my immediate reaction to Praise the Lord! Inc. was 'Over my dead body.'

I summoned all the members of the Residents' Association and got them over tonight. Penny's very loyal. She comes to these things but never says anything, and always agrees with everything we say. That's the kind of committee member I like. Of course I, preferably, would like a committee made up of deaf and dumb people, and then I could fire off my letters in all directions without a by-your-leave, but unfortunately democracy rules in Shepherds Bush.

At the end of the meeting it was agreed I should write a letter of objection on account of the noise, and then, thank God, everyone went home, except Penny who stayed and had supper.

She said that she'd been so miserable after being blown out by Gavin again last time, that she'd gone round to the new young doctor. I think she's panicking that she'll be carted off to the Priory, where she's already spent six weeks of her life in the past.

'When it comes to depression as you get older,' she said, 'the good thing is that you can spot it a mile away as it comes galloping over the hill – but the bad thing is that every time you get hurt it's worse than the last time.'

'Why is that?' I said. 'I would have thought it got easier.'

'My theory is that when you're one year old and miserable, you're just miserable. When you're two years old and miserable, you're not only miserable, but it reminds you of the last time you were miserable so it's worse. By the time you're nearly sixty, any upset rings so many bells in your past that it's like some ghastly bell-ringing competition in your head. Gavin dumping me upsets me, but it also reminds me of my divorce, which reminded me of my father dying, which reminded me of my mother trying to kill herself, which reminded me of the au pair going away . . . and on and on . . .'

'Sounds frightful,' I said. 'What did the doctor say, anyway?'

Turns out she put Penny on some anti-depression and anxiety pill which we looked up in my big book of pills, called *Medicines for All*. We found that its side effects were fits, headaches and, surprisingly, for an anti-depressant, depression.

Nov 4

Woke this morning unable to get the words 'Matabileland' out of my head. Am I going mad? Is there such a place?

Later

Hughie looked in to borrow some linseed oil because James had got it into his head that he wanted to clean and oil all the furniture in their flat. I also wanted Hughie to look at the planning application from Praise the Lord! Inc. to see if he could think up a brilliant legal way of squashing it. I got a bottle of champagne from the fridge.

'It will smell disgusting,' said Hughie, taking the linseed oil as he sat down in the garden. He put his hat on the table.

'Not a cunt's hat, I hope?' he asked.

'Just a touch too small,' I said.

I always feel just a tiny bit odd around Hughie, it has to be admitted. Even though he's sixty-five, he's incredibly attractive and, of course, bright and cynical, which makes him extra sexy. I know he's gay so there's no chance of anything, and anyway I don't want to get involved with anyone, blah, blah, blah, but he did once have a girlfriend and there's something between us. A chemistry. Or is it just affection? I constantly feel that he knows that I know that he knows . . . even when James is around, I always have the hunch that Hughie is secretly collaborating with me behind his back.

What is it about men that makes them attractive? Their movements, I think. Doesn't matter whether they're fat or thin, but they must move elegantly. Their cleanliness – I've never gone for an oily rag of a man. And of course, much as it galls me to say it as it's such a cliché, incredible intelligence and an ability to make fantastically good jokes and laugh uproariously at mine don't actually count against them.

Hughie's got one of those faces that always looks permanently interested, and as if he secretly finds life a huge joke – which I think he does. Hughie is also a smoker, which again I find rather dishy. He always has a fag when he comes round because James won't tolerate him smoking in the flat.

'How's being sixty treating you?' he asked. 'Still enjoying it?'

'Brilliant,' I replied.

'As Bob Hope, I think it was, said: "At twenty we worry about what others think of us, at forty we don't care what they think of us, and at sixty we discover they haven't been thinking of us at all."'

I laughed.

'Old age isn't really very nice, you know,' he said, after a pause. 'Being sixty is fine, perhaps, but after sixty-five, it's downhill. I can feel it. Less sex. Puffing when you go upstairs. Having to mop your mouth all the time in case you've got drips . . . you look so young, my darling, but when I look in the mirror and see those wrinkles . . . I was such a golden boy, you know.'

'You're still gorgeous,' I said. And there was a pause after that and Hughie turned and looked at me for one of those fractions of a second that just said something but I don't know what because he's gay, remember?

'Any news of the MRI?' I asked, rather clunkingly changing the subject.

Hughie paused for a moment, continuing to look me in the eyes and laughed.

'"Gorgeous",' he repeated. 'You're a naughty girl. When are you going to find a nice bloke? You've been single too long.'

'Stop changing the subject,' I said, the teensiest bit flustered. 'MRI. Dates, please.'

'Since you insist, it's in ten days. November 14th. OK? Now back to you and relationships.'

I waved away the question. 'All over. Relationships, *nein danke*. I've made a big decision and I'm never, ever, ever going to have sex again. The whole thing just isn't comfortable any more. Oh, I know you can smear yourself with creams and stuff yourself with hormone replacement pills and the juices will start flowing naturally again, but the last time I had sex I was screaming with pain not with pleasure. And look what Penny went through with Gavin! She's still got cystitis you know. Two months later.'

'Do you really mean that?' asked Hughie. 'I thought that today, even the wrinkliest of specimens are, according to most of the media, meant to be "up for it" till the day they die – preferably "on the job". God, I miss it.'

'Rubbish. We women are always told to "listen to our bodies" . . . and when I listen to mine it goes "Ouch! Ouch! Ouch!" Anyway, sex brings only trouble and misery in my experience. I'm glad to be out of it.'

'And never a thought for poor old Archie?' said Hughie, slyly. 'I saw him the other day and he kept talking about how attractive you are. Come on, Marie. You can't give up sex. You're lovely. You're a sexy person. You're kidding yourself. If it's the last thing I do – and, at the rate I'm going, it might be – I'm going to see you settled with a nice chap. You deserve one. A nice chap deserves you, too.'

'Archie's gone off with a young blonde,' I said.

'No, that's all over,' said Hughie. 'He said he just couldn't cope with the fact that she didn't understand any of his jokes. And she tried to make him eat muesli. And insisted he had a duvet on the bed. You can imagine what Archie's like about blankets. And she kept telling him he had low self-esteem.'

'Archie is groaning with self-esteem,' I said.

'I know, but you know how he pretends to put himself down all the time, while underneath he bursts with confidence. It's an English thing. Very confusing for Swedes.'

'Oh, well, I expect another one will be along soon,' I said. 'He's such a dish and so nice and eligible, he won't be single for long.'

Hughie looked at me. 'You know that Archie is by far the nicest, kindest, funniest person we know,' he said. 'And the richest, but that's beside the point. Why don't you give it a go?'

'I'm hopeless at relationships!' I said. 'At least with Archie I've got a wonderful friendship. Anything more and it would all go wrong. At last I've come to terms with being single and I'm happier than I've ever been before. Don't tempt me!

149

You're like someone who says to an alcoholic who's been on the wagon for years: "Oh, just the one won't hurt!" But it will! I know, darling!'

The 'darling' just slipped out.

'I didn't mean "darling, darling",' I tried to explain, embarrassedly. 'But it *keeps* popping out these days.'

'Oh, a sort of Soho House, Ab Fab kind of darling?' said Hugh, smiling wryly.

'No, oh, I won't be able to make you understand. It's a kind of affectionate, but not *too* affectionate,' I said hurriedly, 'expression, that has come upon me at sixty like a kind of disease. My speech is peppered with darlings. Darlings, not dahlings with an "h",' I added. 'There's nothing I can do about it.'

'Like liver spots?' said Hugh. 'Do you know what Sophocles thought of sex at sixty?'

'I bet Sophocles never called people "darling", even when he was eighty. He was far too cool.'

'Sophocles,' said Hugh, signalling for a top-up for his glass, 'on being asked, when he was an old man, whether he still had sex, replied: "Heaven forbid! I was only too glad to escape from all that, as though from a boorish and insane master."'

'Well, I think the single life is the best,' I said.

'Get thee to a grannery,' said Hughie. 'A joke before I go.'

'Yes?' I said.

'Two old ladies at bridge. One says to the other: "I'm ever so sorry, my dear, and I know we've known each other for years, and were childhood friends, but I can't remember your name. Can you tell me what it is?" The other woman pauses and then thinks. She thinks and thinks and then she says: "How soon do you need to know?"'

Hughie went into a coughing fit, banged his chest and slugged back the final glass in one gulp. 'Time to go. James will think I've run away with a rent boy.' He got up. 'Ugh!' he said, as he did so.

'Why do we say "Ugh," when we get up when we're old?' I asked. 'Did Sophocles have a view on that?'

Hughie sat down again. 'Let me try getting up without saying "Ugh!" he said. He rose, silently.

'Undoubtedly easier with the "Ugh!" sound,' he said. 'Do you think it's like those tennis players who say "Ugh!" when they serve? Anyway, goodbye, my dear,' he added, drawing me up to him for a hug and a kiss. 'You are gorgeous yourself, you know.'

Then he added: 'It was nice when you called me "darling".'

I felt all funny when he went. But soon got over it.

November 5th

For a long time these past few days, fireworks have been let off. When I was small, we had them only on bonfire night. My father would buy a small box of Brocks fireworks, and we would go into the garden in the cold, and he stuffed them into the earth one by one. There was a limited number of choices. Silver Rain – a conical affair which just spurted a silver shower. And Golden Rain – the same only gold. Then there were Roman Candles – shooting different coloured stars into the air at intervals, and Catherine Wheels pinned to trees, which *never* seemed to work. My memory was always of my father, with a long stick, poking desperately at a tiny curled up snake that was spurting sparks in one direction only, usually on to the ground. Occasionally it got going for a couple of seconds, just before it fizzled out. One rocket might have been included – a small affair that produced perhaps two stars. And, of course, there were sparklers. My father taught me to whizz them round and round until they made circles in the air.

I remember the smell so well – it hung in the air, the bitter tang of gunpowder mixed with damp earth. And then, the next morning, we would collect the discarded shells from the garden, squashed and lifeless now, all promise burnt out of them, the sparklers reduced to black and gritty metal sticks.

Now the sky, even a couple of weeks before the actual day, is nightly filled with showers of stars, explosions like bombs, shrieks and screams, and rockets that sometimes seem to spawn their own separate baby rockets once they launch into the night sky – circles of gold, red and blue, half blotted out by the outlines of the trees in the garden. I feel as if I'm in the middle of an attack on Baghdad, rather than in the middle of Shepherds Bush, with shells exploding all around me.

Pouncer is absolutely terrified. He comes in, his ears back, his stomach very low on the ground, as if he has turned into a dachshund; sometimes he touchingly hides under my skirt in the sitting room. He's the same with thunderstorms. As he's an animal and presumably in tune with nature, I always expect him to be in harmony with the thunder and lightning and to sit wisely stroking his whiskers like Buddha while I, ruined by civilization, cower behind the sofa. But no. He's terrified of everything.

November 10th

Wrote an email to Penny which read:

> *Everything going wrong. Pouncer going mad. And have frightful hangover because Maciej gave me a bottle of wine from Poland, which, mistakenly, I drank. All is lost! Grown!*

I got an email back from her which read:

> *What means 'Grown'?*

Embarrassed to find that what I'd meant to write was, of course, 'Groan!' Oh, Lord. Is this the way that old age is striking me? I seem to have no problem with remembering words, but no use if cannot spell ennything. (That's a joke, by the way, a deliberate mistake.)

November 11th

Last night I babysat Gene. I'd suggested it to Jack and Chrissie rather boldly, saying: 'He'll be fine. You go out and have some fun. You deserve it!'

I packed my knitting, a book about an Afghan refugee in the East End I've been meaning to read for ages because Hughie told me it was excellent. And, just in case I didn't have enough to do, I popped in a new address book that I keep meaning to copy my old addresses into. Not that, to be honest, I'm going to copy them all out, by any means.

A new address book has always meant a big spring clean as far as friends go. And I am ruthless about expurgating the ones I don't see that often. Death, increasingly, counts for quite a few excisions, and looking through I found that in the last few years there are no fewer than eight scratchings out due to the arrival of the grim r.

I arrived early, full of good intentions, only to find Jack and Chrissie in such a state of exhaustion that Chrissie was asleep and Jack told me that he didn't think she'd be up to going out.

'I was going to ring you, but then Gene was screaming, so by the time I did, you'd left,' he said. 'I'm so sorry.'

'Why not go round the corner for a drink just for an hour?' I suggested, feeling deeply disappointed but determined not to show it. 'Just to prove you can. Like driving a car after an accident. Not that Gene is an accident, of course,' I said, and then, realizing I was getting myself into knots of confusion, added: 'Well, you know what I mean.'

Our conversation was interrupted by a great hooting outside. We got up and looked out of the big windows of their flat into the street below.

The extremely narrow road is often the scene of a stand-off, but this was worse than usual. A red car faced a small white van in the street, traffic was building up behind each vehicle and neither seemed prepared to budge an inch. Both drivers were hooting loudly, between looking out of their side windows and yelling insults at each other.

'Looks a bit hairy,' I said. Then I thought that perhaps 'hairy' was rather a sixties expression and wondered if Jack knew what it meant.

Jack came over, holding Gene, who looked extremely interested in the scene outside. He was dressed in a little red one-piece sleep suit and had the air of a very clean goblin, sitting very comfortably on the crux of his dad's elbow. He started laughing rather inappropriately.

Outside, in the fading light, we could see the driver of the red car get out and approach the driver of the white van, who immediately got out of his vehicle to get himself into a more advantageous position. They started yelling at each other. Red Driver put his hands on White Driver's jersey, and started pushing him. White Driver retaliated in the same way.

'Darling,' I said to Jack. 'Shouldn't we call the police?'

By now Red Driver had retreated to the boot of his car and produced a hammer and advanced threateningly on White Driver. White Driver raced back to his boot and produced a car jack. As they squared up to each other I could hardly look.

'Jack, we must phone the police!' I squawked. 'This is so horrible! Someone will get hurt.'

Jack and Gene stared down some more.

'No,' said Jack, slowly. 'I think it will be OK. Things like this happen all over London, Mum. It's just that you never get around to see it. It's nothing to worry about. It'll sort itself out.'

Just as I was thinking that perhaps the idea of babysitting was not such a good idea after all, one of the drivers retreated and, with a final screamed insult at the other, got into his car and yelled at the queue behind him to start reversing. Eventually he found a passing place. As the other driver passed him they spat in each other's face, as far as I could see, and peace was finally restored.

Chrissie came downstairs looking extremely pretty and made-up, and eager to go out, so I got my head around this new development, and, while Jack was getting Gene to sleep, she explained everything to me. The instructions lasted for ages. She showed me his bottle, exactly how much milk should be made up, with how many of which level spoonfuls of what, what temperature the boiled water should be. Then there were the nappies, the wipes, the cream and the powder. There were two sorts of nappies, the night nappies and the day nappies and I shouldn't get them confused. There was his dummy, and his bear, and tips on how to get him to sleep if he should wake. In case the bedding in his basket got wet, I was shown where to get fresh bedding, and if he got too hot, I was told, I could pat his face with cotton wool dipped in cool (but not icy) water. I suppose, being a spa person, she knows all about water and its temperature.

If he woke, she said, I should put him back to sleep on his back, not his side or his tummy (completely opposite to how we'd been instructed in my day when Jack was tiny) and he liked the light just so, not too dark and not too bright. What always woke him, she said, was a certain creak in the floor-boards just outside the lavatory, so if I could possibly not step on that floorboard it would be great, and it would be best not to flush the loo, if I had to go, because that also woke him up.

155

If I were to turn on the tap in the kitchen, I should make sure the door was closed because the sound of running water was a sure way of waking him, and although I could watch television, I should put his basket into the next room first, and then assemble the baby monitor.

'Now', she said. 'The baby monitor. You plug it in here and make sure it's on this wavelength, and then turn it to high. Then with the other end,' she added, going into the sitting room, 'you plug it in here, and you make sure those little red lights are showing, and the green light is *off* not on, and it's tuned to number five.'

Finally, if anything happened at all, she explained, they'd be just round the corner in a restaurant literally five minutes away and, as well as making sure I knew both their mobile numbers, she'd taken the precaution of getting the telephone number of the restaurant as well.

My head was spinning, but I pretended, not very plausibly, to take it all in.

'On his back,' I said. 'And monitor at number 3.'

'No, on his side, and monitor at number 5.'

'Of course,' I said. 'Silly of me. And the milk, it's six spoonfuls of powder to four of water . . .'

'Three spoonfuls to three of water . . .'

'And I use this bottle . . .'

'No, that's the bottle we use during the day . . . I tell you what,' she said, looking at me with kind, caring sympathy, as if I were some sort of mad old lady, 'I'll write it all down for you.' Clearly I'd never be able to do her spa-selling job. It obviously requires a brain that can hold whole libraries of information all at the same time.

I felt thoroughly humiliated, but relieved at the same time. And eventually I waved them off telling them not to worry a bit, that Gene would be perfectly safe with me.

I sat down on their extremely uncomfortable sofa – well,

it's uncomfortable for me because it's very low on the ground; once you're in it, you need a hoist to get you out of it accompanied by a Red Indian chorus of 'Ugh!'s – and very quietly got all the things that I'd brought out of my bag. A few feet away, Gene was fast asleep in his little Moses basket, lined with the black and white material that Chrissie had found at a car boot sale. Then I tiptoed over to have a look at him. He was completely peaceful, one little hand lying above him and the other by his side. I went back to the sofa and opened my book.

No sooner had I done so, than Gene made a kind of grunt. After the grunt he made another grunt, and within seconds, he'd woken himself up and started to cry. I tried everything. I picked him up and took him into the bathroom, where it was pitch dark, and sang to him. I offered him more milk – which I had to make with one hand, far more difficult than I imagined. But the minute I offered it to him, he turned his little mouth away from the teat, roaring with tearful rage.

The only way I could calm him down was to walk him round the flat talking non-stop and pointing things out to him.

'Now, let's look at these nice banisters,' I said. 'They're painted white, isn't that nice . . . and look – on the bit at the end there's a big wooden ball . . . *you'll* be playing with big footballs when you're a big boy . . . and now we're going down the stairs, one, two, three, four, five, six, and stepping on the nice red carpet . . . oh, here's a mirror, what can we see in that . . . I can see Gene in there! And Grannie! Gene is in his nice red sleeping suit, and Grannie's looking a bit distraught and knackered, isn't she, it's because she's *very* worried that you won't go back to sleep before Mummy and Daddy get back, and now we're going *up* the stairs, one, two, three, four, five, six, past the nice white banisters . . . and now what else can we see . . .'

I must have continued like this for at least an hour and a

half. My mouth became dry with talking, I kept looking at my watch. For God's sake, when would they return? We looked out of the window and watched all the cars toing and froing in the blackness, with the red lights at the back and the white lights at the front, and we fantasized about where they might be going and what they were up to. Occasionally people would pass by.

'Look, Gene,' I would say in my gentle voice. 'There's a man in a hood. He's probably a mugger. He's a naughty man, isn't he? And look, there's a nice drug dealer the other side of the road. He's making lots and lots of money selling people heroin. And look, here's a man who looks very sad. His wife has probably run off with the drug dealer . . .'

Finally Gene accepted a bottle of milk and I took him into the kitchen where it was very dark, and sang 'Rock-a-Bye Baby' to him, swinging him gently in my arms, while stroking his head at the same time. His eyelids started to droop and I repeated the word: 'Slee . . . eeep, slee . . . eeep . . .' over and over again, like some crazy hypnotist, and finally he dropped off. Tiptoeing along the corridor, remembering the creaky floorboard, I managed to lower him into his basket and sat down, breathing a huge sigh of relief. After a few minutes I thought it safe enough to put him into the kitchen, while I turned the lights up in the sitting room bright enough to read.

Just as I had got started on my book, the phone rang. It was Chrissie. 'Is everything OK there?' she said, anxiously.

'*Fine!*' I replied jovially. I sounded like some dreadful phoney pub landlord from the Home Counties. 'Absolutely fine! He woke up for a little bit but he's back to sleep and there's nothing to worry about at all.'

'Well, we're having a really good time, so we thought we'd go and have a quick drink at the pub . . . is that OK?' she asked.

'Great!' I said. 'Everything's cool! No worries!'

'Do remember, by the way,' she added, 'that if you undo

the blinds, you must hook up the white strings by the side because if he were to lie on the floor by one and pull it down, he might strangle himself.'

'Oh, don't worry!' I said, breezily. 'No strangling round here. Have a lovely time.'

I immediately went round the whole flat checking that all the white strings were tied up beyond reach. I know. It was highly unlikely that Gene would strangle himself when he was asleep, but you couldn't be too careful.

I started on my book again, and had just found my place, when there was a crackle from the baby monitor and the unnerving sounds of a cockney male voice invaded the room.

'Just got in, two minutes to go. Roger!' it said. 'T for Tango, V for Victor and F for 'ow's yer father. Coming up now!'

I leaped up, terrified. For a split second I thought burglars had scaled the wall outside the kitchen, had snuck in through the window and were communicating with each other on walkie-talkies before making off with Gene. Unless, of course, Gene, after all the conversation he'd heard in the first few months of his life, had suddenly learned to talk. I dashed to the kitchen in panic, but there was no one there. But in my haste, I'd trodden on the squeaky floorboard. Gene immediately woke up, howling.

I had to go through the entire routine again. He seemed to get heavier and heavier and as he became more and more wide awake, I got more and more exhausted. Finally, just as he appeared to be flagging a bit, I put him into his Moses basket (On his side? On his back? Who cared any more?) and started swinging him. As I swung, he quietened down. I swung him high, I swung him low. But every time I stopped swinging he started crying. Eventually I stood in the middle of the room, swinging as hard as I could. I swung him so high that I contemplated just whirling the entire basket around above my head, keeping him in place by centrifugal force, but as I got a glimpse of his head as it sped past me on each swing, I saw, eventually, that he was truly asleep. I risked easing up on the swinging. I got slower and slower. Eventually, I stopped, and very gently placed the basket on the floor. And as I did so I heard the key in the lock. Jack and Chrissie were back.

'How did it go?' they asked, as they reeled in, reeking of wine and garlic.

'*Fine!*' I said. 'Absolutely fine!'

'That's great, Mum,' said Jack. 'We've had such a good time! Now we know we can do it, we must do it more often.'

'Any time,' I said, as I gathered up my unknitted knitting, my unread book and my unfilled address book. 'Any time. It's a real pleasure.'

And, of course, in a funny way, it was.

November 12th

Michelle knocked on my door very confused. She'd gone into the local Lebanese supermarket to ask for some pine nuts, and they'd insisted on taking her to a shelf on which were displayed a selection of boxes of aspirin, Nurofen and Ibuprofen. 'I want pine nuts,' she had said. 'Pine . . . pine . . . pine . . .'

'Yes, these for pine,' they had replied, gesturing to the aspirins. 'Tike why pine!'

November 13th

Hughie and James drove me to the Head-Wetting Ceremony, as Jack and Chrissie call it, at a local pub. I'd tried to persuade Jack and Chrissie to put Gene into the long embroidered white lacy dress that Jack wore when he was christened, but they said he wouldn't fit into it (and I'm sure they're right – he's quite a tubby little person) and he wore, instead, a pair of very smart dungarees. Very sweetly they'd put him in the green hat with the purple sprouting on top that I'd finally finished knitting for him.

As a christening present, James had bought Gene a hand-painted mug with 'Gene' written on it. Inside was a special crystal, apparently connected with his birthday. James insisted that this must be kept by his bed to give him good luck. I just hoped he hadn't got it from Gavin's shop in Glastonbury.

It was an oddly warm November day, and the pub was swarming with people I didn't know. I know Hughie hates pubs, so he was very noble in coming along, but he stood outside most of the time, smoking and talking to Penny, who is zombied out with antidepressants. I felt rather gooseberry-like, but I only had to say that I was Jack's mum and Gene's grannie, and the kindness of everyone was amazing.

It was odd, because surely current thinking is that old people are despised and hated because they're ancient and boring, but that day I didn't experience that at all – and have never experienced it anyway. What I did experience was the complete opposite – not a reverence, exactly, but a special kind of protective instinct emanating from all those grunge-dressed people, a kindness and caring for someone not of their generation. Bliss!

We did come across the odd language problem, however. The words 'Andy Pandy' met with complete bafflement as did, oddly, the name Sophie Tucker and, less surprisingly perhaps, Oliver Messel.

I felt rather like my father must have felt when, talking to someone half his age, he referred to someone like, say, Joe Venuti, a jazz violinist apparently well known in his day, but hardly remembered thirty years later. I do *try* not to use the phrase 'Of course you're too young to remember . . .' too often, but it does come up now and again.

There were a few songs, and then a friend of Jack's played 'Danny Boy' on the musical saw. Everything built into a climax, and finally we all raised our glasses to Gene, held high by a beaming Chrissie. James, on my left, I noticed, had to lift up his spectacles to wipe away a tear, and I felt pretty weepy, too. Then James went outside to check on Hughie, and came back to signal to me that he was feeling a bit tired. As I felt I'd had enough, too, I cadged a lift from them.

In the car, Hughie turned back to me and said: 'I had the most extraordinary experience. I met some woman – a parent of one of Jack's friends – who used to know me when I was twenty. She didn't recognize me, of course, but you know what she said? She said: "I'd recognize that voice anywhere." I go to all these lengths to change to become a better person, to mature, to go through hell to twist myself into a new and more noble shape, and all I get, forty years on, is: "I'd recognize that voice anywhere." Depressing, really.'

He then went into a coughing fit and opened the window. Or rather, asked James to open the window.

'God, I wish we had wind-up windows again,' he said, crossly. 'What is the *point* of the electric things? Only good thing about them is that they kill, apparently, the odd toddler.'

Now I *know* his synapses are shrivelling.

November 14th

Today's the day of Hughie's MRI. Don't like to ring because it looks so intrusive. After all, if anything shows up, they'll tell me. And anyway, they probably have to wait a while before they get the results. But can't stop thinking about Hughie, and hoping that everything's going to be all right. Well, as all right as it can possibly be in the circumstances.

Later

'*Hello*,' reads today's bizarre email,

> Let me start by introducing myself properly to you. I am Mark Escrupolo Masilag (junior) from Philippines (The only surviving son of late Sir Mark Escrupolo Masilag)
>
> Me late father was a crude-oil consultant based in Iran until his unfortunate death with my mother as a result of the earthquake disaster that just occurred in Iran killing thousands of people.
>
> As I write this mail, I am still very much in shock and pain. Me reason of contact you is that before me father's death he moved all of his profits he had made so far to Holland just in case there is any war in Iran, the total amount of this funds as we speak is US$28 million.
>
> Please all I want from you is to act as the ESCRUPOLO MASILAG FAMILY personal representative sign the funds release document and have the funds transferred into your account I would be will to share the money with you 50-50 if you can do this to help save my soul from this poverty I am facing now . . .
> I would completely understand if you do not want to help me out in this transaction even though it is of mutual benefit, with the high rate of fraud going on around this days one can never be too careful . . .

December 1st

First Christmas card received. This year, Penny and I have decided not to send out any cards at all. Last Christmas I sent cards only to people who sent them to me, keeping a pile of cards on the hall table, along with a pen, a book of stamps and an old address book. The moment one came in, I'd send one back. Rather cold-blooded.

Of course, Penny and I agreed that we would have to send

cards to absolutely desperate people who are frightfully ill and never get out of the house. Or people who live abroad but whom we still like. Or, as I suggested, those people we can't really bear and try to not see but don't want them to know quite how much we can't stand them because they're not totally horrible.

'But if you include that group,' said Penny, 'we might as well go back to sending them to everyone.'

Later

Met James for mint tea in dodgy Lebanese hubble-bubble café round the corner. Surrounded by dark men puffing away at strawberry-flavoured coals, as far as I could make out. He was extremely upset.

'You know Hughie went for the MRI a fortnight ago, but we *still* haven't had the results,' he said. 'They seem to have lost the notes. I went with him, and it was horrible. Do you think he's in denial about all this? He keeps making jokes about it. I can't bear it.'

'I don't think he's in denial,' I said, honestly. 'I think it's us who are in denial.' I kindly said 'us' though quite honestly it was really James I was talking about. 'I think Hughie has got the hang of death. You live, you die, and it's all fine, that's Hughie's line.'

'I think he's living in his head,' said James.

'No bad place to live,' I said. 'Head, heart . . . whatever . . . But you're the one I'm worrying about. Perhaps,' I added, struck by inspiration, 'you're doing his worrying for him. You're sparing him all the pain and suffering by going through it yourself.'

That's one good thing about having done all this crap therapy. You can spout out any number of psychological models to people which sometimes give them a kind of comfort. Though actually that particular bit of wisdom was from the philosopher Viktor Frankl.

James gulped down this shred of comfort, and I could see, as his face slowly relaxed, that it made him feel better. We all believe that if what we suffer is something noble, something to spare others, we can bear it. If it's just our own measly suffering and holds no greater good, it's simply wall-to-wall grisly.

'That helps,' he said. 'Now we've just got to wait for the results.'

December 2

Ever since that conversation with Hughie in the garden, I've been wondering about sex. I last had sex five years ago, and frankly, apart from the odd unsuitable flare-up of sexual feelings (Hughie (twice), Lucy's dad, curiously, but only once, and, oddly, the eighteen-year-old son of one of my friends who talked to me for hours at a party; couldn't have been more inappropriate), I haven't fancied anyone in the meantime.

So what, I ask myself, is the point of having a tiny bedroom taken up almost entirely with a double bed? After all, the last thing I want is a bloke.

Anyway, to get back to the point. Wondering about sex. I'm seriously considering not having it any more. Penny gave me a book which she said would get me back in the mood. It was called *Better than Ever* by a Dr Bernie Zilbergeld and on the cover was the come-on: 'New brooms may sweep cleaner . . . but old brooms know where the corners are!'

Yucch! The very idea of being fucked by an old broom is totally disgusting!

December 6th

Went to see Gene again today. Talk about better than sex. I may have no one to cuddle me, but Gene makes up for everything. His smell, his soft, new young skin, his little arms reaching round my neck . . . it sounds horribly vampire-like, but it is so, so seductive.

I love having this little boy near me. When we go out, even into the bitter cold and misery of Brixton, I love the feel of him against me. I love his coat against mine, all bulked up, and inside somewhere his warm wrapped-up body. Underneath his outer shell, rumbling with cloth, underneath his dark blue coat and cardigan, his green trousers, and little emerald tights, his teeshirt, his vest and nappy . . . in the middle he is like a hazelnut, all ripe and sweet.

I used to resent the time I had to spend with Jack when he was tiny . . . but now I don't resent a minute with Gene. I can just sit and sit for hours, playing with him, watching him, picking him up, feeding him, putting him down. For me it's not remotely boring. Or rather, as Lucy's husband Roger said (about the only interesting thing Roger has ever said), it is a kind of 'exquisite boredom'.

Is it something to do with boundaries? With Jack I was never quite certain where I ended and he began, we were all hopelessly muddled up. If he cried I was in pain, if he smiled I was happy. But with Gene, I know where both he and I begin and end. It makes the relationship so clear and pure.

It's odd, but every minute I'm with him, I feel my own selfishness and cynicism is being rubbed away by this good and simple little chap.

Dec 7th

I was just about to go to bed, when the bell rang. It was James. His face was ashen.

'I'm so sorry it's so late, but can I come in?' he said.

'It's Hughie, isn't it,' I said. 'You've had the results. Come on, darling, come in and have a drink. Where is Hughie, anyway?'

'He's in such a bad temper,' said James, walking into the sitting room. He was half-crying, choking in the way that men do. 'It's much worse than we thought. He's only got a few months to live, if that, and all he said when we got back from the hospital was: "Just months to live? Well, let's crack open a bottle of champagne!" and I said how could he *think* of opening a bottle of champagne at a time like this . . .' He slumped into a chair. 'And he said for God's sake, he was trying to make the best of things, and I'm afraid I got really angry and of course, darling, I was so upset, and Hughie finally said, really coldly, you know how cold he can be: "For fuck's sake, it's *me* who's got the fucking lung cancer, not you!" and I slammed the door and here I am. Oh, I feel so awful. What will I do without him . . . ?'

What will *I* do without him, I wondered, selfishly, as I downed a large double scotch in the kitchen before going back into the sitting room with the bottle of wine and buckets of soothing sympathy. It's all very well this joking about death, but life would be very empty without Hughie. Will be very empty, I should say.

Eventually I packed James off and rang Hughie while he was on his way, and offered just as much sympathy as Hughie could bear (i.e. about a millionth of an ounce) and reminded him, totally unnecessarily, that James was just a poor mortal and full of kindness.

'I know,' said Hughie. 'Thank God he went to see you. I just suddenly got angry, you know. I mean his reaction was just selfish. If I've only got a few months to live, I don't want to live them with people weeping all around me. I might as well die tomorrow. What did James think was going to happen to me? He must have known this was going to happen. We all die, for God's sake. I don't have some special relationship with death. All the signs that we're going to die have been there from the very day we were born. And as I'm older than James by about fifteen years, the chances were always that I'd die first.'

'Well, do be kind to James, won't you,' I said. 'He's utterly devastated.'

'Oh, I'll be kind to James, don't worry,' said Hughie, rather sourly.

'And I have to say that I'm rather devastated, too, I'm afraid,' I added, rather nervously. 'But I am at least making it an excuse to have a hundred drinks.'

'That's my girl,' said Hughie.

December 10th

Went with Penny to the Estorick Collection. We discussed how difficult it was to get redcurrant jelly these days. As she said: 'I do like jam with my lamb.'

December 11

Great news! When I was round at Jack and Chrissie's, Gene actually rolled over! He giggled with delight at his new achievement. So touching!

Chrissie was going through all her kitchen cupboards and

throwing out everything beyond its sell-by date. I was standing by with a carrier bag into which everything was thrown, and which I was pretending, eventually, I would put in the bin, but secretly kept to take home. Sell-by dates! What a con! When I was young, if the toast was burnt, as it frequently was, it was scraped over the sink and eaten. Mould that developed on cheese was simply cut off, and if the pork smelt a bit peculiar, it was just washed thoroughly and cooked for a rather longer time than usual.

Oh, dear, oh dear, oh dear, reading that back I sound like *such a ghastly old person.*

Got back to put the final touches to my new bedroom plans. I am going to have it completely redecorated, get a much smaller bed – big enough for me to wallow in in luxury, big enough to accommodate one sleeping cat (Pouncer), but small enough to deter intruders. I'm going to shove it up against the wall – and then have a huge space in the middle to dance about in or just stride across or, if I'm really good, do my yoga exercises in.

I also thought that while I was at it, I'd get a new cooker. It seemed dreadfully irresponsible because mine isn't that revolting or hopeless, but the seal on the oven door has gone, and you need a match to light it because all the automatic pilots have got furred up. But Penny said why not? It would 'see me out'.

'See me out'?

There's a phrase I've never heard before!

December 12th

Asked Penny about painters, and she came up with a couple of Romanian characters who cost about £50 a day and work like beavers, as we say these days. I went through the usual agonies of feeling it unfair to hire them at such low rates, and she said that it was ridiculous, that's what they charged and they were glad of the work and if I felt like giving them a bit more when they'd finished the job, fine. She was, however, horrified at the idea of my giving up sex.

'What, never have another man again ever?' she said.

'Yes,' I said. 'It's a wonderfully liberating feeling. Like giving up drink.'

'Not that you'd know anything about that,' she said, rather acidly.

'No, but I can imagine it. You should try it. Why, you're not *really* after another bloke in your life, are you?' I asked her. 'Not after Ghastly Gavin from Glastonbury?'

'Well, it's very unlikely, but I'd like to keep my options open,' she said. 'And who knows? One of the problems is,' she added, 'that ever since I became sixty, I feel invisible.'

I feel *far* from invisible. The moment I became sixty I felt, suddenly, hideously visible. I can crack jokes with green-grocers, address babies in the street in a loud voice, and smile at strangers. It's amazing how many people smile back if you give them a big enough grin, even hoodies and dangerous crack addicts. It's got to be the right sort of smile though. It can't be a half-hearted affair, or one of those nervous, shy sort of permanent smiles you sometimes see on the faces of old ladies as they wander around the streets. It's got to be a big open grin, bursting with warmth.

Luckily, I can do warmth.

'You could always get a dog,' I said. 'Isn't that where you're meant to meet men? Art galleries or in the park with a dog?'

'Actually, you don't need a dog, apparently,' she said. 'You only need the lead. And then you go into the park asking people if they've seen Fido and before you know it men are falling over themselves to climb trees and burrow about in bushes, and then ask you out.'

'Climb trees?' I said. 'We're not talking pandas here, we're talking dogs. And anyway, how do you move from bush-burrowing to them asking you out?'

'I suppose the bush-burrowing gives them ideas,' said Penny.

'Penny!' I said. 'What a ghastly joke!'

'I couldn't help it,' she said sheepishly.

When I got back home I had one of those awful thoughts one occasionally has about friends – how could I possibly know anyone who found the idea of 'bush-burrowing' funny? But perhaps she was thinking: How could I know anyone who *doesn't* think the idea of bush-burrowing funny?

Tried not to think about it.

Dec 13

Have to put a brave face on the fact that Jack and Chrissie and Gene are not, it turns out, coming to me for Christmas. They're going to David's again – but only, they tell me, because David is going to work in Australia for a year, so won't be back next time.

'We'll come next year *and* the following year,' they promise. Probably best, actually. Because it's only when children are two upwards that they understand what Christmas is about. I still feel obliged to get a tree, though, because Jack and Chrissie are coming over one afternoon for their presents, and I thought it would make the house smell nice, but of course I remember from last year that either I have lost my sense of smell, which I think is unlikely, or Christmas trees are now grown smell-free. I miss it so much, that Christmas-tree smell. It used to spell Christmas for me. And now it's gone, along with all the other vanished pongs – the smell of bonfires, burning coal, fog, dirty hair, sweaty suits, the Paris metro and boiling horsemeat, Schiaparelli's Shocking.

Is Christmas trees' lack of smell something to do with the glue they spray on to stop the needles falling off? Not that that made any difference to my tree last year. Only last week, I found a whole cache of needles behind the sofa from last December's tree, which Maciej had missed.

Dec 14

As I was clearing out the bedroom for the painters, I went through all my drawers and chucked out a lot of stuff. Since being sixty, my style of dressing has gone from discreet to preposterous. But I still abide by very strict rules about dressing after middle-age, most of which were given to me by my mother.

1. Never wear white. It makes yellow teeth look yellower.
2. Always keep your upper arms well covered. Those bits of flesh that hang down at the sides (known, apparently, as 'bingo wings') are hideous – and so are those strange rolls of flesh that appear between your underarms and your body.
3. Get a new bra every six months at least and keep it well hitched-up. You don't want to be one of those people whose boobs touch their tummies when they sit down. Or, worse, when they stand up.
4. Don't disguise a lizardy neck with a scarf or polo neck. They always look as if you have something to hide – and the imagination always conjures up something worse than the reality.
5. Never wear trousers after fifty, unless they are ludicrously well cut and slinky, and never wear short skirts.
6. Make sure you possess and wear the most glamorous dress-ing gown in the world.

7. Never wear trainers (especially stone-coloured ones), or any kind of sports clothes, trackie bottoms, tops, etc.

December 15th

The builders came to do my room. I have moved myself into the spare room – and what an education! I think there should be a 'sleep in your spare room' day every year, so that hosts can find out how incredibly uncomfortable the beds are and how the floorboards creak when they want to go to the loo at night. I discovered that the soap I'd put out in the bedroom basin was streaked with grime and stuck to the dish, there was no hook on the back of the door to hang up your dressing gown, and that the fashionable iron-barred bedhead was, while fabulous to look at, hideously uncomfortable. The bedside light worked only if I got out of bed and turned it on at the door, there was no bulb in it when I did manage to turn it on, and, worst of all, there was an old hot-water bottle, stone cold, lurking at the bottom of the bed which must have been there for months. The blind has stuck so you can't pull it down, and the radiator hasn't been bled for years.

The builders are very eccentric. Anghel is very short and very fat with a big black moustache. Sorin is huge, with tattoos, repulsive but weirdly attractive at the same time. Thank God I have no sexual feelings at all, or I would be fantasizing about him. He just has a sweet smile, showing hideously discoloured teeth, and looks you intently in the eyes – either the sign of a wonderful lover or a psychopath in my experience.

He has said nothing except two words. While peeling off the wallpaper, a whole pile of plaster came off at the same time.

'Many dust,' he said.

Was most touched to find that after one wallpaper stripping there was revealed a row of stencilled elephants that I had done for Jack when he was small and it was his room. I stood there almost in tears. What made the elephants even more touching was that for some reason I had stencilled them in dismal grey. Why I hadn't stencilled them in bright yellow or blue I don't know. Took a photograph of them to show to Chrissie. Then felt incredibly silly. Why would she be remotely interested?

Felt very anxious about the builders in general. Although I normally couldn't give a pin about health and safety, I'm slightly worried about the state of their ladder which seems to consist of two sticks held together by the odd wobbly rung. All day they sing loud, wailing mountain songs. Otherwise, they don't speak at all, even though I ply them with coffee, orange juice and even bacon sandwiches. Am starting to feel irrational paranoia.

While working, I hear them talking Romanian next door and shrieking with laughter and banging and pounding. Can't think what they are doing because they are only meant to be wallpapering. I suspect they are digging up the floorboards and hiding caches of arms. Or bodies of dead babies.

The day before they left, they told me, in sign language, that they had got rid of my carpet for me – something I hadn't asked them to do, though I'd told them I was getting a new one. Why? They've left me with hideous dusty underfelt covered with tacks and knots. Had they spilt something on it? Sold it? Surely not – it was so grimy. Was it covered with blood from the man they'd buried under my floorboards? Had they kidnapped Pouncer and sold him for fur coats? They did an incredibly good job and were very amiable, but I was relieved when they went.

Dec 19th

Horrible moment! I was just sitting in my bath thinking how lovely it was the builders weren't there any more, ran my sponge under the hot tap and washed my face with it. And then – my face and hands were red and stung, and suddenly I couldn't see. Tears were pouring down my face. After a few seconds I recognized the smell of Nitromors paint stripper, familiar from years of stripping pine cupboards in my youth and, with great presence of mind, I seized the shower head and sprayed water into my eyes, trying to keep them wide open. Eventually I could see again, but my face still stung and was red, and my hands were raw and tingling.

I was extremely shocked. Obviously the builders had been using the sponge to clean their brushes. Suddenly I thought – what would have happened if Gene had come round for a bath and I had used the sponge on his face? When he cried I would just have thought he was feeling miserable. He would have been blinded. I got so upset that I started to cry proper tears and my head rattled with the horror of the idea.

Dec 20

I made a date to see Hughie when James was out pruning someone's wisteria or whatever he does all day. He was working from home and opened the door in his dressing gown, even though it was eleven in the morning. I noticed he hadn't shaved.

'Amazing,' he said, as he showed me in, 'how when you haven't got long to live, all decorum goes down the drain. Let me make you some coffee.'

'Do they know specifically how long you've got?'

'God knows,' he said, putting the kettle on. 'Months rather than days. But how many? Who can tell? It's a rum old business I can tell you. Not that it matters a great deal to me. I've always been expecting to die one day, and here I am . . . on the threshold. Can't think what those people are doing who are surprised when they're told they've only a certain amount of time to live. Did they imagine they'd last for ever?'

He handed me a cup of tea and we sat down in the sitting room.

'Well, you seem to be taking it very calmly, I must say,' I said. 'You're setting us all a very good example. So far,' I added, darkly.

'I'm not afraid of death at all,' he said. 'And do you know, I feel perfectly all right at the moment. Apart from the cough, I just feel a bit tired. And anyway, you know in one way this cancer thing is rather a relief. It means that I'm never going to get Alzheimer's, which is a real treat. And I'm never going to have to do that whole suicide bit when everything gets too much, which would be incredibly difficult with James around, wouldn't it? I bet he'd never allow me to put a plastic bag over my head and take a hundred sleeping pills. He'd always be there watching.'

'Or, worse, putting holes in all the plastic bags in the house, so you'd never manage to stop breathing,' I said. 'I once bought a book that told you how to top yourself,' I went on. 'It was called *A Guide to Self-Deliverance* and it was produced by a pro-euthanasia group, but it's illegal to publish it now. *But I still have it!*' I added.

'I'll bear it in mind in emergency,' said Hughie. 'In the meantime I'm "being brave" as so many people idiotically describe it. I'm not being brave at all, of course, I'm just behaving like any sensible person would behave. OK: on the minus side, I'm dying very soon. On the plus side, however, I'm never going to get cataracts or have hip replacements.

Someone stuffed a thing about deaf aids through the letterbox this morning and I chucked it away with a light laugh. I'm never going to lose my memory or my teeth. I will never have to master a Zimmer frame – the list is endless, Marie.'

'Couldn't you get a lung transplant?' I said, with a sudden pang of desperation.

'No, they don't do it with cancer patients apparently. I met someone in the hospital who was on the waiting list for a pair, though. Nice man. He has to find a pair that fit, however. He said that because he was big, he was more likely to get some soon, since most of the people on the waiting list for lung transplant cases are cystic fibrosis patients who are usually very small. Odd, isn't it – waiting for the right-sized pair of lungs, like a pair of shoes. Anyway, I'm rather glad I'm not in the running for a pair.' He sucked on a cigarette and looked into the distance. 'The other huge advantage of cancer is that, unlike dropping dead in the street, it means that I can tidy everything up before I go. Make my will. Leave the office neat and sorted out, and organize someone to carry on. Cancer is rather a blessing – not a word I usually use, but it's true.'

'But aren't you sad that you won't . . . um . . .' I suddenly couldn't think of anything to say.

'Live longer? Are those the words you're groping for? Why should I? I've got no children or grandchildren. I was going to retire soon, anyway. Then what? Learn Chinese? Join a bookclub? I can't read fiction. Funny thing about getting old – you want to read only historical facts or biographies. Never could understand why. No, I've always found life a bit difficult, you know, my dear. Bit like wading through treacle. It'll be no bad thing to give it all a break. And I'm lucky. If James were to die before me, I'd find life very hard. I wouldn't have anyone to row with, or to cook my meals for me. No, I'm definitely the lucky one, here. It was a bit of a shock when I was told, I have to admit. But that's about all. I'm quite surprised how I feel about it all. Quite pleased. Everyone's very kind, so I'm being made a great fuss of. Archie is being exemplary. I must say, he is pure gold, that man. And, of course, suddenly I'm terribly rich. I'm cashing in all my pensions and with any luck I will be able to go out with a huge bang.

'And then,' he added, warming to his theme, 'there are all the things I'll never have to do ever again. I will never have to paint a ceiling again. I will never have to go to a godchild's end-of-term concert and listen to her straining away at the oboe. Never have to be driven in some ghastly old banger of a taxi on hairpin bends in the hills of Nepal too fearful to ask the driver to slow down. I will never have to wonder whether it wouldn't be a good idea to see China before I die. Sod China! And South America! My dear, the relief! What liberation!'

I couldn't think of anything to say. 'Well, I'll be very sorry,' I said, honestly. 'You know how I feel about you,' I added, rather clumsily. What did I feel about him? I felt like a daughter, a sister . . . half-fancied him . . .

'And you know how I feel about you,' said Hughie, laughing. 'Now neither of us has any clue what the other is talking about. Let's leave it like that or we'll get mawkish. Everything is as it should be.'

Later

When I got back I was so struck by the idea of death as a jolly good idea that I got out my old euthanasia book. To bump yourself off, apparently, you need 'two plastic bags, approximately 3 feet in diameter and 18 inches in width . . . Kitchen bin-liners are an obvious possibility . . .' And then, describing other methods: 'Drugs and car exhaust require a secure connection between the end of the exhaust pipe and a length of stout flexible hose which should fit over the exhaust pipe –

vacuum-cleaner hose appears to be suitable . . .' Worth knowing if the going gets tough. But in the meantime I think I'll hang around.

Though I have to say that these days I'm always pleasantly surprised, whenever I wake up in the morning, to find that I haven't passed away in the night.

Dec 21

Just read that when he was seventy Dr Johnson decided to learn Italian. Surely not! I mean, it would have taken him about a million years even to get to Italy. He could barely get to Scotland, as far as I remember. I wonder if old people like learning languages for the same reason they like gardening. You can't be made redundant from gardening, and the work never comes to an end, so there's no moment when you feel past it. It's to do with expanding yourself like a sponge, rather than forging ahead.

Though don't speak to me about sponges.

Dec 22

Just remembered that Archie likes gardening. I got a card from him saying that I must come down for a weekend soon. But what does it mean, 'soon'? I can't bear it when people issue vague invitations like this. I actually would rather like to go down and see him, but can't really invite myself.

Later
Said goodbye to Michelle who's going back to her parents for Christmas. As she staggered out of the house with her enormous purple suitcase, covering me with kisses and saying:

'I love you!' I felt it hard to hold back the tears. She's only going for a week, but she is so adorable.

Tears dried rather quickly when, hoping for a soothing cup of coffee, I discovered that yet again she'd used up all the milk.

Dec 23

Went round to babysit Gene for the last time before Christmas. He is just so lovely! He now can stand up with help, and is a total delight. Later, he sat in his high chair, reaching out for the spoon as I shoved his face full of mashed bananas.

I play and laugh more with Gene than I do with anyone. When I put my head back he puts his head back too, and then he laughs. Extraordinary how amusing he is. Far more amusing than most people I sit next to at dinner when I go out. And there is no chance of his growing a beard, which is another great plus.

He has the most adorable face, like a small guru, compassionate, humorous, forgiving. After he'd gone to sleep, I settled down to watch a worthy programme on DNA on telly, hoping to grasp the entire evolution of life in an hour, but had barely watched the opening titles before I suddenly thought I'd have a tiny nap and woke at eleven to find Denis Norden hosting another programme of 'humorous' television goofs at exactly the same time as Jack and Chrissie returned. I couldn't persuade them that I hadn't turned it on specially . . .

Dec 24

Was talking to Penny when I mentioned 'virtuous reality'. 'Don't you mean "virtual" reality?' she said. 'You mustn't let this no-sex thing of yours go to your head.'

Difficult not to, though. My newly decorated bedroom now seems completely huge. I have rehung the pictures, and got a lovely green carpet down, and there is absolutely no room in my new bed for any kind of man, not even a tiny one. In the morning I jump down and run across my vast football pitch of a bedroom, rather in the style of Julie Andrews in *The Sound of Music*. There is room not only for me to do the Sun Salutation, but actually for a whole class of people to do it too. I feel I am living in Versailles. Note the word 'feel'. The room is actually only 10' by 14'.

Dec 25th

Odd that I'm not upset about being on my own at Christmas. Probably because I've had enough family Christmases to last me a lifetime. Anyway, I wasn't on my own. I found myself at the lonely flotsam and jetsam table at Marion and Tim's. Although I had been dreading it all, Christmas Eve and Christmas Day morning, it turned out, as so often happens, to be glorious fun.

Much to my astonishment, Hughie and James were there, having vowed that they wanted only a quiet Christmas at home, and there were also two mad right-wing thinkers, rather a change from the usual lefties, one of whom suddenly said to the other in a very loud voice over the Christmas pudding: 'Now, what are we going to do about Tony Blair?'

There were also several single middle-aged women all of whom looked absolutely *desperate* for sex, and all of whom drank far too much and shouted much too loudly, and were clearly all very unhappy about getting old, which made me feel incredibly smug.

Sat next to Hughie and pulled a cracker with him. Instead of the usual 'What does an elephant pack to go on holiday?'

question, we had gnomic phrases of the kind that Jonathan Cainer comes up with. Mine read: 'This year you will discover the real you.'

Hughie asked if I had any idea who the 'real me' was.

I said I hadn't actually, and it had always worried me. He said he felt the same which is why he asked the question. Eventually we decided that there are several 'real me's inside us.

'Many of whom are in direct opposition to each other, of course,' said Hughie. 'You have the sensitive Marie inside you,' he said, 'as well as the sentimental, the funny and the critical.'

'And the desperate, vile and loathsome,' I added.

'Yes, them, too, of course,' said Hughie. 'I, on the other hand . . . but let's not go into me. Let's agree that we are, rather, collections of personalities, like football teams. Or perhaps more accurately, an assorted rabble.'

'So I am a kind of Marie rabble, talking to a Hughie rabble,' I said.

'If we separated all the "real me"s in this room, we would probably have as many people as there are in, say, Lithuania,' said Hughie, looking round. He laughed. 'By the way – any good presents?'

'Let's say Age Concern have done rather well this year,' I replied, thinking of the huge charity carrier bag I had already stuffed with unwanted gifts. 'Unfortunately, however, I can't give them the wretched goats from Lucy.'

'Goats?'

'Yes, she donated a couple of goats to some African village in my name, without so much as a by-your-leave.'

'But goats are frightfully destructive!' said Hughie. 'They'll probably eat all the villagers' wretched crops! And anyway, you can't give someone a gift to charity as a present. You can ask for someone else to give them to you . . . but not the other way round. How irritating.'

'And you? What did you get?'

Hughie laughed. 'James gave me a book about Gaia,' he said. 'Sometimes I wonder. I've lived with him for twenty-five years . . . does he actually know me at all, at all? But a bit late, I suppose, to ask that question.'

'How are you feeling?' I asked. 'If that isn't too crass a question.'

'Curiously well,' said Hughie. 'A bit tired, and losing weight, of course, but unless I knew it from the test results, I really wouldn't know I'd got cancer at all. That's one of the oddest things. The doctors know I'm dying but, quite honestly, I don't feel I'm dying one bit. And no, I'm not in denial,' he added. 'They're obviously right. But the intellectual knowledge doesn't fit in with the physical knowledge. At the same time, I'm very glad I know where I stand. Or, rather, I know that I'm not going to be standing for very much longer.'

Dec 26th

Penny rang and told me that she'd had a lovely time, and pulled lots of Christmas candles.

Maciej tells me he has just split up with his girlfriend. He is, he says, 'very gloamy'. Rather a good word.

Later

As I dropped my unwanted Christmas presents – an extremely expensive lemon-yellow cashmere jersey from Penny (lemon-yellow! Me!), a boxed set of scented candles from Marion, a photograph of woodland in a clip-frame from Philippa's sister – outside the Age Concern shop, I picked up a free charity newspaper. Glanced inside and this is what I read:

THANK YOU MRS SOUFFLE!!!

Mrs Souffle, a Podiatrist who has worked for the last 15 years in Argyle Place has donated a chiropody chair to the Age Concern toe nail cutting service. Mrs Souffle is now retiring. Age Concern would like to extend warm wishes to Mrs Souffle for her generosity.

When I got home I cut it out and sent it to Hughie to make him laugh.

Jan 4

Very strange day. I am now older than my mother was when she died. She died at the age of sixty plus a few months, and I worked it out that today I am now officially one day older than her.

Strange, uncharted territory. Like most women I've always worried about turning into my mother, but now I have no guidelines, even if I wanted to turn into her. From now on, I'm on my own.

I looked into the mirror and examined my face for signs that I didn't look like her. But it'll take a few years, I think, before I can really feel free of her. What is so odd is that at my age, although very young at heart, my mother did look old. She had thickened round the waist and even, on occasions, walked with a stick. She dyed her hair, but there was a frailty about her that I don't recognize in myself.

Jan 5th

I discovered the other day that I could customize my mobile phone. Instead of the word NOKIA going round and round when it's on standby, it's now the word GENE.

Marion, being a general genius, of course, has a picture of her grandchild on her mobile phone. I am, I'm afraid, not quite up to that.

Nor, I have to say, is my phone.

Jan 6th

Maciej tells me, for what seems like the tenth time, that Polish people celebrate Christmas on Christmas Eve and eat a huge carp.

For what seems like the tenth time, too, I reply: 'How fascinating.'

(Sometimes I wonder: where do they get them from, in London? Do they go and raid the Japanese fish pond in Holland Park?)

When he'd gone, I went to have a snooze, but when I lay down, I imagined being in Holland Park with Gene and a drug addict coming up and attacking us with a knife and saying if you don't give me your money, I'll hurt him. I got terribly upset about this scenario, and started to cry with fear. Then I imagined ringing up Chrissie and weeping . . . the scenario made me quite mad with fright, I felt my heart was going to break. Why do I torture myself so?

January 7th

Latest piece of spam:

Lowest prices: Valor, Xray, Vitality, Super Arrow, Philosophy, moo!
Fearful desire. On preditation requisite.

Fearful desire. Rather a good phrase. As for 'Philosophy, moo' I dread to think what that means. All the more reason to give up sex.

Jan 8th

I drove down with Penny to her bungalow in Suffolk.

According to a doctor friend of Penny's, people who buy bungalows when they're old pop off very quickly because they don't take enough exercise. If you want to live long, he said, stick in your eighteenth-century tall house. Or buy a flat in a block in which the lift is always out of order. Not difficult, of course.

We had supper at a restaurant called The Laughing Cod, a fish and chip joint with pine so stripped and varnished it was orange, dried flowers hanging from the walls, plus assorted souvenirs from Wales, Spain, etc. It's not licensed, so we took a bottle of Chenin Blanc with us, but only drank half of it. As we left, it was extremely windy – a storm was brewing. Penny stuffed the half-empty bottle deep into her coat.

'You won't get blown away with that as ballast,' said a huge man with a beer belly wearing a cardigan with leather buttons, as he reached for another chip. As we closed the door behind us, Penny snapped: 'He wouldn't need *anything* as ballast!'

In the morning we went for a long walk. I am embarrassed by how puffed I get, gasping all the time. Penny kept stopping to look at the view, but I felt she was really stopping to give me a rest. Puff I may but I actually find it easier to stagger on and then sit down than stop and start. We came back to potted shrimps. In the afternoon we walked round the town and I bought Gene a teeshirt. It was a toss-up between one that read: 'I may be small but I am very influential' and one that read: 'I blame the parents.' In the end I got them to make up one that read, simply, 'Gene'. We moved on to the Cats' Rescue second-hand shop where Penny persuaded me to buy the most hideous, beige, but also most incredibly comfortable kind of padded jacket, windcheatery thing that comes down to just above my knees. It cost me £1. When we got home we washed what my mother would have called the 'other people' out of it.

In the evening the gale was gusting. A friend of Penny's popped in for a drink and I showed her some pictures of Gene. Poor woman. She looked at them and said: 'How sweet!' But really all babies look the same to other people. The television news said it was a hurricane, and trees were falling, and it was dangerous to drive. I put on the cats' rescue jacket, now dry, and we walked to an Indian restaurant, our hair and ears blowing behind us like the E. H. Shepard picture of Piglet in *Winnie the Pooh*. When we returned we looked like a Giles cartoon, with hair and umbrellas flying out in front of us.

Came back to watch a documentary about pensions. On the screen was a man holding up a placard which read 'Pension's not Poverty'. Quite unmoved by their plight, Penny commented, rather acidly: 'There's no apostrophe in "pensions".'

Pure joy. Looked after Gene all day. He was sunny and charming and laughed non-stop.

In the afternoon we went to the park and mooched around in the cold, me sitting on a bench and shivering while he sat staring at the trees, and I just felt blissed out. I'm so often impatient, but with Gene I can sit for hours while he sits stuffing leaves into his mouth. Marion says that it took her an hour going down the road with her granddaughter, simply because she wanted to open and shut the gate on every house.

Sitting a few yards away from us on the next bench was a young girl with a baby a little older than Gene. With my repulsive new-found oldie confidence I went up to her with Gene and said hello. It turned out she was a Ukrainian refugee, the father of her little girl had left her, and she was completely on her own.

'Your daughter-in-law, she is very lucky to have you to help with the baby,' she said, sadly. 'My mother back in Ukraine. I have no help. And my baby, she is very poorly. I don't know what is matter with her.'

The baby girl was indeed behaving very strangely. She must have been at least a year old, and she was crawling miserably along the ground howling. Her arms were white and weak and her hair was thin.

'If the doctor says she's OK, then she must be OK,' I said cheerily, staring at this poor little heap of a girl, who clearly was *not* all right at all. 'I'm sure it's just a stage.'

After a bit more chit-chat I went back home.

Oddly I felt far, far sadder about that poor sickly child and her lonely mother than I do about Hughie. Hughie can cope with death. That sad mother can't cope with life.

Archie rang and I was ridiculously pleased. Felt all girlish when I heard his voice and immediately started babbling. This is a very bad sign indeed. But didn't babble for long, because all he wanted to talk about was Hughie.

'Sorry to burden you with this frightful call,' he said, 'but I only heard the news about Hughie just before Christmas and then I was away and now I felt I had to talk to someone *really* sympathetic. Absolutely devastating, isn't it?'

'Hughie's taking it quite philosophically,' I said. 'It's James who's going to pieces.'

'Yes, that's exactly the way I see it,' said Archie. 'Look, as two of their oldest friends, I think we should make a plan. Share the duties. I'll ring James every night from now on, because I'm not in London, and you deal with the Hughie end. Hughie can talk to you. He knows you're sensible and honest and won't fall apart. That's what I *so* admire about you, Marie. Hughie and I were talking about you the other day, and I was just thinking that you are probably the kindest and most sympathetic person we know. And, of course, the most beautiful!' he added, jokingly.

'Kind? Me? I'm horrible! I'm deceitful, manipulative, the niceness is just a pretence . . .' I squawked, not knowing what to say. 'And if you think I'm beautiful I'm glad you can't see me now! I'm in my dressing gown, my hair's sticking on end, I've got a flushed, hangovery face like a blood orange . . .'

'Yes, yes, don't go on,' said Archie, hurriedly, obviously not wanting to hear the truth. 'But don't you think that's a good idea? Let's keep closely in touch, anyway. And you *must* come down for the weekend. I'll give you some dates very soon.'

When I put the phone down I felt utterly confused. What on earth had got into me to describe how awful I was looking?

'Flushed, hangovery face like a blood orange'? That would put anyone off for years. 'Deceitful, manipulative, niceness just a pretence'? Why couldn't I just sit back with a serene smile on my face and say, whenever anyone paid me a compliment: 'Thank you *so* much,' like the Queen.

The more I thought of how stupidly I'd behaved, the more I thought how very nice Archie was, of course. I have never in my whole life so far met a man who would dream, when his friends were in a fix, of ringing up other friends behind their back and making a plan of sympathetic action. He seemed to me suddenly like an old-fashioned knight, full of wisdom and honour.

NOT THAT I AM INTERESTED!

Feb 1

Penny rang saying she'd made an odd discovery in the bath. Her clitoris seems to have disappeared. No sign at all. She wondered where it had got to. Did I think it might come back? Does it just have a little rest when you're not having daily sex? Had I got one still, she asked? Could it explain Gavin's disappearance? When I looked I found that mine, while not having disappeared, had rather diminished, and I have to say I'm not sorry. I always thought the clitoris was a much over-rated part of one's anatomy, which never really lived up to the rave reviews it received over the last twenty years. But I do hope it's seriously on its way out and isn't just pretending. It would be awful if it were to pop up again when I was, say, eighty, with Alzheimer's, gagging for sex with a toothless paralysed old man disabled by a stroke.

I wonder if it happens to everyone at a certain age? I don't move in a group of people who talk about sex – sometimes I wonder if anyone does, actually – and anyway, if I told someone my clitoris was on the wane they might say something awful back, like: 'Oh, mine isn't!' Or, worse: 'I haven't looked recently' in a disapproving kind of way.

I'm always blurting out personal quirks to people in the desperate hope that they will say: 'Oh, I'm like that, too . . . what a relief to hear you also make Nescafé by running the hot tap . . .' or something. But there are moments when I go too far, and my confidante suddenly withdraws. 'No,' she says, edging away, rather, as if she's just realized she's talking to someone with a borderline personality disorder. 'I can't say I've ever done that. And no, I haven't actually ever heard of people doing that.'

Feb 5th

Archie rang and asked me for the weekend again. This time he's given dates. It'll be bitterly cold, but what the hell. He actually asked if I'd like to bring Gene!

'He could ride on the donkey,' he said. 'And there are ducks in the pond. We've still some old toys from our brood. There's the rocking horse. I'd love to meet him. He sounds such an enormously nice chap. But then he must be, if he's got your genes in him.'

Tried to think of a pun about genes, but got a bit confused.

'Are you still there?' said Archie. 'Are you trying to dream up a pun on genes? In the last few seconds, I've failed dismally. I suppose you ought to work very hard and have one glittering one you can use for all occasions.'

'He's a bit young,' I explained. 'But another time, I'd love to. What about Hughie and James? I'm sure they'd be keen to come.'

'I've asked them,' said Archie, 'but James says it might be a bit much for Hughie.'

Since I saw Hughie only yesterday and he seemed fine, I suspected the refusal was more because Hughie, at this stage in his life, simply isn't interested in meeting a lot of new people. What is the point, after all?

Feb 6

Woken last night by a knock on my door. When I snapped on the light I found a distraught Michelle standing in a very short green nightie, looking dazed.

'What's up?' I asked. Oh God. Perhaps she'd smuggled the genius in and he was trying to bore her to death by reading his poetry out loud.

'What does eet mean?' she burst out. 'Life? Why are we 'ere?'

Tears were pouring down her face. I patted the end of the bed, inviting her to sit down, and rubbed the sleep from my eyes. Glancing at the clock, I saw it was 3.45 a.m. I took her hand and tried to pull myself together.

'We are here,' I said, 'just to stagger on. To be nice to each other. To be kind. That's all there is to it. Life is,' I went on, warming to my theme, 'one big mystery. If you ask what it means you just waste time when you could be making some-one else's life happier.'

Inside I was thinking: 'Thank God my "What does life mean?" days are over.'

'But ees zere not God?' she asked, sadly.

'Well, I don't think so,' I said, as kindly as I could. 'Once you stop asking the question, you know, you'll find a great peace descending over you. And everything, paradoxically, becomes clear.'

As I spoke, I could sense a great guru-like clarity come over me. For a brief moment I felt the knowledge of the ancients course through my veins.

'OK,' she said. She shuffled off, and as she tottered out of the room, I detected the distinctive smell of dope coming from her nightdress. She was stoned as a bat.

I, on the other hand, put my head on my pillow and slept the deep sleep of one who feels impregnated with wisdom and goodness. Very pleasant. I felt I had made one of those enormous psychical changes that come only once in a lifetime.

When I woke, all my guru-like qualities had gone down the drain and I was left my usual baffled self.

Feb 10

When I read the papers today I saw that they were chocka with stuff about old people. Are old people the new young people? Seems quite likely, actually. Forget about yuppies, the acronym now (according to the *Daily Mail*, that is, so perhaps rather suspect) is SWELL – Sixty, Well-Off and Enjoying Life. We are, apparently, the most optimistic, most active and highest-spending age group. Of those surveyed, 80 per cent said they enjoyed life, 70 per cent said they felt in control and more than half claimed that their sixties had been the happiest time of their lives.

Yesterday I read about a totally different and totally ghastly group of oldies called SKIs – people who are Spending the Kids' Inheritance. No doubt they blow their fortunes on building golf courses in their gardens, bungee-jumping, facelifts and going to cookery classes in China. *Quel* nightmare, as we used to say at school.

Feb 11

Question: why is it that windscreen wipers always nearly go back and forth in time to the music, but never quite?

Feb 12

This afternoon Michelle knocked on my door and came into my room. I was expecting an apology for the other night and put on my understanding face. But no.

''Arry, 'e ees not genius,' she announced. ''E ees idiot.'

'Absolutely,' I said, very relieved. 'And are you feeling better now?' I asked. 'About the meaning of life?'

'Meaning of life?' she said. 'Life means notting,' she added, finally, with great certainty. I realized she had completely forgotten about coming to my room at all. 'I am stoppeeng smoke,' she said. ''Arry, 'e say I try, but I do not like.'

Later

James and Hughie came round for a drink. Hughie now appears to have developed a lump of some kind in his stomach.

'When you have cancerous lumps, the words "golf ball", "melon", "tennis ball" and "football" take on completely different meanings,' he added, thoughtfully.

'But not, sadly, the word "mothball",' said James, ruefully.

'Oh, for those happy days,' said Hughie, facetiously, 'when "death was but the rumble of distant thunder at a picnic". Auden,' he added.

When they left I felt sad. But in an odd way I can't believe it. Partly because although he's a bit thinner, Hughie seems just the same as he always has done. The idea he'll die soon is very hard to take in. And, anyway, you can't really imagine someone's gone when they're not gone. It's afterwards, when you're alone and they're never coming back, that the pain starts stealing through.

But I do feel regret. It's not just sadness at the absence of Hughie, it's his take on everything. And at this particular period of life, that take is increasingly difficult to share with anyone.

When Hughie dies, there will be fewer people who recall the things of my father's generation. Who remembers now the Quinquireme of Nineveh, John Masefield, Longfellow's *Hiawatha*, 'Albert and the Lion', Gussy Fink-Nottle, what a cohort is . . . who will one be able to talk to who one can assume has read all the Russians? Oh, I know that academics have, but I mean just ordinary daily people. Fewer of them about.

Expect for Archie, actually . . .

Marion, who sometimes does reviews for the *Tablet*, being a Catholic, told me that she wrote an email to a literary editor there about a book by some bishop, saying: 'If you have no one to review it, Barkis is willin'.' The editor wrote back saying: 'I haven't . . . but who is Barkis?'

That's the sadness of getting older. No one younger knowing who Barkis is, or, presumably, who Dinu Lipatti or Peter Watson were or what the Light Programme was or where Schmidts used to be, and all of us oldies having no clue who Sade, Jade and Beyoncè are. (Beyance? Beyence?)

Archie'd know.

Feb 13

Chrissie has asked if I'll babysit Gene one day a week because she's going back to spa-marketing part-time. I am so flattered I can hardly speak. It is just so extraordinarily lovely to be trusted with such a precious person. When I told Lucy she laughed in rather an unpleasant way. 'You do know,' she said, 'that according to my *Guardian*, four out of five families rely on grannie to work and cope, and around 7 million grannies in England are involved in childcare? You're being taken for a mug,' she added, surprisingly harshly for her. 'What about what *you* want to do?'

What *I* want to do is look after Gene one day a week.

When I got to the flat, Jack and I had some coffee before he went off to some psychology course. He's doing something – whether it's research, a PhD or an MA I'm not sure. Whatever, it means that next year he can start practising. He told me about a friend of his who was madly in love with the girl who lived in the flat upstairs, but couldn't think of how to get to know her.

'He could always go up and ask her for a cup of sugar,' I said.

'Cup of sugar?' he said, in a puzzled way. 'Why should anyone ask anyone for a cup of sugar? I've heard that expression before, actually,' he added, 'but I've never understood what it meant.'

I thought for a bit before I realized where it came from. 'It must come from the war, with rationing,' I said. 'Neighbours would ask each other for cups of sugar or bits of butter or dried eggs if they ran out before their next week's rations arrived.'

'Dried eggs?' said Jack. 'What are they?'

Honestly! Sometimes I feel like some ancient old duck being interviewed by schoolchildren for their oral history project. What are dried eggs, indeed!

He washed up but when he turned to say something to me, he saw me transferring all the contents of my bag into my Cats' Rescue jacket and asked me what I was doing.

'I'm putting everything in my handbag into my coat

pockets,' I said. 'I feel nervous going out round here with a bag over my shoulder. Easily snatchable.'

Jack laughed. 'Oh, don't worry. You'd never get mugged in that coat.' He picked up his bag, kissed Gene, said: 'Byee!' and went off.

Was the coat that bad, I wondered? I'd been beginning to kid myself it was rather smart, in a beige kind of way. Perhaps I should dye it.

In the park, I pushed Gene in the winter sunshine and sat down on the grass. Gene cuddled up to me, and a man in a baseball cap who was passing by said: 'There's a little lad who loves his mum, ain't it?' I simpered and, I'm afraid, didn't correct him.

Only once he'd passed did I notice he was clutching a large can of Special Brew.

Near by a huge dark gang of sinister hoodies were lurking with their bicycles. I felt frightened. Surely they wouldn't take advantage of an old grannie and her grandson? Then I had fantasies that a knife would be held to Gene's throat and I would have to give up his plastic ball, cloth book, and push-chair before they'd release him. I was managing to divert my anxieties with this silly scenario until I saw a policeman in a bullet-proof vest behind a tree, talking to someone on a walkie-talkie. Gene was sitting, picking things up from the ground and putting them in his mouth – a crisp packet, a leaf, one of those weird black seed balls to be found only in London parks.

I swooped on him, and we hurtled home.

That evening I came back feeling sated and bloated with loving and caring. A wonderful feeling, almost disgusting, like eating too many strawberries.

Later
Tonight was consumed with anxiety that Gene's socks might be too small for him. From time to time I get worried . . . it's

because of the powerlessness of being a grannie. Is he getting enough to eat? Is he getting too much to eat? Is he dehydrated? Is he getting enough? Too much? There is no way that any of these ideas can, of course, be expressed directly to Jack or Chrissie, because they'd rightly think I was being a gross interferer, but I don't know a single grannie who doesn't have these weird fears. Marion is always worrying that her granddaughter doesn't get enough vitamins, and slips her mashed salmon and broccoli behind her mother's back. Lucy is terrified because her daughter-in-law wants to put her grand-child in a nursery, and she says she's read that nursery for under-fives makes children anxious and unhappy.

'But what can I do?' Lucy said worriedly to me when we bumped into each other in Waterstone's at the board books section. 'Perhaps,' she added, looking around the New Books laid out on a table, 'I should try this.' She picked up a book called *The Good Grannie Guide*.

'You don't need that,' I said, putting it back on the table. 'There is only one piece of advice that grannies need to know and that is their twenty-four-hour mantra.'

'What's that?' asked Lucy.

'"I say nothing."'

'Well, come on, tell me,' she said. 'Don't keep me in suspense.'

'"I say nothing,"' I said. 'That's it. The advice. "I say nothing. I say nothing. I say nothing." Again and again and again.'

Actually I did say something the other day, and it sort of backfired on me. Gene was ill with a temperature and Jack was trying to get some Calpol into him, which he was resisting vociferously. I was so upset when I saw Jack forcing his head back, opening his jaws and jamming the stuff down his throat (rather like me stuffing Pouncer with pills) that I went out and bought a small carton of Ribena with a straw.

'Why don't you put the Calpol in here and then let him suck up the juice?' I suggested. 'He likes straws.'

'Does he?' said Jack rather suspiciously. He peered at me crossly. Whoops, I thought, I've let the cat out of the bag. I'm sure I'm not meant to buy him the occasional carton of Ribena, because it's full of sugar, but I do. Well, twice I have, feeling very guilty.

Anyway, he looked annoyed and said it was a ridiculous idea. I then realized that I hadn't been following the mantra. I drove home repeating: 'I say nothing' again and again, hoping that I would never make such a mistake again.

So when it came to socks, I couldn't say anything. And no one I know has ever had the socks panic, anyway.

I rang James for reassurance. Well, not just for reassurance, but when you're as low as James is, it's always nice to feel needed. Makes you feel more in control.

'Socks too small?' he shrieked on the phone. 'You think a growing child's feet are going to be deformed by small socks? Hughie!' he called out. 'Marie thinks Gene's socks are too small! Marie, you do know that grass can grow though Tarmac, don't you? It would take more than socks to stop Gene's feet growing. If you think his socks are too small, go out and buy him some new, big ones!'

Feb 14th

Most odd. Maciej, who usually arrives at about ten past nine when he's meant to come at nine, suddenly appeared at eight o'clock.

'Well, this is very nice,' I said, as I made a cup of tea. 'Couldn't you sleep?'

He mumbled something and then Michelle came down and he busied himself washing the kitchen floor.

Later

Rather odd. Got a rather nice Valentine card from Archie! Inside he said: 'Well, someone's got to send you one, haven't they? Keep up the good work! Archie x'

One 'x'.

Feb 15th

Bought some new socks at Green Baby and took them round to Chrissie.

'Oh, great,' she said. 'They'll go marvellously with the new shoes I just bought him. His present ones are far too small, aren't they? I keep worrying that his feet will be deformed.'

'Oh, no,' I said, cheerily. 'Grass can grow through Tarmac, you know.'

She looked at me as if I were utterly mad, and then made me a cup of tea.

'How's Gene?' I asked, picking him up and putting him on my knee. He is *so heavy*! I can barely carry him now, so heaven knows how I will be able to lift him when he's two years old, and yet I seem to remember being able to lift Jack up until he was about seven years old. 'Oh, I never asked how he got over his flu the other day . . .'

'Oh yes,' said Chrissie. 'Oh, by the way, we found a way to get Calpol down him. Jack got a carton of Ribena, injected some of the Calpol into it, and he sucked it all up through a straw!'

'How brilliantly clever you are!' I said.

Feb 16th

James and Hughie picked me up and we went for tapas round the corner and Hughie ordered, at once, two bottles of *vino verde*, which I thought was rather bold. 'One for me, and one for you two,' he said, as he helped himself to a gigantic tumblerful.

For the first time, he looked really ill. He was incredibly thin, and gasped a lot. His clothes hung on him baggily, like the skin on an old cat.

'No,' he said, noticing my face as we sat down. 'I'm not the debonair devil-may-care boulevardier of old. More of a wreck.'

'He hasn't been out for days,' said James, and that use of the third person brought it home to me how ill Hughie must be getting. 'He's been resting all day to come out tonight.'

'How's Penny?' asked Hughie, clearly rather eager to get away from the subject of his illness.

'Still miserable about Gavin,' I said. 'Who has, of course, dropped her again.'

'What was that book he read?' asked James. '*Death in Venice*?'

'Never managed to finish that,' I said.

'One of Thomas Mann's worst,' said Hughie. 'I find so often that if everyone goes on and on about how marvellous a book is, ten to one you've got a cold dead fish on your hands.'

'You two are talking as if you've joined a bookclub,' said James, helping himself to a huge portion of prawns in oil and chilli.

'Nonsense, we're being much more interesting,' said Hughie. 'What's that you've got there? *Patatas bravas*? Let's get some more. Brave potatoes. That's us. Brave old potatoes.'

Feb 17th

Was going to the shop in my nightdress under my coat, as usual, when I met Sheila the Dealer, looking very mad indeed. Her face was covered in the kind of scabby spots you see only on cocaine-crazed top models, and she was so thin and anorexic-looking it was impossible not to entertain the idea of simply taking her arm and breaking it in half just to hear it snap.

She stared at me like a terrified cat. Clearly she wasn't aware of ever having seen me before.

'You look just like Celia Imrie,' she said, harshly.

'Celia who?'

'Celia Imrie. On the telly,' she said. I had never heard of her, being, like Vivienne Westwood apparently, in complete ignorance as to who the latest celebs are.

'Well, I hope she's wise and beautiful,' I said, rather charmingly and patronizingly. Hoping to make my escape.

Sheila inspected me for a few seconds. 'She's not *too* bad,' she said, and tottered on.

Feb 18

Things with Maciej have become even stranger. Got up this morning and bustled out of my bedroom door only to find him what I can only describe as tiptoeing down the stairs.

'Oh, hi!' I said, feeling, quite honestly, a bit freaked out. It wasn't his day. Surely he wasn't popping in with his key to burgle a few small items? A Polish friend of Hughie's had warned me about Poles. 'They are all scum!' she had said, most disloyally, I thought. But Maciej wasn't scum. He was brainy and beautiful. 'What are you doing here today?'

'I so sorry,' he said. 'I come round, actually, I left something here yesterday, I no want to disturb you, actually. My mobile,' he added, producing it from his pocket.

Extremely odd.

Feb 19

The phone rang and who should it be but Baz, an old friend, who only wanted to know someone else's phone number. 'And what's all this I hear from Hughie that you've given up sex?' he asked, rather irritated, I thought. 'I'm very upset about that.'

'Hughie has no right to go around telling anyone that,' I said. 'It's private.'

'Hughie's dying, love. He has every right to do what he wants.'

'No, he hasn't. Just because you're dying or old, doesn't mean you can be bad mannered and disloyal.'

'Oh, shut up, Marie,' he said. 'What I want to know is why you've given it up. Wouldn't you just have a little try with me? You know how I've always fancied you.'

I never knew he'd always fancied me and since he's married and notoriously faithful I was rather astonished to hear it. But he went on and on, being so flattering that I wasn't sure whether he was flirting with me or teasing me or whether he was deadly serious.

'I want to take you out to dinner,' he said. 'To discuss this.'

'I'm going away,' I said firmly. And I was. I was going to stay with Archie. Only for the weekend, mind you, but I wasn't lying.

'So when will you be back?' This time I did lie. There was a scratching sound at the other end of the phone. 'Can you hear me? I'm writing this down,' he said. 'Well, I look forward to that. I'll ring you when you get back. And we'll go out and have supper.'

I was so staggered by what sounded like an invitation for a real 'date' (having not been asked out on a date for years and years) that later that afternoon, when I went to fill the car up with petrol, I opened the boot up instead of the petrol tank.

Feb 20

'How's the boyfriend situation?' I asked Michelle, when I bumped into her at breakfast today.

She looked amazingly coy and simpered. 'I have met nice Polish boy,' she said, shyly.

'A genius?' I said, laughing.

'No – yes, he ees genius. He could not finish studies in Poland to be teacher, so he here cleaning.' She looked at me conspiratorially.

'Not Maciej!' I said. She nodded.

'We hope you do not mind. We very quiet.'

'But that's lovely!' I said. I couldn't think why I hadn't thought of it before. A perfect match. 'I'm so pleased for you!'

'Maybe we move in flat together soon,' she added. 'And you have to get new lodger?'

February 21

Went down to Archie's by train. I even took a minicab to the station, which was, as usual, driven by a man who had a dreadful story to tell. He had been some kind of big cheese commander in the Ethiopian Air Force, running a department of 350 men, big pal of the king and so on. Suddenly he was thrown into jail with twenty-three comrades, where he rotted for two years. All of them were killed by the guards except him, and he somehow got to England and now lives in some ghastly two-roomed flat in Wembley, utterly miserable.

Honestly, in the past all these stories were so very far away, the sort of thing you only read about in newspapers. Now they are coming closer and closer, like grandmother's footsteps. I feel it's only a matter of time before my crazy worries about bunions and arthritis and Gene's feet are going to be last on my list of worries, not first.

Very nice to be driven, anyway. Can't be doing with driving, as these days I get so panicked on motorways, always having to work out the route on paper – M 25, exit 5, on to A 362 and so on. It's totally pathetic, considering I've driven single-handed across Europe and America in my time, and once even on the roads in India. Though I have to say, after my train journey, I was starting to wonder whether it wouldn't be better to go back to the old driving method, frightening as it is.

Behind me was a man on a mobile shouting: 'I'm on the fucking train, that's where I am! Forest Hill? No, I won't fucking meet you for a drink in Forest Hill. Forest Hill, Forest Dump, Forest Gump! I'll meet you in Victoria tomorrow . . . six o'clock!'

At the table to my left was a young mother who looked as if she might be a personal trainer, with her three-year-old daughter. They were staring at colours in a book. The child was saying: 'Blue . . . red . . . brown . . . green . . .' And the mother was correcting her. 'Aquamarine . . . cerise . . . burnt sienna . . . duck-egg . . .'

Meanwhile, ahead of me was a gang of girls reading out problems from a teenage magazine. 'Listen to this: "I've been with my bloke for seven years now and since I had my baby he doesn't want sex with me. He cuddles up but nothing happens and he won't talk about it. I can't go on like this . . ."'

'What's the answer?'

' "Whatever the reason, you've got to get to the bottom of this. Cook him his favourite meal, relax him, then give him a big hug and gently explain how you feel . . . Perhaps he'll open up . . ." Who writes this fucking shit anyway?'

Archie lives in a kind of mini-stately in Northamptonshire. Well, it used to be Northamptonshire. Could be anything now. Could be Clwyd for all I know. If that's how you spell it. Or that strange place called Cumbria. Oh, for the days when Westmorland existed! There are lots of open fires, which is all very well, but it's usually a sign that there is no central heating at all, and I realized the minute I arrived that this was going to be one of the coldest weekends in my life.

I'd brought a fantastically smart black-and-white glittery skirt and a very sexy top from Zara (only £25) but would have preferred to have worn about eight woollen dressing gowns with a hottie strapped to my middle.

Why is it that other people's houses are freezing? I've noticed that even in my house, other people start to shiver . . . and I shiver in theirs. It's so funny because when I was young, it was far, far colder than this. I remember having to brace myself to get out of bed at my grandparents', on to the cold linoleum floor. Then I used to crouch in front of a convector heater, and dress, first encasing myself with a huge undercoating of vests and long woolly pants. Now I am cold even with the central heating on and we all complain bitterly, yet none of us wears hats or gloves. I remember going to country houses when small where everyone wore mufflers, hats, jerkins – in the house! My aunt Angela used to wear mittens, a scarf and a hat while she cooked!

A huge array of parties had been arranged, and, it seemed, dozens of other people were staying, and as I dressed for dinner, my heart sank. I would have to meet People from the Country. They hear you come from London and before you know it they're asking if you've been to the theatre recently.

In my experience hardly anyone in London ever goes to the theatre. The theatre is full of tourists, Americans and People from the Country who think that going to the theatre is a sophisticated London thing to do. Like lectures on Chinese glazing at the Royal Academy. Most of my friends in London rarely go to the theatre or lectures, but People from the Country can tell you whether Simon Russell-Beale's performance of Hamlet at 'the National', as they call it, was better than Ian McKellen's Lear at 'the Vic', and, worse, take a whole evening explaining why.

Sometimes I feel like asking if they've mucked out any good pigs recently, or turned over any fields to arable. But I, unlike country people talking to Londoners, am too polite.

Luckily no one like that at supper, and a good time was had by all, even though I was sitting on a seventeenth-century chair that swayed like a lily. I was next to Archie who said weren't young people so lovely to talk to, but didn't I feel sorry for them, having to talk to us.

'We must seem such *frightfully* boring old ducks,' he said. 'Just like old people did to us when we were young.'

I disagreed. I am really fed up with people who are old putting themselves down as if they've got some kind of disease.

'I think young people are jolly lucky to talk to you – or me!' I said sharply. 'We're funny and amusing, and we've had interesting lives – well, I'm not, and haven't, but you have. Hold your wrinkly old head up, Archie, clench the liver-spotted fist and wave it in the air!'

When I told him, after the pudding wine, that I probably had a date waiting for me in London, he asked: 'Blind?' And I'd already responded furiously, saying: 'Certainly not at all blind. He knows exactly what I look like and that's why he's asking me out!' before I realized what he meant.

He looked rather puzzled and said: 'But I understood from Hughie that you were giving all that a bit of a rest! Seemed a terrible shame to me, frightful waste if you don't mind my saying so.'

'You must remember, Archie,' I said, gulping, 'that Hughie is *terribly* ill.'

I'd seen him a couple of days before coming down, and now he can hardly leave the flat he's so weak. But all the same, what on earth does he think he's doing, telling everyone about my private life?

When I got up to bed, full of champagne, white wine, pudding wine, liqueurs and such deliciousness I could barely speak, I found an odd phenomenon in my bedroom. The floor seemed to be heaving, like the sea. I first wondered if it was a drunken illusion, but I discovered pretty quickly that it was the wind, howling through the floorboards, and making the carpet rise in waves. I had never been so cold in my life. I put on my nightdress and then realized that I would have to put my slip on first, then my nightdress, followed by my tights, and a jersey. Even then I was freezing. I desperately wanted to go downstairs to get the cats' rescue, but unfortunately I suspected the burglar alarm would have been put on, so I was stuck, with my teeth chattering, reduced to wearing a skirt around my neck like a scarf, and pulling up the Turkish carpet beside my bed and putting it on top of me. I finally fell into a fitful sleep.

English country houses. So strange. The towels always have holes in them, the surface of the bath is often like fine sandpaper, sometimes with patches of green showing through, the bedroom curtains never meet in the middle. And the lavatory! Every time I went, at Archie's, I had to lift off the lid and adjust the ballcock to get it to flush properly. Then what happens if you get night starvation and want to sneak into the kitchen for a glass of milk? Quite apart from the burglar alarm problem, there's the Laura Ashley dilemma. The famous designer of the sixties and seventies was in someone's country house and, as far as I know, went to the loo in the middle of the night; politely, she didn't turn on the light, and fell down her host's stairs, killing herself in the process.

Sometimes I wonder if all the other guests in the house party are battling with the same demons as myself. And yet we all troop down to breakfast, after, probably, a night fighting the cold, intransigent ballcocks, lights that don't work, dripping taps and gurgling noises in the bath, and, when asked whether we've slept well, we all reply: 'Oh, *fine!*'

I think there'd be a market for a Guest Room Kit which you could take from house to house for your stay. It would consist of earplugs, a silken sleeping bag (just in case the sheets were last slept in by dogs), a clothes peg for keeping the curtains closed, a powerful torch to guide you to the bathroom and to read by, an electric blanket and extension cable in case there are no sockets near the bed, and an eyeshade in case the curtains are made of such fashionable muslin that you're woken by the sun at five in the morning. A comfortable pillow would help, too. And a blow-heater.

In the morning, Archie showed us round the house. Odd. Because usually I wonder whether anyone really wants to know that the old coach-house once stood where the new library is now built. Are we really interested in the fact that the thickness of the wall between the conservatory and the kitchen shows that it was once part of a sixteenth-century ice-house? Do we really wish to be told that the roof was made of oak until Charles I forbade the making of oak tiles and insisted on slate instead? Or that the limestone to be found making the lintel in the pantry came originally from Wales, a left-over from the ice-age?

Usually the answer, in my case at least, is 'Absolutely not.' But this time, I found it all strangely interesting. Archie was at his most charming and when all the houseguests were staggering downstairs with their suitcases, preparing to take their leave, he mouthed to me: 'Could you bear to stay for a cup of tea?' So I did.

'I hope you weren't too *frightfully* bored,' he said, as he poured out the Earl Grey in his huge sitting room. I nearly sat down on one of his dogs, but luckily it scampered off before I could squash it. 'These weekends are such fun for me, because to be honest it's jolly lonely down here without Philippa. She was so good at organizing. Did you notice that the entire supper yesterday was Marks and Spencer? Fourteen King Prawn and Asparagus Risottos, and eight Lemon Tarts, not to mention fourteen portions of Ratatouille . . . rather shameful really, isn't it? But I'm just hopeless at cooking. I can make a piece of toast, and that's about the beginning and end of my repertoire.'

We gossiped about the guests and about retirement and death, and, of course, Hughie and James. Surprisingly, Archie said that he thought Hughie's attitude to death was absolutely spot-on. 'I'm going to see him next week,' he said. 'He's a real Trojan, isn't he?'

There was a slight pause and then he said: 'I hope you didn't think I was putting my foot in it yesterday when I said what I said. But you know Hughie made it sound so drastic, that I was rather alarmed for you.'

'Archie,' I said, 'it's for the best. I'm simply hopeless at relationships. It's something I've learned as I've got older. I'm good at lots of other things, but not that. Either I fall madly in love with people and they don't fall in love with me, or the other way round. It's horrible for everyone.'

'But surely you could overcome that if you just got together with a friend,' said Archie, sitting back in his chair. 'A friend is all we really want in life these days. Not sex, especially, though it's jolly good fun, or can be, but really what we all want is a pal, a number one supporter. That's what Philippa was to me. Only connect – wasn't that what that bloke, who was it –

E. M. Forster – said? I don't like to think of you not connecting. It sounds as if you're making the best of a bad job, if you don't think I'm being *frightfully* patronizing.'

For a moment I felt touched by a huge sense of loneliness and, to my great surprise, tears came to my eyes and I could hardly speak. Then I recovered myself.

'We're all lonely, Archie, and once we admit that to ourselves, we're happier,' I said. 'Without relationships, and I mean sexual relationships with the opposite sex, we have nothing to lose. It's friendship alone for me from now on.'

'That,' said Archie, looking horrified, 'is one of the saddest things I've ever heard you say. Well, all *I* can say is that I do wish you well on your blind date. I rather hope he makes you change your mind.'

'Fat chance,' I said. 'Anyway, this isn't really a date. He's not serious. I just said it to make conversation.'

'We've known each other long enough,' said Archie, looking at me very kindly, 'for you to know that you don't have to make conversation with me.'

And it dawned on me slowly that I was actually having a proper conversation – with a grown-up man who wasn't married or gay. Or weird. But the minute I thought that, a shutter came down inside me. The territory was far too dangerous. Anyway, there were probably platoons of Swedish bimbos in the bushes, waiting to pounce on Archie the moment I got out of the drive. In the cupboards, hiding in the great big stone urns in the garden, shivering inside the lavatory cisterns, concealed in the walls of the old ice-house . . . all lying low till they heard the door close and then springing out, like a Busby Berkeley chorus.

'I must go,' I said, looking at my watch.

'I'm very sorry,' said Archie, who'd now got up and had perched himself on the arm of the sofa and was looking down at me. 'Let's meet in London, anyway. I've loved having you.'

'As the actress said to the bishop,' I said, automatically, as I got up, then quickly added: 'I'm sorry, that was silly.'

Coming back to London in the train, I found myself thinking how very nice Archie was. And then I remembered the sight of him in his beautifully cut overcoat outside Pulli and then . . . Marie! None of that! That way madness lies.

Feb 25

For the last couple of weeks I've been dropping in on Hughie every other day. Not for long, because he can't cope with too much visiting. But just for about twenty minutes.

I find it very difficult to know what to talk to him about. We can't really discuss the future, because, of course, he has none. He is not remotely interested in Gene, but that's not surprising, since he's never had children and doesn't really like them anyway.

I sit, rather awkwardly, in the comfortable sofa, and get him cups of tea or drinks, while he sits in his big chair, sometimes breathing in additional oxygen through a plastic tube wired up to his nose, which is attached to a huge canister by his side.

'Have to say I rather wish I could get all this over with,' he said, the other day. 'But it's odd how one's body just hangs on, fighting away for life, even when you don't want it to. It's like being attached to some primeval force over which you have no control. I keep telling it: "Give up, you fool, give up", but it goes on blindly fighting, like some bone-headed soldier in the trenches, obeying the orders of some force over which I have absolutely no control.'

'You're not turning religious, are you?' I asked, rather nervously.

'Marie! Of course not. It's just the way our bodies are designed genetically, nothing to do with God.'

'Thank God,' I said. Then we both laughed.

Feb 26

After I'd got back to London and waited a week, it was clear that Baz wasn't going to ring, and I'm curiously disappointed. But, really, thank God he didn't. Because if he'd pounced, I would only have pushed him away, he would have been humiliated and I would have felt like a creep. Keep telling myself how great it is to have given up sex, anyway. I hate that clawing feeling below my stomach, aching with want. I'm relieved at not having to clamber into bed with some slightly pissed pal or a young, naïve pick-up, just to satisfy a craving. Sex is no longer my be-all and end-all, and when it was it took over so completely it damaged friendships, my career, my sanity.

And all I feel now is great relief that I don't have to worry any more about faking it or not faking it, or asking for it, or pushing him away, or whether I've come or he's come . . . and what a relief it is not to care any more about whether he will ring when he said he would. What a relief, too, to be able to flirt shamelessly without any risk of it going any further.

March 4

Went to the library to get out a talking book – oh, what bliss! I thought I'd try À la Recherche du Temps Perdu. Proust. Might finish listening to it by Christmas. Never managed to get past the madeleine bit when I was young.

When I went to the cashpoint, I inserted my library card

into the slot and was very irritated when it refused to give me any money. Oh dear, is this the beginning of the end?

March 6

Penny rang me up in great excitement. It turns out that Lisa has remet her first boyfriend ever and they've decided, within about three weeks, to get married.

'He's such a darling! I always liked him best!' she said. 'And now I'll have grandchildren!'

As a result, she had her financial adviser round to tell her how best to manage the paltry savings she has, and also to tell her how much – or how little – she has in pensions. 'Or,' she said rather crossly, on the phone, 'pension. Why do they always make it singular?'

'No idea,' I said. 'But will you be able to exist in your old age? Your even older age, I mean? Without selling the house?'

'Apparently. He said that I should look at my financial investments as a cake. Why do they always say that? I've never looked at a cake and thought of it as my financial investments, have you?'

March 10

To my utter fury, Praise the Lord! Inc. has got planning permission. But after that fury had passed, I realized that the best thing to do is to make friends with the pastor, a giant Jamaican man called Father Emmanuel, who has already started painting the outside of the building. As I passed by today, Father Emmanuel grinned down at me from the top of his ladder.

'I will come and have tea with you,' he said, beaming. 'We are so pleased to be here to spread the word of the Lord. And you will not hear us, I give you the word of the Lord. Everything is soundproofed. Thank the Lord. We are lucky to have such wonderful neighbours.'

Since he must know that I am the person who initiated all the objections to his getting the property, I am inordinately touched by his generosity of spirit, and go back home wondering if there might not be something in this Christianity business after all. Then give myself a sharp slap on the wrist and tell myself to pull myself together.

April 2

Went with Gene to the park in Brixton. There was no one in the playground except one small black boy of seven. His name was Tom. There we were, the three of us, standing on the rubbery Tarmac, in the cold wind. Gene was holding on to the inside of some kind of coloured piece of wooden construction and toppling over, and Tom, who was far too big for it, was clambering all over it, calling him. 'Gene! I'm here!' Tom was very kind to Gene, and lifted him up the steps and guided him down the slide.

When I spoke to him, it turned out that he was spending the whole day alone because his family had gone to hospital with his mother. He had, apparently, no father. When I asked what was wrong with her, I discovered that she was in a wheelchair, unable to move, or speak. His sister lived with them as well. She was sixteen and had a baby. Also his auntie who is on benefits. They all live together in a two-roomed flat on one of the grimmest estates nearby. Eventually I took Gene back in his comfortable pushchair, sucking his bottle, to Chrissie and Jack's centrally heated, spacious, happy flat, and we put on a DVD and watched Boobah. Thinking of that lonesome little black boy, I felt my heart would break.

215

Only connect, I thought. How well I connect with Gene. And I connect with that sad little boy, too. Yet how badly I connect with men.

Archie's voice came floating into my head. 'We've known each other long enough,' he was saying. 'You don't have to make conversation with me.'

April 3rd

Lisa came up to London, determined to buy a retro wedding dress. Penny insisted I come to help them choose something from Steinberg and Tolkien, a shop in the King's Road, with an amazing basement vault bursting with beautiful – and slightly smelly – retro clothes from the forties, fifties and sixties. Penny and I rushed about clutching at skirts and tops saying: 'But didn't you have one like this in the sixties?' 'I remember trying to copy that Ossie dress by getting a vest from Pontings and dying it . . .' 'Oh, look, a Bazaar skirt! Always far too expensive for me!' 'But didn't you have this Biba trouser suit? I'm sure I remember you wearing it . . .' 'Could it be mine?' 'Oh, look at this Courrèges mac!'

Finally Lisa picked a very nice dress by Zandra Rhodes, and Penny and I were oohing and aaahing and remembering the parties we used to go to dressed in the same clothes. It was all utterly bizarre. Or Bazaar, as Penny said. 'Pretty quaint – or Quant, too,' I said. When we rolled about laughing Lisa said to her mum in a low voice: 'Oh, do keep quiet. It's so embarrassing!'

Determined to wriggle out of the wedding. I used to love weddings, but now I find them utterly miserable affairs. Firstly you're fairly sure the couple's going to get divorced pretty snappily and secondly, it's so grisly having to meet all those other relations and godparents. The last time I was at a wedding, I sat next to the wife of the second cousin once removed of the groom's father, who was madly in favour of the Iraq war, and on the other side was just an empty space – some creep who hadn't turned up. And we were all sitting! Couldn't escape.

Funerals, on the other hand, are much jollier affairs. They're a coming together of people to fill the space left by the dead person. We are all warm to each other, warm with sadness, not prickly and suspicious like we are at weddings. Well, I am.

Soon Hughie will die, of course. And I will be at his funeral. Must ask him what he wants. It'll give us something to talk about.

April 5th

Hughie was better today. At least he was dressed and coping without the oxygen. It didn't seem the moment to bring up the subject of funerals, but he brought it up himself.

'You wouldn't do the address, would you, Marie?' he said. 'James says he's too shy to ask you.'

'Of course I will, Hughie,' I said, putting my arms round his shoulders. It's so sad. He's all bony under his clothes, like a skeleton.

'You can be ruthlessly honest,' he said. 'I won't be there to hear it.'

'If you were, I promise you, your ears would burn,' I said. 'Are you arranging it all in advance?'

'Yes, I am, actually,' said Hughie. 'Normally I think it's a bit unfair, don't you, to plan one's funeral in advance? When someone's died, the people left behind like having something to do, wondering which tune to sing Psalm 23 to, things like that. But for us, it gives James and me something to talk about. Conversation's very difficult when you're dying, you know.

You suddenly realize how much of it is dependent on the future. Anyway, I have got a future, and it's funeral-shaped, so James and I spend long hours in the evening reading out suitable passages from Cicero and Tacitus, and listening to the most wonderful pieces of Monteverdi, and he cries and I just lie back and enjoy it all.' There was a pause. Then Hughie said: 'You know what James said the other day?'

'No.'

'He asked if I wanted the funeral to be a celebration of my life! *Imagine*! Fuck celebration! I want everyone to be crying their eyes out!'

'Quite right!' I said.

'And none of that Canon Holland crap, either,' he said. 'How does it go? "Death is nothing at all? All is well? I am only in the next room?" I can tell you, I will *not* be in the next room if I can possibly help it.'

April 20

Penny's been told by the financial adviser that, like a surprising number of old people, far from owning only paltry savings, she is actually rolling in money ('The grey pound,' I said to Penny. 'The silver pound,' she snapped back). So now, desperate to get a better-shaped body with which to attract younger men, Penny has got a personal trainer called Friedrich. He is a muscular German with hair in a pony-tail who, apparently, turns up dressed only in shorts and a vest and puts her through the most gruelling routines.

'He wanted to go jogging round the block,' she confided. 'But I said no, I couldn't face it. It's so humiliating to be seen trying to get fit. I might meet someone I know in the street. I might meet *you*!'

April 21

Went shopping with Marion in Kensington High Street, and found a toyshop. Funny that a while ago Marion and I would be shopping for clothes or antiques, and now all we do is go into toyshops looking for amusing presents for our grandchildren.

We looked at everything in the under-two age range, and I bought Gene a plastic thing that makes all kinds of noises. There are red, yellow, green and orange buttons and when you press them a frightful, raucous American voice yells out 'RA-A-AD! YALLO! GRAIN!' followed by a peculiar colour (or perhaps 'color' would be a better way of describing it) called 'ORNCH!'

We had a cup of coffee in the local horrible Starbucks, and she showed me a picture of her and her granddaughter. Very sweet but, naturally, since she isn't mine, it left me completely cold.

'Oh, what a darling!' I cooed. 'And look at you, too!'

'Yes,' said Marion, wryly, putting the photograph away. 'Funny, isn't it, how you can come to terms yourself with being old, but never come to terms with photographs of yourself looking old. Still, we're so lucky. That joy – it's so utterly surprising. Did you hear that grandchildren are the reward you get for not killing your children?'

I laughed politely but actually I've never felt like killing Jack – except a couple of times when he was about Gene's age, of course.

'What I love about being a grannie,' she added, enthusiastically, 'is being able to do more for my daughter. When children leave home, you've got all this pent-up nurturing love inside you. It's left waiting, behind a big dam. Then, a grandchild arrives! Out flows all the love, like from a river that has got all clogged up with middle-age, bits of old bracken, muddy scum, odd pieces of flotsam and jetsam. Now it bursts through, clear and sparkling again. I love feeling suddenly that I can give something to the future!' she added, her face glowing. 'I love it, I love her! When I look at her tiny face I can already see in her the old lady she will become!'

Don't know how Marion manages to do everything. I love her, but she's one of those old people I *don't* want to be. She's on the board of her local health committee, raising money for a school in India, caring for her crippled mother, looks after her granddaughter when she can *and* she's doing a degree in philosophy and eighteenth-century pottery through the University of the Third Age ('Third Age' – there's a euphemism! Why not just call it University for the Old?).

What I say is: Hasn't she got anything better to do with her time?

Got back to find this email:

University Diplomas

Obtain a prosperous future, money-earning power, and the prestige that comes with having the career position you've always dreamed of. Diplomas from Prestigious non-accredited universities based on your present knowledge and life experience.

If you qualify, no required tests, classes, books or examination.

Bachelors', Master's, MBA's, Doctorate and PhD degrees available in your field.

Confidentiality assured

Call now to receive your diploma within seven days.

Strongly tempted to buy one and tell Marion: 'I've got a PhD in a week. So ner!'

April 22

Hughie's had to go into hospital for some kind of treatment. A blood transfusion? I went to see him. On the way, I passed a huge giant of a man, covered in dirt, standing on his head in the middle of the pavement in the street, chanting the Lord's Prayer.

Felt rather faint and peculiar as I walked into the hospital, past all the people in wheelchairs and patients on crutches, frantically grabbing as many smokes as they could before heading back into their various wards. I went up in the huge lift – huge enough to transport prone bodies. Hospital is such an alien place for most of us, and usually signals the existence of an unpleasant problem, that we view it all with greater clarity than most things in our lives. The grey colour of the walls. The frantically jolly artworks, put up to raise morale. The strange bins for mysterious objects called Sharps. (Hope I won't end up in there one day.)

Then the ward itself. All those coloured patterned curtains, a landscape like a picture by Vuillard. And then the way you scan the beds. Could that yellow-looking skeleton be Hughie? Could that grey-faced corpse be him? Or would he be looking jovial and twinkly, assuring us that it was all a mistake?

I only recognized him because James was sitting next to him, holding his hand. He wasn't really Hughie, more of a shape. He was sitting in a chair, completely covered with a yellow-grey blanket, which was draped over his head. He was breathing through oxygen tubes, his mouth scabby and parched, and his eyes sunk right into his head. Breathing was difficult for him, and although he recognized me, he could hardly manage more than a glimmer of recognition.

I sat down and James smiled at me. I could see he had been crying. I kissed Hughie's forehead and felt bad about finding it rather repulsive, because it was so thin and greasy.

'They say he might be able to come out tomorrow,' said James. 'They've monitored everything and if his various levels get back to normal, which they should do, then he'll be able to come home. For a while at least.'

James and I sat there quietly for about ten minutes, either side of Hughie, neither of us knowing what on earth to say. There was no sound but the rumbling of hospital bustle in the background, and the relentless beeping of the heart monitor behind Hughie. Then I said to James: 'Do you want to get some coffee? I'll stay, if you like.'

James got up and I was left with Hughie alone, staring at the shell of the man, holding his hand and trying to imagine what it might be like without him.

Suddenly Hughie tried to speak. He made grunting noises. I put my head to his mouth. 'Getting rather past my sell-by date, I'm afraid,' he said, hoarsely. Then he gave a kind of gasping laugh and closed his eyes.

April 23

Just got back from babysitting Gene. He has a bouncing machine that hangs from the doorframe and spends about ten minutes in it at a time, leaping up and down laughing, looking like a mixture of a leprechaun and Michael Flatley.

He can now put a blanket over his head and take it off. Which I think is *tremendously* clever.

He has a little cloth book of animals and we go through it again and again, me making all the animal noises. The only one he can do is the fish noise which is a kind of 'pu pu' sound made simply from opening and closing your mouth. I am overjoyed. I feel totally responsible for having taught Gene to read. I am bowled over by his brilliance.

Later

James rang and said Hughie was much better and back at home. But it's only a matter of time. James said it was probably weeks rather than days but might even be days. Oh dear, oh dear, oh dear.

May 5

When I went round to Gene yesterday, I found that there was no sign of his special book, so he couldn't go 'pu pu' at the fish. I drew a fish for him, but it unfortunately elicited no response, just a pointed finger and a: 'Bah!' When she got back from shopping, Chrissie said they'd lost it. I went home cast in gloom and spent the whole of this morning going round children's bookshops trying to get another copy, but needless to say none of them had heard of it.

Finally I went down to Daisy and Tom's in the King's Road, but the only cloth books they had were all done up in cellophane, so you couldn't read them, and there was nothing, as far as I could see, with a fish in it. Only dozens of black-and-white books.

'Why black-and-white?' I asked an assistant, and she told me that according to the latest research, babies respond to black-and-white better than colour.

Sounds bonkers. Suppose it's publishers' way of saving money – babies, after all, can't shout: 'We want colour!'

Felt very gloomy on my way out, but as I passed the crayon section, what should I see but the book! Admittedly packed in a set of four, for £10, but a grannie's love knows no bounds. I was so delighted by this that I had to find the saleswoman I'd spoken to, and show her.

'When he gets to the fish bit,' I said, expecting her to faint with admiration and call her colleagues over, asking me to repeat this amazing story, 'he goes "pu pu"!'

'Oh, really?' she said, edging away slightly.

Found my car clamped when I got out so book in total has cost me approximately £280. Worth every penny, I say.

May 7

Penny rang me in a panic. She sounded tearful and desperate. 'I've got VD,' she said. 'That wretched man has given me VD! Can you credit it! I've only just got over the cystitis and I'm bleeding!'

'But you can't have VD,' I said, sensibly. 'He must have used a condom anyway. Everyone under the age of forty-five uses a condom these days. It's compulsory. Anyway, they don't call it VD these days. It's a genito-urinary infection. At least it was when I last . . .'

'Well, I've got it anyway,' she said. 'I've probably got AIDS, if he's gay. Oh, God. Just when I thought I might be going to be a grannie! You can't be a grannie with AIDS! I mean it's totally out of order!'

'Shape up, Pens!' I said. 'It's incredibly difficult to catch AIDS. Or rather,' I added, to show that I knew what I was talking about, 'to contract the HIV virus which leads to AIDS.'

'Well, if it's not VD, then I've got cancer of the uterus,' she said, calming down. 'I've looked it all up in the BMA book of *Complete Family Health*. There's no getting away from it.'

'Go and see Dr Green,' I said. 'Find out exactly what it is. I'll come with you, if you like.'

'No, it's fine,' said Penny. 'I'm probably going to die. And before Hughie, too! If they put my body in the freezer, we could have a joint funeral!'

'Nonsense,' I said. 'Ring me when you get back.'

Later

Penny has just rung. 'Well, I went to see Dr Green and she prodded and poked inside me,' she said. 'And then she said: 'I suppose you couldn't have . . . by any chance . . . still got a coil in, could you?' I'd forgotten all about it, Marie! Then she said: "Well, I think it's a bit redundant considering you're sixty, don't you?" and she yanked it out.'

I suppose everyone nowadays is on the pill. It seems weird to think that when I was young I used to go round with a Dutch cap in my handbag. Funny solid round bit of rubber that we bunged up ourselves before sex and then pulled out with a big pop six hours later. Surely Dutch people didn't wear caps like that? Awfully hot and uncomfortable.

Honestly, sex. Is it worth it? I used to know a wonderful old lady of sixty (well, she seemed like an old lady then, though now, of course, being the same age myself, I am rather staggered to imagine that I would describe her in those terms). A few months after her birthday she suddenly confided in me: 'You know, darling, I have decided to give up sex. I think it rather *undignified* for any woman of my age to have sex, don't you?'

Anyway, I read the other day that a third of women over the age of sixty no longer sleep with their husbands – older women prefer separate rooms to what the paper euphemistically called 'close encounters'. It was 'snoring' and 'fidgeting and uncontrollable libidos' which forced them out. Apparently Evelyn Waugh said that he'd rather visit his dentist than share the marital bed.

May 8th

Just read about someone who boasts that her mother was still doing the hokey-cokey with two false hips at the age of 101. Is that marvellous, admirable and splendid? Or is it, as I think, simply barking mad and crackers?

Later
Finally dyed the cats' rescue jacket black. I haven't dyed anything since I was about twenty, when Penny and I used to go to Pontings and buy old men's vests and dye them purple and wear them as mini-dresses. This time the dying was fantastically successful. The cat's rescue jacket came out amazingly cool blue-grey and expensive-looking. Wish I'd done it ages ago. Unfortunately, however, my fingers have gone the same smart shade of grey and no amount of pumicing will get them clean.

Then went to have my frightful toes chopped about by the chiropodist, a rather sad woman from Yugoslavia. She told me she was so depressed a couple of weekends ago that she'd had a bath, put on her best make-up, dressed herself up in her nicest clothes, and gone down to Paddington station to throw herself under a train. 'But then I felt so stupid, I came home again,' she said.

I seem to be the recipient of so many weird confidences. What the hell. Someone has to be.

May 17th

Chickens came home to roost tonight. Had a dinner party of my own which was a complete disaster.

First of all, Hughie couldn't come at the last minute because he felt so terrible. James said he was going downhill fast. So, obviously, James couldn't come. Penny had some relative to stay who I'd generously said could come, thinking that one extra woman wouldn't be too bad, but at the last count we had seven women and two men – a nightmare. In desperation

I rang Archie, hoping that perhaps he might be in London, and, amazingly, he was, and seemed very keen.

Penny's relative, a sallow widow from Wiltshire, was, as my father would say, 'perfectly nice'. How I hope that no one ever describes me as 'perfectly nice'. There is something about that word 'perfectly' that sums it all up. Anyway, much to her credit, and unusual in a perfectly nice person, she smoked. But when I insisted that she be allowed to have a fag, there was a ghastly silence all round, and she said that no, she'd have a cigarette outside.

As an ex-smoker I am fiercely pro-smokers' right to smoke, and got extremely cross that my guests had exerted such social pressure that the poor woman was forced into the rain in the garden. Dangerously, I said that it was preposterous not to allow guests to smoke, and how would they like it if I started banning deadly topics of conversation from my house? For instance, I said, I would like to ban from my table all conversations about alternative medicine, Films I Have Seen, how dangerous London is getting these days, and moans about old age, because they are so fantastically boring, but I am too polite to do so.

There was general laughter and then over the main course Tim said that talking about mugging and danger, he'd been mugged recently, and then after general mugging talk, with everyone topping each other with tales of hoodies, the pale widow said that after she'd been mugged in Salisbury the only way she got over it was to go to a healer in Wells, and then everyone told their alternative medicine stories. After going out to get the pudding, gnashing my teeth with rage, I got back to find that one of them was trying to tell the plot of the movie she'd seen last Saturday.

'The actress was . . .' she said. 'Oh, dear . . . I can't remember . . . not Nicole Kidman, not Meryl Streep, the other one . . . rabbits . . . obsessive love affair . . .'

'Senior moment,' said someone. And then everyone started talking about how we're all losing our memories.

It's true that I can never find where I have parked my car. But I could *never* find where I'd parked my car, even when I bought my first Fiat 500 at the age of eighteen. I can't even distinguish one car from another and can only remember which is my car by reading the numberplate. And if a couple of years ago I lost my room in a hotel in Italy and was found wailing on the wrong floor, that's about the sum total of my recent forgetfulness. If anything I find my memory has got considerably sharper as I get older, partly because it was so appalling in the first place, partly because I am so much less anxious than I used to be and partly, possibly, because I stuff myself with fish oils, remembering that Jeeves's mighty brain was due to the huge amount of fish he ate.

Thought: have I written all this before somewhere?

After that we got on to the last cliché dinner-party subject, how time speeds up as you get older. I explained the theory that when you're three, the next year is a third of your life, but when you're sixty, the next year is a sixtieth of your life, which gives it the impression of shortness, but everyone looked at me blankly and then Marion said that Christmas came every five minutes, hardly worth taking down the tree, until Archie, who was all too aware of what was going on, managed to wrench the conversation round to 'the worst meal I've ever eaten' which was, if not totally original, at least entertaining. Changing the conversation round, though, took a huge amount of psychic power. Helping Archie maintain the topic, I felt like a HGV driver doing a U-turn, everyone dying, really, to talk about age and alternative medicine.

I went out to make the coffee and, blow me, when I got back they'd all returned to the same old tram-lines. (No doubt Jack would say: 'Tram? What is a tram, Mum?') Now they were talking about whether there was life after death. The perfectly nice woman from Wiltshire turned out to be a great believer in God, and stupidly, though I should have kept quiet, I said that I believed in absolutely nothing at all, and thought that science would eventually explain the entire meaning of life, if indeed there was one which I doubted. After the chilly silence that followed I tried to ameliorate it by saying how Richard Dawkins is an enthusiast about everything, how he says science is so much more exciting, mysterious, awesome, blah, blah, than religion, but I felt I had said the wrong thing.

Everyone looked at me pityingly (particularly the women and, worst of all, Archie, who I think has been known to set foot in a church now and again), as if I were a cold-blooded amphibian who had never experienced "joy". I tried to explain that indeed I did feel joy as I could feel all my DNA and micro-molecules dancing in tune to their counterparts in trees and mountains and rain and Scottish lochs, but the damage had been done. Those spiritual clearly thought I was a horrible, insensitive kill-joy. I felt distinctly unfeminine, as I heard myself reply, when Marion asked if I didn't think I'd see my father again when I died: 'Absolutely NOT! And he was certainly convinced he'd never see me again. Although it would be lovely to meet him again, it would be a very unpleasant surprise for both of us to find that our views about the existence of an afterlife had been wrong all along.'

After that they all left, saying they'd had a perfectly wonderful time, and I knew they were lying their heads off, and I was left to do the washing-up feeling a complete idiot. Even Archie went early, saying he had a train to catch, which I'm sure was an excuse. Oh, dear. I bet the scales have fallen from his eyes and he thinks I'm just a loud, shouting, horrible person.

Later
Glenn Close.

May 27

Latest mad piece of spam:

> *No more Traffic Camera tickets!!*
> *SAFE and EASY to use. Unlike license plate covers – Photo blocker*
> *is legal in all countries around the world.*

If only.

Midnight

Huge commotion in the street, so loud that I went out in my dressing gown. A dark shape was slumped against my neighbour's wall two doors down. A police car whined down the street. Then an ambulance. Some kind of knifing, apparently.

May 30

Turned out that the man I'd complained about, whose radio had been playing so loudly, had been stabbed to death by a friend over a £10 loan. Curse of Sharp, I'm afraid. It always works.

June 2

I've been looking in on Hughie most days recently. Some days he can get out and says he feels reasonably OK for a couple of hours; others he gets too tired and has to go to bed or sit in a chair at home. He has got rather hooked on daytime television, and raves about programmes like *Richard and Judy* and *Countdown*. When I last saw him he was so deep into an old black-and-white movie, something with Richard Todd in it, that I had to sit through it with him as he wouldn't switch it off.

'If I'd known how good television was in the afternoons,' he said, 'I'd have never gone to work.'

Later
When I was in the kitchen today, I noticed Michelle dropping a teabag of green tea on the floor, and then picking it up and throwing it away.

'Why on earth are you doing that?' I asked. 'It's perfectly usable. The tea hasn't touched the floor, and it's going to be sterilized by boiling water anyway.'

Michelle looked at me with disgust. 'No, eet ees dirty!' she said.

I once cooked a whole stew for six people which fell on the floor. I simply scraped it up and served it. But I suppose it's the old wartime frugality that shows through, with me. Waste not, want not.

I find it extraordinary to think how much change I have lived through during the past sixty years. When I was young we had no car, no telly, no supermarkets, no frozen food, no mobile phones, no central heating (the doors were always closed in winter to keep the heat in) and the lights were always turned off whenever we left a room, to save on electricity.

It seems incredible to me, as I sit here, stifled by central heating, listening to the whirring of a dishwasher in the background, that when I was small, a man used to come round every evening on a bicycle with a long lighted stick to ignite the gas lamps in our London street. There was still a working granary in the London street which I passed on my daily walk down to the river to feed the seagulls. Rag-and-bone men drove by at weekends with their carts and nose-bagged horses, shouting their strange stylized cry: 'Ragnbooooone!', and the roads were covered with steaming piles of horse manure. And in the summer I would collect huge blocks of ice from the fishmonger to keep in our 'ice-box', a lead-lined substitute for a fridge. Nearly everyone in the streets was thin and white. Their teeth were often bad, their hair was, like mine at the time, washed only once a week, and everyone smelled, it being long before the days of deodorant. We were living in post-war London, where, as George Orwell wrote, austerity ruled and everything smelled of 'boiled cabbage and sweat, of grimy walls and dirty clothes'.

June 4

I can tell that already Jack believes I'm losing my mind, but I think he has thought me fairly barking for the last few years because he always assumes I've lost my keys, and helps me across the road. Today he said as we were sorting out the pushchair for me to take Gene to the park: 'Why did you just say "bugger"?'

'I didn't say "bugger",' I said.

'Well, you did.'

'I didn't, darling. It's not the sort of thing I say.'

'Well, you did say it. I don't mind if you said "bugger" or not, but you definitely said it.'

Did I say it? Did he mishear? Am I going mad, old?

June 7

I have Gene while Jack and Chrissie go away for a night on their own. I am so lucky! I keep looking at his little cup and plate; I've got all the toys out and his cot's all ready. I feel quite skippy inside, as if I had a new boyfriend coming over. How Jack and Chrissie will be able to cope without him for two days I don't know.

When they dropped him round he was wearing a little blue tank top I had knitted him, and looking like such a tiny little man, even though he can't walk yet.

We got to Holland Park OK. Jack and Chrissie had fixed his car seat in the front of my car. But getting Gene and the pushchair in is as difficult as doing Rubik's cube with a blindfold on. Eventually I managed to click all the straps into place without him screaming too much and about an hour later, we arrived at the park and fed the birds, an activity he'd like to do all the time, as far as I can see.

It's odd how happy I can be just standing about feeding birds, while Gene watches from his pushchair. When Jack was young and we mooched about in Holland Park, I'd scream internally with boredom. I had the washing to do, I had friends to ring. Oh, I'd be thinking all the time, *I want to get a life!*

These days I don't want to get a life. Or, rather, I've got a life. Looking after Gene.

We walked round a mysterious wooded bit at the back of the park. I got very nervous when we saw three extremely sinister hoodies on a bench in the distance, clearly involved in some kind of drug deal. One of them had an iPod (I think) plugged into his ears; one held a pit-bull terrier on a chain. Unfortunately Gene spotted the dog and, yelling: 'Do! Do!', insisted we walk past. When we came up to the group, he grinned and shouted, pointing to the dog, while I maintained my usual petrified Don't-you-dare-lay-a-finger-on-me! I-am-a-feisty-old-bat-with-a-killer-handbag! expression. As we paused for Gene to look, the hoodies instantly burst into wreaths of affectionate, friendly smiles, each of them gave Gene a high five, and the one with the iPod let him listen to the music on his earphones. I felt horrible being so suspicious. I suppose it is possible to be a creepy drug dealer and charming with small children at the same time.

Finally got back to the car after Gene had examined what seemed to me every single blade of grass in the entire park, and it was a case of so far so good. But then I had to fold down the pushchair, and after about twenty minutes trying to pull and push at all the catches, I finally gave up and just rammed it, open, into the back. Then, once I'd put Gene into the car seat, I couldn't get his straps to snap shut. Manoeuvring everything is like trying to put up a deck chair while wearing boxing gloves.

As I couldn't possibly drive him home with no safety belt on at all, I improvised by tying a plastic bag to one side of the seat, and then tying that to the finger of a glove, and knotting the whole thing up with a rubbery thing with hooks on the end that you use for keeping luggage on the top of your car. In the end, poor Gene looked like one of those strange and sinister parcels you sometimes see on the luggage carousel at Stansted, a parcel that has, apparently, been there for years and looks like being there for another few years to come. I drove back very slowly indeed, one hand on the wheel and the other on Gene's tummy in case he should suddenly propel himself through the windscreen.

When we got back, he tucked into some pasta, peas and ham, all mushed up. I gave him some fizzy water, and as he felt the sparkles, he let it all run down his front, roaring with laughter, as if it was a huge joke played on him by the water.

He went to bed peacefully, and I felt so happy sitting downstairs, watching telly, knowing he was upstairs in his cot. I could hear his sweet soft breathing on the monitor, and I thought: Well, Marie, if your cup doesn't runneth over now, I don't know what.

Having said that: what would it be like if someone else were in the same room as me, also contentedly listening to the monitor? Someone friendly. Like Archie. Have to admit that it would be rather nice. Then realized that he probably was, at this very moment, entertaining the Swedish bimbo team at the Ivy, and stuffing their faces with gravadlax.

Later
I was right. I couldn't have said 'bugger'. I must have said 'buggy'.

June 8th

I took Gene back to Brixton in the evening, and put him to bed, because Jack and Chrissie were coming back after supper. I stayed over, so they could be late. I went to bed at eleven, but there was no sign of them at twelve, and by one o'clock I was panicking. By two o'clock I was desperate.

What would I do if anything had happened to them? Had they been killed in a car crash? If so, should I move to Brixton to live with Gene and care for him, or should he move in with me? What school should I send him to? Jack and Chrissie are committed to state education. What should I do if they were both in comas? If I'd sent him to a private school and then they both suddenly woke up, would they be furious and never speak to me again?

Suddenly heard the sound of a flushing loo and, convinced burglars had invaded, I nervously pottered out of my room and said: 'Hello?'

It was Jack. Turned out they'd been back since 11.30 but I'd been asleep and hadn't heard them come in.

June 9

Having bitten my nails ever since I was born, I've now managed to grow them at last. They're turning into uncomfortable claw-like talons, and my fingers feel all stuffy and hot underneath them. What are long nails actually for? Retrieving dropped coins from the floor, picking my teeth, repairing damaged earrings? Scratching out the eyes of mine enemies? Must be more to them than that.

June 10th

As I walk down to the river to see Marion, the seagulls remind me of my own youth, suddenly, walking down with my grannie to feed them by the river. I remembered my tiny hand in her big hand.

When Gene is older, I wondered, will he dismiss his grannie in the same off-hand way that I dismissed her? Will he behave as badly to me as I did to mine? I was so troubled in my twenties that I had no time for her, this woman who meant so much to me in my childhood. I don't even remember going to her funeral.

It is only now that I appreciate her and remember her with such waves of love. I hope she is looking down from wherever she is – not that, actually, I believe she is anywhere but you never know – and knows how much I loved her, and how she shaped so much of my life.

And how will my son behave to me? Will he be impatient when I'm old and ill, like my father was with my grandmother? Like many sons can be with their mothers when they start to crack and crumble?

June 11

Penny rang. She's been looking at a book on feng shui and has found a compost heap in the 'relationship corner' of her garden. Would clearing it and putting in some wind chimes bring Mr Right along, she asks?

Later
Archie rang saying his thank-you letter had been returned to him because he'd got the postcode wrong. Curiously insulting, that, to think that he didn't even know my address. However, at least I was able to apologize for frightful evening which he didn't seem to think was frightful at all. He is *so* polite.

June 15

Oddly overcome with concerns about Gene. Each morning I am up at four, white with anxiety and fear.

Desperate, I emailed Marion. I told her all my worries – that he'd get bullied at school when he went, that he'd take drugs when he was fourteen, that he would become overweight and be teased. I wrote that I worried about Jack and Chrissie suddenly moving to Australia, that they'd just ring up one day and say: 'Sorry, we're off. Tough tittie. Goodbye!' How, I asked her, can you stop the thoughts?

Within minutes she'd written back:

Dearest Marie,
This is all, I am sure, connected with the impending loss of Hughie. My sister (grannie of five) speaks to me almost every day and so very often we prop each other up, trying to allay fears about the latest anxious preoccupations surrounding these heavenly little

creatures. We are so blessed really to be involved with our young – and their young – but I suppose it's bound to have a cost, following the punitive and universal rule of no good without the grind. I have been known to cry so much as I drive back home from my grannie duty that I can't see where I'm going – the parting, the missing. And she and others rather a lot more sensible in general than us, feel equally bereft as they say goodbye. As usual, all to do with loss, isn't it? Fear of losing yet another person who matters . . . The joy, though, the sheer unqualified joy of shared time with these littlies makes it all worth while, even the 2 a.m. angst, I reckon – and as soon as your Gene is on the phone with his 'D'you know what, gran . . . ?' stories and discoveries, I'm sure there'll be far more on the plus side. Makes me weep just thinking about the trust, the unconditional love that flows from these lovely babes, and being able to give the same love back to them – also unconditionally – makes all the anguish fade away.

I am so, so lucky to have such friends.

June 16

Jack and Chrissie asked me to Sunday lunch. When I arrived they were convulsed with laughter.

'Gene has got a name for you!' they shrieked.

'Oh, really?' I said, immensely flattered as I took off my coat.

'Who's that?' they said to Gene who was staring at me, smiling. They pointed at me. 'Who's that?'

'Gaga,' he replied. 'Gaga. Gaga.'

'Thanks a bunch, Gene,' I said, with mock resignation. 'I come here, I love you, I look after you, and all you can do is reward me with a name that clearly defines me as a barking old bat. You'll go far.'

But inside I felt as pleased as if I'd been given a Damehood. Gene recognized me. 'Gaga.' Oh, dear. I think I'm going to cry.

Got back to find message from James. Hughie back in hospital. And this time it seems unlikely he'll get out.

June 17th

Today Hughie lies on his back in what hospital staff call, apparently, the 'end-of' ward, a place from which there is no return. All he can do is breathe, in and out, in and out. And stare. Terrible sight. Hardly alive. He looks like some awful kind of Damien Hirst installation.

James was sitting, wearing a blue plastic apron, by the side of the bed. And by other beds, other families also sat or stood, all dressed in their blue plastic pre-mourning clothes, nervously touching bits of their swollen or emaciated relatives, serious-faced, whispering, moving slowly with anticipatory grief.

Hughie kept making gurgling sounds, and there was no way he could communicate with anyone. Now he has a tracheotomy in his neck.

When James went for a break I stood by Hughie, dipping a sponge into water and putting it on to his lips. I asked him if he was in pain, one blink for yes, two for no, but Hughie made no response and by the time he did blink, I'd forgotten which was yes and which was no. What a time to have a senior moment.

I ended up standing there for three-quarters of an hour, sponging his sweaty, oily head, stroking his few days' growth of beard, and, oddly, whispering sweet nothings to him. I told him that we all loved him, I loved him, he loved us – occasionally breaking off to say what gibberish it all was, and telling him to try to feel peaceful and relaxed.

'We are all doing our best, everyone wants the best for you, come what may . . .' I said. Everything I said seemed to include the possibility of death. I felt it would make him feel happy to know that we weren't all just hoping for him to recover when it wasn't possible.

Occasionally he would open his eyes, with a look of terror and suspicion, but then he seemed relieved to see me there, and went back to his struggle with breathing.

Of course he's going to die. I feel angry only that they are keeping him alive for the moment. It is so unfair. All they are doing is maintaining him in a state of misery, between life and death. They could probably keep him like this for ever.

The nurses came and went, all through the day, monitoring, writing, staring at the machines, fiddling, twisting knobs . . . it is a macabre scene.

June 18

James rang this morning saying they were going to turn off the machines that are keeping Hughie going. Apparently it is a situation known as 'power off'. They anticipate he will die by four o'clock.

As I had an appointment to have my hair cut at ten this morning, I kept it, but knowing I had a date with death in the afternoon was a strange experience. I felt very peculiar, with constant spells of dizziness. I kept putting off going to the hospital. Tidied the house. Had lunch. Even mowed the lawn. I really couldn't bear it. Finally went, hurrying, and there was James on one side of Hughie's bed, under a television monitor which showed Hughie's heartbeat and blood pressure dwindling away in front of our eyes.

Occasionally a nurse came in and looked at the monitor and pressed a few buttons. James said: 'It'll all be over in quarter of an hour' – and sure enough it was.

All three of us were surrounded by large plastic barriers, to shield us from the other people. I sat on one side of the bed holding Hughie's hand; James sat on the other, his arm resting against Hughie's paper-thin skin. 'It's like being in a swimming pool,' said James. He kept turning away to cry. Poor old Hughie. He already looked like a corpse, gasping away with his mouth open, the yellowing whites of his eyes showing. Some of the tubes had been taken out of his hands, and he was covered with sticking plaster to protect the wounds. Very, very slowly, he faded away and all the machines came to a halt.

And as he died, I had the most curious feeling. I was aware of dying being the most natural thing in the world. It was as natural as – as, well, going to the lavatory. Dying was just something one did. The only different thing about it was that we do it just once in our lives.

As Hughie died it was as if a light chiffon scarf had been thrown into the air and – poof! – he'd gone. In an odd way it wasn't sad at all. Just a normal part of a day.

July 1

The funeral took place in Golders Green Crematorium. I am now so dreadfully familiar with the place that I no longer have to get out the map to find it. On the way there, I had a strange experience. I allowed a huge container lorry to pull in in front of me, having overtaken me, and as I followed behind, the driver put on his winking lights as thanks. I was suddenly overcome with emotion. It seemed to signify all the kindness of strangers in the world. This great big dirty lorry, from God knows where, a grisly warehouse in the suburbs of Rotterdam perhaps, and yet this sudden burst of human warmth emanating from it. I found myself starting to cry with gratitude.

Hughie's death is making me so tender.

This great sadness, what a treat it is to feel like this . . . what a kind of honour. Grief isn't a curse, it's a blessing. To be so connected that you feel true loss – what is there to commiserate about that? Why should you want to make anyone 'feel better' when they're unhappy in this way? This grief is only another side of loving, one part of what it is to be human. I can't help being angry with people who try to claim sympathy when they are feeling bereaved. This deep fruitcaky, purple pain is a sort of joy, such a luxury.

When you are feeling the pain of being bereaved, you are still connected to life, you still want the dead person to be alive, you still believe life is worth living.

Though on second thoughts, I bet James wouldn't agree with me.

The moment I left the car and walked towards the group of mourners outside the chapel, I saw Archie. Tall. In his lovely dark coat. This time he was wearing a black scarf as well. He towered among the rest, a quiet group, all looking dazed, with their sad faces on, speaking in low voices.

When I reached him, 'I'm so pleased to see you,' he said, hugging me. 'Let's sit together.'

We went in, and the funeral started. James read out a lovely piece by Cicero which went:

The death of the old is like a fire sinking and going out of its own accord, without external impulsion. In the same way as apples, while green, can only be picked by force, but after ripening to maturity fall off by themselves, so death comes to the young with violence but to old people when the time is ripe. The thought of this ripeness so greatly attracts me that as I approach death I feel like a man nearing harbour after a long voyage: I seem to be catching sight of land.

I got up and spoke about Hughie, feeling rather like Tony Blair because I left significant pauses between phrases and adjectives. I am becoming sickeningly adept at this kind of thing, having now given four funeral addresses in my time. I find that after each point I make, I have to wait a bit to let a speck of emotion rise up in me. It does the whole drama thing good for the tears to fill the eyes. Indeed, so affected was I by my own words, that when I left the pulpit, grey-faced, I kissed my hand and pressed it to the coffin. I kept finding myself saying to myself: 'Goodbye old boy. Poor old chap. Oh, you poor dim ducky. Oh, you brave old potato.' Just bits of rubbishy, affectionate nonsense. Returned to my seat next to Archie, who was blowing his nose violently. He said: 'You certainly know how to get us all going. And five minutes max. I timed you. Perfect length. Brilliant.'

For one moment I looked at the coffin. My connection with Hughie had been so special, I felt it was something that no one else had. And then I was aware of the fact that everyone else in the congregation almost certainly thought the same. They imagined that they all had some unique relationship with Hughie. And that was what made him so extraordinary. His ability to make each of us feel privileged to have such an intimate relationship with him.

I turned to look at Archie and smiled, but as I did so, I caught his eye. Then something very odd happened. I was suddenly overcome with a strange longing to kiss him. And felt extremely embarrassed about it. It's awful how, the minute you fancy someone, you imagine that they must be aware of it. I hardly knew where to look. Then I remembered from other times how sexy funerals make you feel. Loss is such a turn-on. So I tried to dismiss the flicker of attraction as a passing mistake.

At the party in the flat afterwards, all the sadness was temporarily gone, and we talked in relieved burbles, as if we were at a great reunion cocktail party. I had a long chat with James, drank a couple of glasses of wine and ate about six smoked salmon sandwiches.

Penny was there with, oddly, Friedrich, the trainer who had been persuaded for once to get out of his vest and put on a suit. He looked about thirty years old. Penny appeared blissfully happy.

'Have you ever seen *The Wizard of Oz*?' I asked him casually, as we passed in the corridor.

Luckily, he looked utterly baffled.

There was a bit of a scrum by the kitchen. And as I was squeezing by towards the front door – I was feeling a bit funeralled out – I noticed Archie was squeezing by in the opposite direction.

'You're surely not going, are you? So soon? We shall all be totally bereft,' he said. 'Have another drink with me. Won't you? We haven't had a chance to have a real chat.'

He took me, strangely, by the hand, and pulled me into the sitting room.

As we sat down, I felt utterly confused. It was true. Archie was looking particularly dishy. His hair might be white, but it was very silkily white, he had a nice mouth . . . and with a lurch, as we looked at each other, I realized that I fancied him just as much as I ever had done when I was fifteen. Not only that, but it crossed my mind that he fancied me. We didn't talk for a second, just looked at each other.

'I have to tell you something,' he said. 'Hughie and I had a chat before he died. And he said that you once had a schoolgirl crush on me.'

What was I to say? I felt like an overblown rose, petals flying in all directions. I didn't know whether to giggle or get all stuffy. Instead, I said, blushing: 'Oh, rubbish. He was raving. Terribly ill. Full of chemotherapy. Went to his brain.'

'He seemed OK to me,' said Archie, smiling very slightly.

'Anyway, I thought he didn't have chemotherapy? But look: the thing I have to tell you is that when I was fifteen, believe it or not, I had a crush on *you*.'

'Oh, ha ha,' I said, completely beflustered. This couldn't be happening to me, I told myself. I'm the one who's got the single bed, remember, Marie? I'm the one who's hopeless at relationships. I'm the one who's renounced sex after sixty for good.

'Forty years too late!' I heard myself saying foolishly.

'If I promise not to take you to Pulli, would you have dinner with me the week after next, when I'm coming up again?' he asked. 'We could talk. We could – ah – talk about old times.'

And then: 'Oh, *yes!*' I heard myself saying, all defences finally completely down. 'Any day would be lovely!' Inside I was cursing myself and saying: 'Marie, how could you? At least play it cool!'

'What about Thursday week? Pick you up at eight?'

'Lovely!' I said, gulping and blushing. I realized that I meant every word. Even if I'd asked fifteen people to dinner that night, I'd happily put them all off.

Archie got up, reached down and took my hand, giving it a squeeze. Then he leaned over, put his mouth to it and kissed it.

'Good-oh,' he said. 'I'll count the days.' He looked me in the eyes, then turned away and left me, reeling, on the sofa.

Later

Of course I just couldn't stop thinking about him. I tried to focus on the funeral, or puzzle about Penny's relationship with Friedrich and even tried to tidy up Gene's toys, which were scattered about the room from his last visit, but my brain seemed completely taken over by Archie.

'We could talk about old times'! He'd 'count the days'!

I'm afraid I found the whole thing utterly thrilling and goofy-making, and tender and lovely all at the same time, one moment feeling like dancing inside and the next berating myself for breaking my resolve about relationships.

When I turned on the computer I found I had an odd piece of spam, so odd that I wondered if it hadn't come from the Other Side, sent by Hughie:

> *tying finished conduct silence clock intelligent*
> *from shoulder imagine*
> *fill control enough by*

July 2

I sat in the garden, thinking about Hughie and how lucky he was, in a way, to suffer only for a few weeks. I have a Living Will stashed in almost every room in my house, in my wallet, with my doctor, with my solicitor. Jack has been told so many times how much I want him to get rid of me if I become a burden, I'm sometimes surprised he doesn't seize a cushion and do it now, just to shut me up.

But here I am. With a date on the horizon. A proper one. With a friend. With, it seems, a grown-up. With a lovely bloke I've known for years and years and years. My only worry is what on earth I'm going to tell Penny. Not to mention everyone else to whom I've been banging on smugly about my chosen state of celibacy. I feel such a total idiot.

Later

In the garden, staring at my roses which are blooming bright scarlet, I was feeling pretty blissed out, when a loud drumming started across the way. Suddenly the sounds of 'Amazing Grace' came bursting into the garden, great roaring live music with tambourines and a choir. All the blackbirds and pigeons flew into the air with horror, and Pouncer's ears went distinctly back. I became extremely irritated. I *knew* Praise the Lord! Inc. was a dreadful idea.

Later

I was just going out to the shops to get some more loo paper – Michelle had taken the last two rolls up to her room to do unspeakable things to her face with her 'products' – when I bumped into Father Emmanuel, coming out of church after the service. A surge of resentment filled me as I said crossly: 'You know, Father Emmanuel, whatever you say, I can hear all your hymns in my garden. All the words, everything.'

He broke into a smile and clasped my hand with his, all black knobbly fingers.

'Oh, Mrs Sharp,' he said. 'That is wonderful news! I am so glad you can share in our joy! That is jost wonderful!'

I was about to burst into a grouchy tirade, but looking at his beaming face, it was impossible not to respond with a smile.

'Just wonderful,' I repeated, trying it out. Then I found myself – corny or what? – giving him a hug.

Because it dawned on me that there are worse things than sitting out in the summer sunshine, in your sixties, with the sounds of 'Amazing Grace' drenching the garden, with a real date with your first love on the horizon.

I know that seeing Archie will be friendly and funny and sexy and loving all at the same time. We both know it. Indeed, if there's a slight blip it comes only when I think of the size of my minuscule bed. But as I write this, I remember. Michelle is moving out. And in her room there is a *very* large double bed.

So would I go so far as to say things are 'jost wonderful'?

Well, I jost might.

He just wanted a decent book to read ...

Not too much to ask, is it? It was in 1935 when Allen Lane, Managing Director of Bodley Head Publishers, stood on a platform at Exeter railway station looking for something good to read on his journey back to London. His choice was limited to popular magazines and poor-quality paperbacks – the same choice faced every day by the vast majority of readers, few of whom could afford hardbacks. Lane's disappointment and subsequent anger at the range of books generally available led him to found a company – and change the world.

'We believed in the existence in this country of a vast reading public for intelligent books at a low price, and staked everything on it'
Sir Allen Lane, 1902–1970, founder of Penguin Books

The quality paperback had arrived – and not just in bookshops. Lane was adamant that his Penguins should appear in chain stores and tobacconists, and should cost no more than a packet of cigarettes.

Reading habits (and cigarette prices) have changed since 1935, but Penguin still believes in publishing the best books for everybody to enjoy. We still believe that good design costs no more than bad design, and we still believe that quality books published passionately and responsibly make the world a better place.

So wherever you see the little bird – whether it's on a piece of prize-winning literary fiction or a celebrity autobiography, political tour de force or historical masterpiece, a serial-killer thriller, reference book, world classic or a piece of pure escapism – you can bet that it represents the very best that the genre has to offer.

Whatever you like to read – trust Penguin.

read more
www.penguin.co.uk